RADCLYFFE HALL

(1883–1943), was born in Bournemouth, Hampshire. She was christened Marguerite Radclyffe-Hall but in adult life called herself John. Radclyffe Hall was educated at King's College, London, and in Germany. She began her literary career by writing verses, collected into five volumes of poetry. Many of these, notably 'The Blind Ploughman', were set to music by popular composers of the day and sung in drawing rooms and on concert platforms all over Britain up to and during the First World War.

In 1907 Radclyffe Hall met Mrs Mabel Batten, the society hostess, under whose influence she became a devout Catholic. She lived with her until 'Ladye' Batten's death in 1916 and through her met Una, Lady Troubridge, who was to become her lifelong companion. Radclyffe Hall published seven novels. The first two, *The Forge* and *The Unlit Lamp*, were published in 1924. They were followed by *A Saturday Life* (1925), *Adam's Breed* (1926) which was awarded the Prix Femina Vie Heureuse and the James Tait Black Memorial Prize, *The Well of Loneliness* (1928), *The Master of the House* (1932) and *The Sixth Beatitude* (1936). She also published a volume of stories, *Miss Ogilvy Finds Herself* (1934).

In 1930 Radclyffe Hall received the Gold Medal of the Eichelbergher Humane Award. She was a member of the PEN Club, the Council of the Society for Psychical Research and a fellow of the Zoological Society. Her friends included Elinor Wylie, May Sinclair and Rebecca West in England, and Colette, Romaine Brooks and Natalie Barney in Paris. Between 1930 and 1939 Radclyffe Hall lived in Rye, Sussex but she spent much of her time in Italy and France in pursuit of a lover, Evguenia Souline. Radclyffe Hall died in Dolphin Square, London.

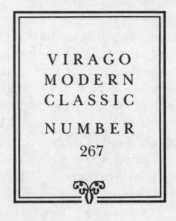

VIRAGO
MODERN
CLASSIC

NUMBER
267

RADCLYFFE HALL

A
SATURDAY
LIFE

WITH A NEW INTRODUCTION BY
ALISON HENNEGAN

DEDICATED TO
MYSELF

Published by VIRAGO PRESS Limited 1987
41 William IV Street, London WC2N 4DB

First published in Great Britain by J. W. Arrowsmith Ltd. 1925
Virago edition offset from The Falcon Press 1952 edition
Copyright Radclyffe Hall 1925
Introduction Copyright © Alison Hennegan 1987

British Library Cataloguing in Publication Data
Hall, Radclyffe
   A Saturday life.—(Virago modern
   classics).
   I. Title
   823'.912 [F]   PR6015.A33

ISBN 0-86068-794-5

Printed in Finland by Werner Söderström Oy

INTRODUCTION

To those who associate the woman with a nobly suffering profile and her work with the proudly tragic martyrs of *The Well of Loneliness*, the discovery that Radclyffe Hall first made her name as the author of a comic novel comes as something of a shock. But thus it was.

As early as 1915 William Heinemann, one of the canniest and best of publishers, had rejected some of Hall's short stories, saying that he'd prefer to wait until he could publish the novel which he knew she could—and one day would—write. Although she did not tell him so then, Hall had already embarked upon and abandoned one novel. Her development as a novelist was to be painful, slow and late. Five more years passed. Then, throughout 1921 and 1922, when she was already in her early forties, she began and laboured over *After Many Days* which, renamed *The Unlit Lamp*, was to be her first completed novel: completed first, but published second.

The Unlit Lamp was a large book and a sombre one: a difficult and dangerous combination for a first work by a comparatively unknown writer. It's true that some of her songs, written under her baptismal name of Marguerite Radclyffe-Hall, were popular and one, 'The Blind Ploughman', had become a national favourite during the Great War. But many things had happened to Marguerite Radclyffe-Hall between 1906—when she had paid for the publication of *'Twixt Earth and Stars*, her first volume of poems—and 1922 when *The Unlit Lamp* was seeking a publisher. In that time she had recognized and accepted her homosexuality and had become the lover of an older,

v

sophisticated and demanding woman. Mabel Batten, or 'Ladye', was well read, well educated, an outstanding amateur musician, a generous patron of the arts and an exigent, if loving mistress. That word, however jarring to present day lesbian-feminists, is appropriate to the two women's sense of their own relationship. Marguerite had long been 'John' in her own eyes and those of her friends. She was already elaborating her passionately felt identity as a 'congenital invert', one whose biologically female body was at odds with an essentially male mind and spirit. She was Male to Ladye's Female, Pupil to her Teacher, willing Squire to her Domina, Lady, Mistress.

Rapidly Ladye set about filling the gaps in her gauche young lover's erratic formal and social education. Above all she made it quite clear that any lover of *hers* was expected to work, and work hard, in the pursuit and attainment of excellence, preferably musical or literary.

The affair began when John was twenty-seven. Over the years developing tensions were exacerbated by Ladye's increasing ill health. A motor accident in 1914 left her a permanent invalid. A year later the relationship was already foundering when John met Una, Lady Troubridge, for the first time. The result was the wretchedly precarious triangle which developed between Ladye, John and Una, who was at that time the unhappily married wife of a high-ranking naval officer. When Ladye died in 1916 John was racked with remorseful guilt: her long desired freedom to build the new partnership with Una had been purchased with Ladye's death. Eventually, and painfully, the two surviving lovers found a way, via Spiritualism, to incorporate the dead Ladye and make her a living partner in their shared daily life. By the end of 1920, when John began work on *After Many Days*, she and Una had successfully negotiated an unusually perilous and protracted Beginning to what was to be for both of them the central relationship of their lives.

In the sixteen years which separated the publication of *'Twixt Earth and Stars* and the completion of *After Many Days*, their author had undergone a considerable metamorphosis. Marguerite had become John. Sexual inexperience had been replaced by confidence in her powers as a lover; sexual confusion and guilt had been replaced by combative pride in her membership of an honourable, admirable and much abused sexual minority. Early, if slightly ambiguous involvement with Ethel Smythe, the ardently suffragette composer, with Emmeline Pankhurst and The Women's Social and Political Union, had brought her into contact with organized feminism. Paradoxically her own male-identified sexuality and self-image made her strongly and hostilely aware of social and economic privilege automatically accorded to those born biologically male. Her own male persona, so often harshly condemned as sexist or misogynistic by latter-day feminist commentators, in fact helped to make her a keen-eyed critic and chronicler of male injustice and absurdity. Her conversion to Roman Catholicism in 1912 had given her a temperamentally sympathetic framework for the strong religious impulses which were always to shape her life and work. The rather slapdash dilettante of her youth had been schooled by Ladye to accept more disciplined ways, more clearly defined goals. The years of arduous and demanding labours which she and Una had undertaken for the Society for Psychical Research had completed her training in long hours of continuous and concentrated work at her desk. From the agonizing intricacies of her *ménage-à-trois* she had acquired a great store of painful and compassionate wisdom about jealousy, loss, need, fear, cruelty and self-deception. It was a store she would draw on constantly for her novels. And, perhaps most important of all, she had found in Una a partner who was prepared to devote most of her energies to John's work, to subordinate the demands of her own personal needs, and considerable talents, to her lover's. When, late on

Christmas Eve, 1922, John made the truly final correction to *After Many Days*, much of the triumph was Una's.

But would it ever find a publisher? Heinemann was dead. Various publishers' readers expressed gloomy doubts about content and length. John's agent, Audrey ('Robin') Heath, suggested that if John wrote something 'light and short', something less frightening to wary publishers worrying about whether to take a plunge on a first-time author, it might prove more tempting than the first novel. Once the second book was safely sold, the first could be offered again with a stronger chance of success. John accepted her advice and, in mid-January, 1923, set to work just three weeks after completing the previous novel.

Most remarkably, this author who was usually so utterly dependent on inspiration and for whom writing was almost always a long drawn-out agony, completed the commissioned work in a mere five months. By late June the publishing house of Arrowsmith had accepted *Chains*. Heartened by the faith shown in her, John began work on a third novel almost immediately. In January 1924 *Chains*, or *The Forge* as it had become, was published. It appeared under the name M. Radclyffe Hall (John did not want her gender to be instantly apparent), was immediately acclaimed, sold well and was in its second printing by March. Reviewers hailed a new comic talent. Now, just as Audrey Heath had hoped, a publisher came forward for *The Unlit Lamp*. Cassell accepted it in the middle of June, 1924 and, just three months later, it appeared as the work of 'Radclyffe Hall'. The book established her reputation with reviewers, bookshops, libraries, readers and fellow-writers. John found herself a slightly bewildered celebrity, admitted on terms of equality to the company of authors whom she had long held in awe.

Just as *The Forge*'s success had made possible *The Unlit Lamp*'s publication, so now *The Unlit Lamp* eased the passage of John's third novel, *A Saturday Life*. Nearly seven

viii

hundred advance copies had been sold when Arrowsmith published it in April 1925: the jacket was designed by Una. John had been writing voluminously since she was four or five years old but not until early middle age was she able to conceive and carry through to fruition a full-length novel. Then, in just sixteen months, she published three. It was a feat as dazzlingly spectacular as any of those achieved by Sidonia, the wilful, enchanting, exasperating and ultimately ambiguous heroine of *A Saturday Life*.

Just as Hall's 'serious' novels contain far more wit, humour and sheer warmth than second-hand accounts of them allow, so too both of her comic novels have serious, and connected, purpose. Both *The Forge* and *A Saturday Life* explore the nature of artistic endeavour and the human cost at which artists pursue or abandon their calling. Central to each novel is the vexed question of what distinguishes genius from talent, geniuses from the talented. Are they distinct, or is genius simply the name we give to supreme talent? Do 'artists' really differ in some essential way from other human beings and, if so, how? Equally important, how, if at all, can we compare the inanimate work of art— the painting, the book, the sculpture—and the living one into which some highly skilled, dedicated and gifted human beings can fashion themselves, a relationship, or a way of living. Must we always choose between living for our Art or learning the Art of Life?

On the face of it, *A Saturday Life* tells a very simple tale. Sidonia, the young and only daughter of the widowed Lady Shore, is an enormously gifted child of remarkable precocity. Her gentle and absent-minded mother, who desires only to be left in peace to pursue her scholarly Egyptological studies, finds her days endlessly disrupted by her volatile child's dizzying progress. With passionate enthusiasm Sidonia takes up one interest after another, almost mastering each before abandoning it for its successor. Dancing, the piano, wax modelling, sculpture, singing—over the years all are embraced with rapture, discarded with indifference. Utterly scandalized, upper-middle-class Kensington looks on, aghast with deeply pleasurable horror. Hopelessly out of her depth, Lady Shore early on enlists the aid of her closest friend, Lady Frances Reide. For almost two decades Frances prompts, counsels and supports both mother and daughter until, at last, in marriage and maternity Sidonia finds her true destiny. Or does she?

It sounds the very stuff of romantic fiction: a heroine allowed her brief moment of illusory (and anyway unwanted) freedom, before a firm tug on the rope brings her (gladly) back to the last page and Happy Ever After. In the event, it turns out to be something rather different . . . .

Serious though its purposes are, this is a gloriously funny book. From the very first paragraph, with its mock-pomposo repetitions of the adjective 'Queen Anne', we realize we are in the realm of High Comedy. The writing is crisply confident, the tone dead-pan. For the reader irresistible laughter keeps bubbling up. Devastatingly well-chosen adverbs are devastatingly well placed so that a character's own statements are endlessly undercut, reversed or denied. Marvellously deft portraits and psychologically acute observations abound.

Much of the assurance comes from Hall's own personal knowledge of her subject and setting. Uniquely amongst her books, *A Saturday Life* is 'Dedicated To Myself'. As a child she, like Sidonia, astounded eminent musicians and composers by her precocious facility in extemporizing and playing by ear. (Like Sidonia, she read music very badly.) She too scribbled verses and songs almost as soon as she had learnt to write. Her early formal education, like Sidonia's, was patchy and unreliable. Her early childhood also was passed in a fatherless household ruled by women. The 'At Homes', drawing-rooms, dancing schools and governesses of Kensington had been as familiar to her as to her heroine.

She, unlike Sidonia, did not model wax or sculpt clay, but Una did, well enough to earn her a reputation as a child prodigy and a scholarship—at the age of thirteen—to the Royal College of Art. Marriage halted a career which had looked extremely promising to the many critics who were deeply impressed by the marble portrait bust of Nijinsky which she had exhibited in 1913.

Hall makes her way equally confidently through the ideas which frame the book. Many of them she had already pondered for years and would continue to explore throughout her writing life.

Time; age; heredity; the formation of identity; the evolution of morality: all these fascinated Hall and all of them help to form the very substance of *A Saturday Life*. Many of them are encapsulated within the title's meaning. Lady Frances, long bewildered by Sidonia's lightning changes of mood and direction, comes across an English book on a Florentine stall. It is a commentary on Eastern religious ideas. Much of it leaves her unmoved until she reaches a description of certain souls destined to live through seven reincarnations on earth. Those who have reached the seventh incarnation carry with them all that was learnt, suffered and experienced in the previous six. Life for them is a perpetual and unsatisfying *déjà-vecu*. Nothing is truly new, truly interesting, truly vital. Everything has been done before, every relationship is exhausted before it begins. Such a soul is said to live a Saturday Life (or, in Sidonia's words, to be 'serving a kind of Saturday Lifer'). Is this the key to Sidonia's passionate enthusiasms and abrupt rejections?

Hall herself never directs us to believe that reincarnation 'explains' Sidonia, even if Sidonia, Frances and Lady Shore find the belief comforting. Rather, she uses the idea to symbolize and explore connections between Time, identity and morality. Lady Shore finds time troublesome. Certainly, if forced to choose, she prefers BC to AD, but how much better it would be if time were not. 'Time does not exist', she tells her cat desperately, faced with yet another of Sidonia's very present excesses. Yet sometimes it seems as though Time *causes* Sidonia's excesses, or, rather, in a different time they would not be excessive. Morality itself is strongly contingent on time: one age's virtue is another's vice. Time has the power to determine decency, beauty, morality and value. Kensington is shocked to the core when the eight-year-old Sidonia dances naked in the cloakroom of her dancing academy but, as Frances says: '... perhaps it's in her relation to time, she's improper because she's NOW'.

For Miss Valery, the luckless dancing teacher, a pale shadow of Maud Allan and Isadora Duncan, Sidonia's cavalier disregard of Present Time's proprieties certainly brings problems. Irate parents threaten to remove their children and, as Miss Valery herself admits,

It was one thing to worship the Greek in marble, always a modest medium; it was quite another to see it dancing minus clothes on linoleum in a Fulham cloakroom.

But usually Time is Miss Valery's ally. By believing in her own earlier incarnation as an ancient Greek she creates for herself a personal history which transcends the stifling inhibitions of her Fulham world:

The story she had woven for her own consolation made her blush whenever she thought of it. It dealt with her life as a Greek courtesan, and was very completely satisfying.

The theory of reincarnation gives Miss Valery permission to dream forbidden dreams, fulfil forbidden desires. It also offers Lady Shore a way of coming to terms with the perennial maternal question of 'How on *earth* did her father and I produce this child?'

No [Lady Shore] could not comprehend Sidonia as the outcome of so discreet a mating. She almost began to doubt her own virtue, in view of present events.

Age plays as many tricks as Time. The number of years we've lived bears no necessary relation to the age we feel and are. 'Childishness' pursues us all our lives and children frequently astound us by their maturity and wisdom. Hall returns to this confusion of human chronology again and again in this book. Sidonia's father was 'an old infant'. Lady Shore and Frances treat themselves to cinema matinées and cream teas like a 'pair of elderly children'. The adolescent Sidonia weeps tears which fall slowly, 'like the difficult tears of the old'. At sixteen she spends an excruciatingly boring evening with the twenty-two-year-old Joe Poulsen and thinks 'I must be older than he is . . . I feel like a great-aunt or something.' In the rapturous days when the teenage Sidonia is falling deeply in love with Frances and insists that Frances spend each afternoon with her,

Frances was startled at herself.

'Am I fifteen years old,' was her fierce mental comment, 'to enjoy tea and hot buttered toast in an attic?'

Radclyffe Hall was always fascinated by Time, by the arbitrary and constantly shifting distinctions between past, present and future. For many years she was vulnerably involved with Spiritualism, which claims to transcend the barriers between the living and the dead. Roman Catholicism, to which she was a convert, teaches that the dead have power to intercede for the living and that the living may, by prayer, improve the lot of the dead. Other aspects of Christian teaching emphasize the presence of Christ, in the world, now. Hall herself published in 1932 *The Master of the House*, her own version of the Christ story, set in present-day Provence.

Over the years she became increasingly aware of the part Time plays in defining supposedly absolute values: 'moral', 'natural' and 'perverted', for example. *The Well of Loneliness*, still the book for which she is best known, challenged her age's definition of all of those. In *A Saturday Life* it is not

Sidonia but Frances who suffers most 'because she's NOW'.

Frances is quite clearly an invert. The word never appears in the book but the message is clear for those with eyes to see. Long before Hall attempted to publish *The Well of Loneliness* her work had been filled with implicit and coded lesbianism. In *The Unlit Lamp* homo-eroticism, between mother and daughter, pupil and teacher, is overwhelming. *The Forge* contains throwaway descriptions of anonymous minor lesbian couples. Its heroine, Susan Brett, is briefly and ambiguously involved with the painter, Venetia Ford—a character so recognizably modelled on Romaine Brooks that she broke off her friendship with Hall. All these intimations were not lost on lesbian readers, as their appreciative letters to Hall reveal. Frances found a particular place in their affections, claimed immediately as 'one of us'. All very well for Hall, in disingenuous vein, to write that Frances 'elected, and no one ever knew why, to be Lady Shore's Guardian Angel': her lesbian readers knew why all right.

Everything about Frances—her 'masculine' house, 'gentlemanly' greying temples, androgynously aquiline face, 'mannish' clothes—declares, codedly but unmistakably, her inversion. As does her passionate devotion to Lady Shore and the residual guilt which impels her to work so hard for the thing she most dreads, Sidonia's marriage:

And because she was conscious of a little empty feeling at the thought of Sidonia engaged, being Frances, she stubbornly redoubled her efforts to bring an engagement about.

For Frances, women are Other. She

had never been able to regard herself in the light of an average woman. It was no good, she simply could not judge them (the other female millions) from a purely feminine standpoint. [Other] Women, she considered, were far safer without money. God intended them to marry and have nice little babies. She herself had never married; but then that was different. Why? Oh! well, because it was.

Frances has quite a lot of money. And, when she attains her majority at twenty-one, Sidonia will have some, too— about one thousand pounds a year, quite comfortable. Economic pressure alone need not force her into marriage. This Frances knows. But the next paragraph gives us the clue to her own self-denying determination that Sidonia shall marry. In her thoughts Frances turns from the 'nice little babies' whom God intends women (*other* women) to have, and thinks instead of the women themselves: women heavily pregnant, proud but vulnerable, clumsy yet dignified; women suckling their children in the open air, indifferent to the grubby claims of false modesty, entirely oblivious to everything but the unique bond which links the lives of the suckling woman and the suckled child.

Both image and reality are intensely potent for the unchilded Frances, evoking a complex and many layered response. Woman and child embody the mysterious continuum of life and death, of the generations' endlessly recurring cycle of growth and decay. But for what purpose do the generations, each so pathetically weak and stumbling, so little able to learn from its predecessors, succeed each other? In their mutual self-absorption mother and child embody both the question and its partial answer: the purpose of living is to make life possible. To Frances, gazing on them, their significance is partly spiritual. ('She had felt that she wanted to pray.') But they are also deeply erotic in their unabashed physical expression of passionate tenderness. For Frances, who looks on, they paradoxically appease and arouse longing in her. Empathy with the child brings her vicariously a lover's warmly reassuring contact with the beloved female body. Empathy with the mother brings her a bitter sense of loss for her own unconceived children. And those children were indeed unconceivable—not because of age or infertility, but because of the framework of beliefs and assumptions within which Frances has formed her sense of her own self and sexual identity.

Traditionally, maternity is the essential expression of womanhood. The theory of congenital inversion confers normality upon inverts, but at a price. The inverted woman's desire for members of her own sex is 'normal' because she is 'really' male. For the male to bear children constitutes a true perversion of the Natural Order. The inverted woman may not be a mother. For Frances, as for so many women of her period, inversion entails a cruel choice between sexual identity and motherhood—a choice reinforced by the legal and social sanctions enacted against unmarried women who bear children. If Sidonia is to fulfil her womanhood, she must be a mother. To do so, she must marry. Conceptually and socially there is no alternative, as far as Frances can see. In part, as Hall makes clear, this is because Frances refuses to see. In fantasy she imagines

Pictures of rooms looking out on old gardens; pictures of gardens folded up in twilight; pictures of evenings beside a pleasant log-fire; pictures of nights filled with soft, contented breathing; pictures of a woman with a child at her breast.

The language keeps carefully ambiguous the identity of the woman. Is it Frances who breathes softly and suckles her child? Is it Sidonia? Is it some perfect She? In the fantasies of women who love and desire other women the boundaries between Self and Other constantly blend and blur. This particular woman's identity is unclear. What *is* clear is Frances's rage at the knowledge that, for her, the fantasy will never become reality. The knowledge stirs in her

a feeling of longing . . . a sudden rather fierce resentment against life, a vague, uncomprehending pity for herself, a desire to lift up her voice in protest and ask, 'Why? Why? *Why?*'

But Frances, as Hall goes on to tell us, 'was not a dreamer, nor was she introspective, by choice at all events'. If unwelcome thoughts crash in, unbidden, she hurls herself into mundane activities. If they come at night, she'll 'switch on the bedside lamp and read Sax Rohmer'.

Frances has many fine qualities: loyalty, spirit, ironical self-awareness, humour, compassion and endurance. With sturdy independence she furnishes her 'masculine' rooms, wears her 'mannish' clothes, rides the snubs and insults of those who (like Sidonia's eventual husband) find her 'eccentricities' painful, distasteful or indecent. But she lacks certain forms of moral courage. Sometimes her 'gentle-manly' concern for good form replaces independent moral judgement. Class and convention trap her as surely as theories of inversion. She does not question the traditional links between heterosexuality, marriage and maternity. Not for her the rebellions of Miss Ogilvy and Hannah Bullen, two of Hall's other fictional heroines who do begin to doubt. Sidonia must and does marry.

Yet we need not lament her marriage too bitterly. Hall gives us no reason to believe that Sidonia is now securely moored. Doubt hovers over all. Sound until the last. Constant pointers suggest that if Sidonia *is* settled for life, it's an appalling tragedy. If she isn't—then heaven help everybody because the storms already weathered are as nothing to the ones that lie ahead. Sidonia sees her new husband through the eyes of love: Hall does not. Sidonia sees his strength and beauty: Hall sees, and makes us see, his eternal 'boyishness' (so charming in youth, so wearisome in maturity), the arrogance with which he condescends to the woman he claims to love, the basic contempt and fear he feels for everything which affronts his aggressively conventional sense of normality. A strange mate for Sidonia. But even as we leave her, we realize that her infant son has already displaced her husband in her affections. In the best comic tradition, *A Saturday Life* ends with a marriage and a baby. In life itself, that isn't the end of the story. Una knew that. Once Sidonia discovers it, anything may happen.

Alison Hennegan, Cambridge, 1987

CHAPTER ONE

I

IN the Queen Anne drawing-room of a Queen Anne house, in a Queen Anne square in Kensington, a child of seven years old was dancing slowly with concentrated solemnity. Her eyes were closed, her lips slightly parted, and she hummed a queer little melancholy tune in rhythm to which she moved. The light in the room was subdued yet golden, filtering in beneath the sun blinds from the hot summer day outside. Splashes of sunshine lay on the carpet, and fell on the body of the dancing child as she swayed from side to side.

A tall and elegant Queen Anne clock chimed four with staccato precision. The voice of the clock sounded somewhat surprised as it broke in upon the child's humming. The whole room looked unusually sedate with its stiff walnut furniture and formal chintz; it formed in no way a suitable setting for the little girl's strange performance.

The child stopped dancing, and opening her eyes, surveyed herself thoughtfully in a long mirror. Except for a wreath of artificial leaves, she was unashamedly naked. The wreath was jammed down low on her forehead, and bound in a mop of auburn hair which curled short and thick on the nape of her neck. Her eyes were green and very wide open, their expression habitually questioning. Her small, pale face was slightly triangular, wide across the cheek-bones and pointed at the chin. Her nose was straight and blunt at the tip; her mouth rather large and well shaped. But the most remarkable thing about her, as she stood there looking at herself in the glass, was the faultless line of her strong little body, the luminous glow of her skin. She suggested something perfect in freedom, that belonged to the youth of the world.

She lifted her arms and studied the pose, which apparently did not please her, for she changed it to that of drawing a bow, letting fly an imaginary arrow. A new sound came from her parted lips, a lively, aggressive tune this time. She raised her right knee and then her left, and throwing back her head she danced again with a series of stampings and prancings. The dance was a strange convincing thing, wilful, a little cruel. She frowned as her bare feet stamped out the rhythm, drawing her thick brows together.

'Miss Sidonia!' exclaimed a horrified voice. Her nurse had come in unperceived.

The child looked round. 'Go away!' she hissed. 'Go away! Can't you see I'm dancing?'

'I never saw such a sight, no never! What *have* you done with your clothes?'

Sidonia pointed to a corner of the room. 'Over there. Now please go away.'

'You naughty, heathenish little girl! Have you gone off your head, Miss Sidonia?'

The humming grew louder, the dance more violent.

'Stop that this instant!' commanded the nurse.

Sidonia laughed a triumphant laugh. 'I can't stop; I'm sort of wound up!'

'You *will* stop. Whoever saw the likes, taking off your clothes in the drawing-room in broad daylight? Supposing the footman was to come up. You're a very immodest child.'

'I'm dancing, and no one can dance properly in clothes,' remarked Sidonia in passing.

'Well, of all the bold and brazen talk! If you don't stop at once I'll go and fetch your mother.'

The nurse stepped forward to seize her charge, who, however, evaded her skilfully.

'I don't advise you to touch me,' warned Sidonia. 'If you do I shall have to bite you.'

'We'll see about that!' said the angry nurse, catching the child by the wrist.

Sidonia's head made a downward sweep, and her small,

white teeth struck viciously. 'I'm sorry,' she remarked, as the blood began to flow, 'but I warned you what would happen if you touched me.'

The nurse turned pale. 'Miss Sidonia!' she gasped; and then, 'Now I *shall* fetch your mother.'

But Sidonia waved her lightly away, as though the incident were closed.

2

Lady Shore was sitting at a very large table in the room at the back of the hall. Since her husband's death, three years before, this room had become her refuge and her comfort. It had been Sir Godfrey's particular sanctum; the casket of all his dreams and imaginings. In it he had planned his journeys to Egypt, his battles with the secrets and sands of ages, and his ruthless and interminable digging. She had stood beside him, his wife and his friend, his faithful and ardent fellow-worker. These two had shared the heat of the day in no merely metaphorical sense, for the sun of the desert had sallowed her skin and weakened her eyes.

She had always accompanied him, ever since their marriage, on all his expeditions; until gradually, something in her that belonged to the present had died, and been buried in the dust of Egypt. She and her frail, somewhat small Sir Godfrey, with his retrogressive yet adventurous mind, had turned, as it were by common consent, to the past for romance and freedom. They had sought among the ruins of a dead civilization for the beauty they missed subconsciously in their own. When they had unexpectedly produced a child, their feelings had been a mixture of pride and dismay at the advent of this very lively link with the present.

'Time does not exist,' Lady Shore had remarked, staring down at the new Sidonia; 'the past and the present and the future are all one,' and Sir Godfrey had nodded wisely.

And the longer she lived the more certain she grew that time in fact did not exist. She could never see events in the light of to-day. Why trouble since they equally belonged to to-morrow, as they had done to the reign of Amenhotep I?

9

She let her eyes dwell on the hard little scarabs that lay scattered on the table before her. She fingered them tenderly, reverently even; the Shore Collection was famous.

'Come in,' she called absently as someone knocked. 'Yes, Blake, what is it? I'm very busy.'

'I'm sorry me-lady, but just look at this!' extending the wounded hand.

'Dear me, it's bleeding! Have you hurt yourself, Blake?'

'I've been bitten!' remarked Blake, and waited.

Lady Shore pushed back a lock of grey hair which had fallen across her nose. It had always fallen across her nose, and for years had been prematurely grey. Her short-sighted eyes strayed towards the table, but remembered themselves in time.

'Surely not Ptah?' she inquired rather anxiously. 'Ptah's such a gentle cat.'

'It's no cat that has met its teeth in my hand,' said Blake in an ominous voice.

Lady Shore gave a sigh of genuine relief and looked up at Blake with her kind, vague smile. 'It's Horus, of course! I'm so sorry, Blake. I know he's irritable, I think he's still grieving for Sir Godfrey.'

'It's no parrot neither, neither parrot nor cat. It's a human bite, this is, me-lady.'

'A human bite?' Lady Shore was startled. 'A *human* bite?' she repeated.

Blake drew herself up. Her moment had come, she felt that she had been subtle. She felt, moreover, that she was fully entitled to make the worst of most things. Had she not followed Sir Godfrey and his lady to the haunts of bugs, heathens and mosquitoes, serving Lady Shore in the capacity of maid for years before Sidonia was born? Had she not risked her health in that service, refusing two proposals of marriage at least, and finally consenting to be nurse to Sidonia, with all that that post entailed?

'It's Miss Sidonia, me-lady,' she announced. 'She's dancing round the drawing-room stark naked!'

Lady Shore blinked furiously several times. 'Nonsense!' she exclaimed, almost with animation.

'If you don't believe me, come and see for yourself,' said Blake, now thoroughly offended.

Lady Shore sighed gently, a patient sigh, not very appropriate to the occasion. Blake watched with stern, disapproving eyes, while her mistress tidied the scarabs. Lady Shore collected a sheaf of notes which she put in a neat little pile; then she closed an imposing-looking reference book, having carefully marked her place. Intensely untidy in everything else, she was quite the reverse in her work. It was almost as though her instinct for tidiness belonged exclusively to some period B.C.

'We will go to the child, Blake,' she said.

3

That evening Prudence Shore put aside her manuscript (she was writing a life of Sir Godfrey) and abandoned herself to the consideration of her daughter's extraordinary conduct.

Of course, she had always known that Sidonia was a very unusual child; from an early age this had been apparent, Sir Godfrey had often remarked it. Sidonia had shown abnormal aptitudes from the time she was three years old; she had varied between periods of complete idleness and periods of acute activity. At three years old she had seized a pencil and drawn Adam and Eve, fig leaves and all. No doubt the result of the 'Biblia Innocentium', but remarkable nevertheless. Moreover, from that moment, for six months at least, she had drawn with a kind of frenzy. They had bought her blocks of expensive paper and had sharpened innumerable pencils. When the six months had come to an end, however, Sidonia had begun to stare blankly at her block, or to scribble mere infantile inanities.

At five she had taken another spurt, this time in the direction of somewhat morbid poetry. At five she had written:

> '*I am dying—I am dying—*
> *Oh, Lord, help me in my pain!*'

This poetical epoch had lasted until she was six, at which age, for a short time, Sidonia got religion.

'God sat on the foot of my bed last night,' she announced with conviction one morning.

'What did He look like, dear?' asked her mother absently; she had just been studying a fresco of Anubis.

'I don't know; it was something shadowy and tall, with a bright light all round its shape.'

'Are you sure you were not just dreaming of God? Were your eyes really open when you saw Him?'

'I didn't see Him with my eyes at all, I saw Him out of the side of my head.'

What might have been a genuine psychic impression became tainted with distressing rapidity. The housemaid at the time was from the South of Ireland, hence the ornate reconstruction.

'Have you seen God again?' inquired Lady Shore rather less than a fortnight later.

'I saw Jesus last night, He had on a red cape with gold stuff all round the edge.'

'Did He speak to you, dear?'

'Oh yes, we talked. He told me to get a Rosary like Kathleen's, then He patted my head and went out.'

'Went out?'

'Yes, like a candle when you blow.'

'I see,' said Lady Shore, bewildered.

4

Lady Shore was reviewing these things in her mind as she sat in the Queen Anne drawing-room. To them had been added a curious remark, made that very afternoon. She had reasoned with her daughter as gently as she could regarding the biting of Blake. Sidonia had said that she was sorry for the bite, though it went very well with her dance. But when told that to appear naked in a drawing-room might be considered somewhat odd, since it was no longer the custom, she had argued that our bodies were very unimportant, only there so that people might perceive us.

'We couldn't see each other without them, you know,' she had said, smiling up at her mother.

And poor Lady Shore had been too much impressed to pursue the subject further.

She sighed and rubbed her short-sighted eyes that itched after long hours of writing. 'If that dance had only been Egyptian!' she thought, and was conscious of distinct disappointment. 'But it wasn't Egyptian, it was purely Greek,' she murmured aloud, with distaste. 'And yet where has the child ever seen Greek dancing? We've no Greek vases or pictures of frescoes; there's nothing Greek anywhere in the house. I'm sure she's never been to the British Museum—it really *is* very extraordinary!'

Ptah, the enormous blue Persian cat, rubbed his side against her leg. His yellow eyes stared up into her face unflinchingly, coldly wise. A long, low purr vibrated through his frame; it had neither beginning nor end. It might have started at the tip of his nose, or, conversely, at the tip of his tail. The sound penetrated to Lady Shore's consciousness; she felt soothed without knowing why.

'Time does not exist,' she said, dropping her hand till it sank into Ptah's thick fur.

Then she sighed yet again. Her remark, she felt, was inadequate under the circumstances. She often made inadequate remarks, a habit which caused her much worry. She got up and went to the study for comfort; she wished that Sir Godfrey had not died.

CHAPTER TWO

I

THE Greek dancing caused considerable trouble, but at last a teacher was found. A lady not lacking in pioneer courage had opened a school in Fulham. There, to the amused astonishment of the neighbours, who were not yet fully educated in such matters, the pupils of Rose Valery disported themselves in strange garments conspicuous by their abrupt terminations. Such an exhibition of bare young thighs, calves and feet had never before been seen, at all events in Fulham. The pupils ranged in age from five years old to nineteen, or thereabouts; and twice a week, with the assistance of an upright piano, they endeavoured to recapture the soul of ancient Greece. Some years later the Rose Valery Classes won for themselves much well-deserved praise and produced some excellent dancers, but when Sidonia first made her appearance the scheme was barely in the bud.

Lady Shore had consulted her friend Frances Reide. She always consulted Frances Reide; it saved trouble. And Frances had seen Sidonia dance, and had laughed and had recommended Rose Valery. Precisely why Frances Reide had laughed Lady Shore had not understood. Frances had screwed her tortoiseshell eyeglass into her eye, after breathing on it hard and then polishing; she had sat with her hands pressed down on her knees and her head stuck forward inquisitively. She had murmured, 'Good Lord!' and then 'Great Scott!' and finally she had laughed.

'Well?' Lady Shore had inquired nervously.

And Miss Reide had given a non-committal whistle.

'Shall I take it up? I mean, should she be trained?'

'You can try it; no harm in trying.'

'But how? Where? It's not like ballet or ballroom dancing.'

'It certainly is *not*!' said Frances Reide, twitching out her eyeglass with a jerk.

Sidonia had invented a costume for herself, since nudity was forbidden. She had managed to contrive a tunic effect by wearing an outgrown linen chemise and a pair of very short drawers. Blake was still shocked, but Lady Shore had felt it wiser to compromise.

'You see,' complained Lady Shore to her friend some days later, 'she's at it from morning till night; she's for ever tearing off all her clothes and putting on those ridiculous garments. The child will end by getting pneumonia. She's like a creature possessed.'

'Perhaps she is possessed,' murmured Frances. 'Yes— she probably is possessed.'

Lady Shore looked startled; they were sitting in the drawing-room, and she glanced quickly round it for comfort. 'Oh, no!—Not here. I mean, not Sidonia. Now if it had been Egyptian——'

'If it had been Egyptian you'd have been rather pleased; I know you!' said Frances, smiling. 'If Sidonia were to turn into Set or something, you'd be rather thrilled than otherwise. You're just an adorable, muddle-headed baby; Sidonia's much older than you are, Prudence.'

'I'm terribly anxious about the child. I only wish Godfrey were here,' sighed Lady Shore.

'A lot of use he'd have been!' remarked Frances. 'He was just another old infant.'

'But so brilliant, Frances, so clever, my Godfrey.'

'Yes, clever, but B.C., my dear.'

'And so is Sidonia,' said Lady Shore, brightening. 'Do you mean to tell me that her dancing is modern? Now, what have you got to say, Frances?'

Frances looked as though she could an' if she would have said a great many things; instead she asked for a cigarette and obtained permission to smoke. She smoked in silence for a minute or two while Lady Shore sat and blinked at her, struck as always by her friend's personality, by her wonderful, shining sprackness. Her dark hair shone, especially on the temples, where there appeared a gentlemanly greyness. Her black eyes, flat set and Oriental looking, were almost as bright as her eyeglass; even her thick eyebrows looked well-groomed and glossy. Her skin, the colour of the very best vellum, was drawn neatly over her face; her nose was austere; her mouth hard bitten, but redeemed by a sense of humour. She was well above the average height and as trim about the flanks as a racehorse. She gave the impression of perpetual fitness; you felt that she was always in show condition and would certainly win in the ring. Even Lady Shore did not know how old she was, she changed so remarkably little. They had met in Egypt ten years before, and Frances looked much the same now as then.

It was not until after Sir Godfrey's death, however, that a real friendship had grown up between these two women.

'Grown up' is perhaps hardly the way to express what had happened, there had been no gradations in this friendship; Frances Reide had just dumped it down fully grown, an accomplished fact, as it were. The friendship was as trim, as sprack and as decided as was Frances Reide herself. She elected, and no one ever knew why, to be Lady Shore's Guardian Angel. She was also her confidante upon every subject, and sometimes her adviser. The better to carry out her self-imposed task she had left her beloved Chelsea, and had taken a small house in Young Street, not one minute's walk from the square.

'You're a dear old, addle-pated mummy-chaser, and I've got to see that you don't get run over or walk into the Round Pond by mistake.' That was how Frances had put it.

Not a very inspiring declaration, it is true, but it stood for quite a deep devotion. Lady Shore had peered with her short-sighted eyes, and had finally said, 'Thank you, Frances.'

She was peering now with her short-sighted eyes, waiting for her friend to speak. Her lock of grey hair had fallen again, and was tickling her nose rather violently. She pushed it back clumsily into place; Frances was looking at her.

'It'll fall down again, I suppose you know.'

16

'Yes, it's always coming down,' agreed Lady Shore humbly.

'My dear Prudence, why don't you wear a net? I've urged you to buy some hair nets.'

'I have bought hair nets, I bought six at Barker's,' retorted Lady Shore quickly.

'Then why don't you wear them?'

'Well, you see,' said Lady Shore, 'I can't get them on without making a rent, and my hair bulges out through the holes, when they're torn.'

Frances Reide took the cigarette out of her mouth and smiled an indulgent smile. On seeing the smile Lady Shore plucked up courage.

'We were talking of Sidonia,' she reminded. 'I said that Sidonia was B.C.'

'And she is B.C. I agree with you there, she is quite disconcertingly B.C. at times, only—well, she's terribly modern too, in fact she's more than modern. What I feel about Sidonia is difficult to express, I can't find any words that fit it; she's a sort of a backward and forward proposition, possibly an omen of some future product. She makes me feel both stimulated and uncomfortable; it's that B.C. touch with the ultra-modern, a heady sort of combination. The child attracts me, she always has, she's got a weird fascination. Sidonia's like a rather outrageous cocktail, I'm never quite sure it's very proper.'

'How can a child be improper?' laughed Lady Shore.

'How, indeed? But she is, at least I think so.'

'*Improper?*'

'Oh, not in your sense of the word, Sidonia's too young for that.'

'Well then, how?'

'I don't know—I can't make out—perhaps it's in her relation to time, she's improper because she's NOW.'

'Ah!' said Lady Shore, thinking backwards with some avidity. 'Ah, yes, things were purer then.'

'I don't know about things being exactly purer. I didn't mean that, in any case.'

'We must surely realize from *The Book of the Dead*——' Lady Shore began again, thoughtfully.

Frances held up a warning hand. 'Never mind that, Prudence; "Let the dead bury their dead". What you've got to do now is to tackle the present.'

'Oh no,' said Lady Shore absent-mindedly.

'Yes, Prudence, you've just got to tackle the present; in other words, Sidonia.'

'But if she belongs to the past and the future, then there is no present,' Lady Shore remarked hopefully.

'Then you'll have to make one, to give her a present; you'll have to force it on her somehow.'

'She loves gooseberry fool and jam roly-poly; that's a very present taste, don't you think so, Frances?'

'That's hopeful; yes, dear, that's distinctly hopeful; your problems seem near solution.'

'Frances, you're making fun of me.'

'A little,' Miss Reide admitted.

'Then don't. I'm terribly inadequate, I know. I can't get a grip on Sidonia somehow; it's like trying to hold a bit of quicksilver. And then there's my work,' she finished plaintively; 'that life of Godfrey takes up so much time.'

'There is also the life of Sidonia,' said Frances. She got up to go. 'Try the Rose Valery School; I don't know of anything better.'

'I will, indeed I will,' Lady Shore assured her, pressing her hand in gratitude.

2

Sidonia's first appearance at the Rose Valery School was positively melodramatic. To begin with, she looked so extremely unusual, with her pale face and shock of auburn curls. She was little and quiet and immensely self-possessed, not at all put out by the groups of gaping students. The moment Rose Valery set eyes on the child she had, or so she said afterwards, great difficulty in stifling a scream of pleasure.

'Now, my dear,' said Miss Valery, controlling her emotion, 'we must see just how much you know of dancing. That lady over there is going to play the piano, and I want you for the moment to dance anything you like; just make movements in time to the music.'

Lady Shore pushed her offspring forward.

'Don't do that!' said Sidonia, scowling.

Lady Shore desisted, and the piano began.

'Now then, dear!' encouraged Miss Valery.

'I don't like the piano,' said Sidonia firmly.

'Oh, but you must have music, you know. Miss Robinson, again, please!'

Sidonia stamped her foot. 'I won't have a piano, I hate the sound, it's wrong!'

'Wrong!'

'Yes. I want a big harp thing, like I heard a man play at a concert the other day.'

'She wants a harp!' cried Miss Valery in rapture. 'A lyre! She's not Greek, she's Greece!' She turned to Sidonia, 'Quite right, my dear, they always danced to harps.'

'Who's they?' asked Sidonia with interest.

'The ancient Greeks, they always danced to harps.'

Sidonia looked vague.

'Who were they?' she inquired, with her head a little on one side.

Rose Valery smiled across at Lady Shore, then she stroked Sidonia's hair. 'Haven't you heard of the ancient Greeks?'

'No,' said Sidonia, 'I don't think so.'

'She's a little backward,' Lady Shore explained; 'but she's not quite eight yet, you know.'

'Backward!' murmured Miss Valery; 'backward, and she wants a lyre!'

The piano began again.

'Oh, stop!' cried Sidonia. 'I hate it! It's hard and wrong.'

'Then what shall we do? Can you dance without music?'

'I'll hum,' said Sidonia firmly.

She hummed in a loud, self-reliant voice, moving rhythmically as she did so. The students whispered together and tittered, but Sidonia danced on, all unconscious. She changed the rhythm several times, fitting her steps to each new tune.

19

By the end of ten minutes, when she had stopped dancing, Miss Valery was pale with excitement.

'She's not Greek, she's Greece!' she repeated ecstatically.

Sidonia wandered unconcernedly away to a group of children at the far end of the room. 'Why are you wearing those ugly clothes?' she demanded. 'I like to dance naked, don't you?'

The children were silent, then one of them said: 'It's immodest to take off your things.'

'Immodest? What rot! That's what my nurse says, but she's an old ass!'

'Sidonia!' called Lady Shore rather sharply, as though some telepathy had reached her.

Sidonia turned. 'That's my mother,' she explained, 'she doesn't understand things either.'

'But it's perfect, quite perfect,' Rose Valery was saying. 'I hope you'll let me train her professionally.'

'Well, I hadn't thought of that yet,' said Lady Shore nervously. 'I should have to think that over, Miss Valery.'

'Good-bye, little Artemis, I shall see you next week,' said Miss Valery, kissing Sidonia.

'Good-bye,' said Sidonia coldly. She was feeling rather cross; she hated being called by names that she did not understand.

3

'They were awfully shocked when I told them I liked dancing naked,' Sidonia confided in the brougham going home.

'Oh, darling, you didn't tell them that! Oh, no, darling! And after mother explained that it was never done.'

Sidonia was silent; she sat back in her corner feeling foolish and shy. Had she done a dreadful thing in telling the children? She couldn't for the life of her see why. But now she foresaw that she might feel awkward at meeting those children again. Doubtless, like Blake, they considered her immodest, one of them had actually said so. She sat up suddenly, stiff and defiant. She didn't care a rap what any of them thought. She knew that she knew something they did not know, though she couldn't find a name for it even to herself.

'I will, I will, I will, I will, I will!' she murmured softly.

'Will what, my darling?'

'Dance naked,' said Sidonia.

And Lady Shore was silent with the silence of despair.

CHAPTER THREE

I

By the time Sidonia had had eighteen lessons Rose Valery was bewildered and outraged. It was all very well for a child to be pure Greek, but one must consider public susceptibilities.

Sidonia had proved herself to be a born dancer—oh, yes, Sidonia could dance! She had also proved to be an incorrigible rebel, and a proficient worker up of all the other children. Take, for instance, that matter of the cashmere tunics. Sidonia, aged seven, had disapproved of them, and had said so with complete disregard of people's feelings. Then again, she had laughed extremely rudely at the costumes at the students' performance, costumes made by mothers for the most part. It had given the greatest offence. The children were divided into those who cried resentfully and those who adored Sidonia. The former told their parents, who complained to Miss Valery; the latter aped Sidonia's disobedience. For Sidonia disobeyed as a matter of course whenever she thought she knew best, which, unfortunately, was often. She took her own poses and invented her own steps, and what was worse, refused point-blank to do the special limbering exercises upon which Miss Valery prided herself. True, Sidonia did not require to be limbered, but then the other children did; and since the exercises were not popular in any case, it soon became apparent that progress was at a standstill.

'Bend down! Lower—lower! And now jump!'

Sidonia pretended to fall flat. Her satellites giggled and also pretended.

'Attention!' thundered Miss Valery. 'Now! left arm forward and right knee up. One! Two! Three!—Spring!'

But only four sprang, the other five were satellites, and, like their leader, they remained standing in their awkward and wobbly pose.

'Spring!' screamed Miss Valery, hysterical with temper.

'Why?' inquired Sidonia mildly.

'Why? Because I say so!' shrilled Miss Valery.

'But it's so awfully ugly,' said Sidonia.

'Sidonia, be silent! I insist on your obeying.'

'I won't when I know it's ugly and wrong.'

'What do you mean by "wrong" I'd like to know?'

'Not right,' Sidonia said gravely.

She had gradually submitted to the sound of the piano, on finding that no harp was forthcoming, but she still insisted on singing loudly to herself, and this threw the other children out of step.

'Stop that humming at once, Sidonia.'

'I can't, it will come. It comes as I move my legs.'

A burst of laughter had greeted this sally, which, however, Sidonia had meant seriously.

Then, of course, there had been that remark about clothes, or rather the joy of the lack of them. The children, shocked at first, had gradually become amused, until one day Sidonia, stripping in the cloakroom, had given a demonstration of how to dance naked. Naturally the children had talked at home, with the result that three mothers and one uncle had written. The uncle had been particularly emphatic, he harped upon the word 'corruption'. He pointed out that although England was an island, it was, thank God, a very different island from one that he might mention. (An allusion completely lost on Miss Valery.) He stated at some length that the era was not pagan, but eminently Christian in all respects. He even went so far as to condemn the Valery School, comparing it to a cesspool of ancient iniquity. In conclusion he said that the prospectus was misleading, purposely so, no doubt; that he might feel it his duty to bring the matter up in the proper quarters, and that he wished to withdraw his niece immediately from further contamination.

Rose Valery was sadly considering these things in her third floor flat in Fulham. She did not want to lose the brilliant Sidonia, upon whom she had built such high hopes; at the same time, she could not afford to lose pupils because her school got a bad name. The letter of the uncle had upset her very much; he was quite an important uncle.

'Ridiculous!' she murmured. 'Utterly ridiculous! Stupid, prurient-minded old man!'

Still, she herself had been rather shocked; yes, she undoubtedly had been. It was one thing to worship the Greek in marble, always a modest medium; it was quite another to see it dancing minus clothes on linoleum in a Fulham cloakroom. Ah, that was it, the cloakroom was to blame, with its ugly and sordid personality, its dangling corpses of shabby coats, its rows of worn, misshapen shoes. Out in an oleander grove the child would have looked quite perfect. Blue sea, an Alma-Tadema fountain, and perhaps a potted lemon shrub or two, that was another charming alternative. Sidonia would have been wonderful in such a picture.

'It certainly was purely Greek,' Rose Valery repeated for the twentieth time that day. The repetition seemed to bring comfort, of which she felt sorely in need. 'Adorable Greece!' she murmured, letting her eyes stray round the room. They fell on Maple's second best suite, disguised now by one or two cheap goat-skins. On a mattress on stumps, masquerading as a divan, and loaded to repletion with gaudy cotton cushions. On a very inadequate pendant light muffled up in a pink silk handkerchief. On some photographs of Athens, the Acropolis and the Erechtheion; and last, but not least, on a plaster cast of the Niké of Samothrace standing alone with an ancient Greek lamp burning soulfully in front of it. Miss Valery believed that the lamp was ancient, she felt acutely the necessity to believe; the more she had doubts the more she believed, she was busy at believing now.

'I *am* a Greek reincarnation,' she said doubtfully; I feel that I simply must be!'

The story she had woven for her own consolation made

her blush whenever she thought of it. It dealt with her life as a Greek courtesan, and was very completely satisfying. The lamp was in some way connected with the story, that was why it had to be a genuine antique. She was never quite certain where she had kept it; probably in her bedchamber.

Her father had been a parson, of course, not more than ten years ago; but death had gathered him in rather suddenly, thus releasing his daughter to come to London and reconstruct classic postures. She thought of her father in this hour of trouble, a placid, imperturbable man; a helpful creature in serious emergencies, though lacking in imagination. She could never have mentioned her secret to her father, the secret of her Greek incarnation.

'Ah, well,' she mused, looking guiltily at the lamp, 'he knows it all now—all! all!'

But whether the Reverend Walter Valery knew all about it or not; whether or no death had convinced him, as life had failed to do, that reincarnation was a fact; whether or no in the light of his vaster, grander knowledge he was able to look with charity on his daughter's past career, there still remained the problem of Sidonia to tackle; Sidonia, who bid fair to wreck the Rose Valery School.

Miss Valery wandered over to a small looking-glass, and began to finger her hair. It bore a resemblance to scrambled eggs slipping out of a ribbon fillet. She had modelled this coiffure on sundry Greek friezes studied at the British Museum. It contained a slight suggestion of each one of these friezes, it also suggested the parsonage. Her pale blue eyes looked distinctly worried, and so did her worn, lined face; but she twitched down the fillet and puffed out her side-locks, after which she felt rather better.

'In those days we should not have minded at all,' she thought, returning to Sidonia, 'and yet, now——'

She paused. How she hated that 'Yet, now,' it was always popping up to fret her. For side by side with the Greek courtesan there marched the Pauline Christian—the creature of hymn-books and family prayers who had played the organ on Sundays; the creature who had carried soup to the poor, organized work parties and Mothers' Meetings. Hard to have to organize Mothers' Meetings when you yourself might be for ever unwed! She remembered having felt this very often in the past, but of course she had never mentioned it.

She shook herself impatiently and took up her pen; she really must write at once to Lady Shore.

'It is not that I, personally, minded,' she lied. 'I'm a pagan at heart, I fear, but what am I to do when people complain? I have my school to consider. Please don't misunderstand me, dear Lady Shore. I know there is no harm in Sidonia, no one could be with the child for five minutes without realizing her innate purity. But Sidonia is very self-willed indeed, which makes her difficult to teach. For one thing she refuses to do my set exercises, and they are so extremely important. Quite apart from the incident in our cloakroom last Monday, I have other causes for complaint. Sidonia puts the children up to grave disobedience; she herself, of course, will never obey. I cannot keep the class together much longer unless I can check this insubordination. At the same time, I do not want to lose Sidonia; she is a wonderfully beautiful dancer for her age, and I cannot but feel that she might easily be one of my best pupils. Would it not be better if I gave her private lessons?'

CHAPTER FOUR

I

As was only to be expected, Frances Reide was sent for. The message had been urgent: 'Come at once,' it had read. But when Frances arrived, somewhat shaken out of her usual composure, it was to find her friend examining a scarab through a large magnifying glass.

'I'm very uncertain about this one,' Lady Shore remarked. 'I suppose Godfrey wasn't deceived?'

Frances sat down abruptly. 'You sent for me, Prudence.'

'Yes, of course; it's about Sidonia.'

'Ah!' said Frances, lighting a cigarette, 'I guessed it might be about Sidonia.'

Lady Shore picked up the magnifying glass again, and flicked the scarab on to its stomach. 'I don't quite like the look of these cracks, they feel new; don't you think so, Frances?'

Frances gently pushed away the outstretched hand. 'And Sidonia?' she demanded quietly.

'Oh, Sidonia! Oh yes, she's a very naughty child. You'd better see what Miss Valery says.'

She began to fumble about among her manuscripts. 'Now where did I put the thing?' she complained. 'I'm always losing something in this house. Oh, by the way, Frances, Professor Wilson says he'll be only too delighted to write a preface for my book, that is, if it's ever finished! I've warned him that I'm always a very slow worker, and of course a life of Godfrey—be careful of those scarabs with your sleeve! Now where on earth have I put that letter? It was here a minute ago. Oh, well, it's gone,' she finished complacently. 'Wait a second, and I'll tell you all about it.'

Her hands strayed towards her immense reference book; she began turning over the pages rather guiltily.

'Hum!' remarked Frances, moving in her chair.

'Just a moment,' said Lady Shore, making notes.

Five minutes elapsed, then ten, then fifteen, at the end of which Frances rose. 'Come back!' she commanded, towering very tall, 'Come back at once, or I go.'

'What—what?' cried Lady Shore, in the voice of one roused suddenly out of deep sleep. 'Oh! Yes, of course. I'm so sorry, dear. Sidonia, it's about Sidonia.'

'The letter, please,' said Frances firmly.

'Yes, the letter—oh, here it is! It was under my blotting paper all the time. You'd better read it for yourself.'

Frances read the letter through without making any comment, then she said, 'We must send for Sidonia.'

'All right, but what are we going to say? Have you thought what we're going to say?'

' "*Don't*", that's what it occurs to me to say; just "*Don't*", and again—just "*Don't*".'

'Oh, it's all too tiresome,' broke out Lady Shore, 'at this moment it's really too bad. Why can't my child behave like other children? That's not much to ask of her, surely?'

Frances considered. 'I suppose,' she said, 'it's because she's not like other children. I think private lessons would be the right thing; she's obviously upsetting the school.'

'Yes, and now Miss Thomas has given me notice,' went on Lady Shore, almost tearful. 'She finds Sidonia impossible to teach except in those subjects that she likes.'

'Will you leave Sidonia to me for once?' inquired Frances, ringing the bell.

'Yes, oh, yes; if you can make any impression I shall be only too thankful, I assure you.'

'I want Miss Sidonia,' said Frances ominously.

'Yes, miss,' replied the footman, and presently Sidonia's head appeared thrust inquiringly round the door.

'Come here!' commanded Frances.

'Oh, hallo, Frances!' chirped Sidonia brightly, scenting a rising storm.

Frances surveyed her from head to foot. 'You're a nice one!' she remarked reflectively.

Sidonia fidgeted, and then she scowled. 'I'm busy at lessons,' she said.

'Yes, I'll bet you are. Well, I'm getting busy too, only it's going to be with you.' She glanced down at the letter in her hand, 'This is from Miss Valery, Sidonia.'

Sidonia flushed an uncomfortable pink, but the smile she gave was angelic.

'She's bored with you,' went on Frances calmly. 'She finds you a plaguy little bore; a most unpleasant child, I gather.'

Sidonia's eyes flashed. 'I like that!' she muttered.

'I'm glad you like it,' said Frances. 'Now suppose you just listen carefully to me. Do you know the meaning of "*Don't*"?'

Sidonia laughed rudely. 'Well, rather!' she scoffed. 'Who doesn't at my age, I wonder?'

'That's good,' said Frances, 'that's excellent, my child; understanding is half the battle.'

Sidonia looked uncomfortable again. 'You're laughing at me,' she remarked.

'Not at all, I assure you I was never more serious, as I hope soon to make you understand. And now for the first of my series of "*Don'ts*". We'll begin first, I think, with Miss Thomas. You refuse to study except when it suits you; you defy and persecute your governess.'

'I only choose the things I like best to do.'

'Then *Don't*,' said Frances quietly. 'And now about your dancing; you're rude and you're pert, and you set yourself above Miss Valery. She writes that you break up the class by refusing to obey her rules. She complains that you make the other children just as boring and as silly as you are yourself, that you take your own line regardless of orders; and, moreover, that your own line is quite idiotic. She says she feels sorry for you in her heart, because your behaviour is so babyish and stupid. She says you remind her of the pantomime clown, always trying to be clever when he's really only there to make people laugh at his antics.'

Sidonia gave a stifled cry of rage. 'Damn! Damnation!' she shouted.

'Sidonia!' It was Lady Shore, thoroughly shocked. 'What language! Where did you learn it?'

'And Blast!' cried Sidonia, now comfortably launched, 'and Swine and Bitch and Bloody!'

Lady Shore sank back in her chair with a moan.

Frances held up her finger. 'This is very interesting, Sidonia,' she remarked. 'Where did you learn those words?'

'Outside "The Three Bells", where we wait for the bus. I've been storing them up!' said Sidonia triumphantly.

'Just so, I see; you've been storing them up. Do you admire the men who use them?'

'No, I don't; they're beastly, dirty, common men. Why should I admire them, Frances?'

'Because if you store up what they say you must want to be like them, dirty and common!'

'I'm not, I'm *not*!' Sidonia stamped furiously. 'I'm not a bit dirty or common!'

'Do you think you'll want to use those words again?'

Sidonia considered, then she nodded.

'Then *Don't*,' said Frances. 'I merely say *Don't*. If you're wise you'll refrain from swearing. And now about the dancing. As I've said, Miss Valery is thoroughly bored. Do you know what it means to be a bore?'

Sidonia shook her head.

'Poor child,' said Frances pityingly, 'she's a bore without knowing what it means.'

'Then you tell me what it means!' commanded Sidonia.

'Of course I will, only I'm so sorry for you. A bore is a person who tries to be clever when they're really intensely stupid. Bores are the stupidest people on earth, because they don't realize that they're stupid. They think, as a rule, that they're very amusing and that what they do makes people laugh. Of course, people laugh, but it's not at what they do, it's always at them for doing it. And then, because they're so very stupid and think themselves so clever, they fancy they know better than everybody else; that's the greatest sign of the bore. It's quite enough to tell a bore to do a

30

thing for him or her to refuse you on the spot. They think, you see, that it's grand to refuse, that it makes them seem more important. A bore always wants to tell you their reasons for constantly being disobedient, but of course they never listen to yours when you try to explain why you want obedience, they're so sure that you must be in the wrong. They can't think things out like other people; poor dears, they've just got to do almost everything and anything that comes into their heads. In fact,' she concluded, sighing a little, 'they're ill, like the old man we saw last summer, the man they called "the village idiot".'

Sidonia stood petrified as though turned to stone. Then, 'You think I'm like that?' she asked softly.

'Oh, yes, you're a bore, so you must be like that. I thought it only fair to tell you.'

And then the storm broke. 'It's a lie!' shrieked Sidonia. 'It's a beastly lie! It's a lie! I'm not a stupid idiot like that man last summer! I'm not what you'd call a bore! I'm clever! I dance divinely, I tell you! Miss Valery herself said "divinely". I heard her! Of course, I don't obey, because I *do* know better. What she wants me to do is ugly! Ugly and stupid, stupid and ugly! She's a damned stupid old geezer!'

Frances smiled coldly. 'And why do you think you know better than Miss Valery?'

'I don't know, I don't know! I only know that I do. I feel all alive and queer when I'm dancing, it's like pins and needles all over; and I hate their piano, it ought to be a harp —and I hate Miss Thomas upstairs—and I hate the exercises and I won't, *won't* do them—and I hate sums and spelling and grammar—and I hate my clothes, they're ugly and hard, I want to tear them into strips!' Her face took on an inspired expression. 'Like this!' she screamed, tearing a large rent in her overall. 'Like this and this and this!'

Frances watched her quietly. 'I'm glad you mentioned clothes, I was coming to them,' she remarked.

Sidonia stopped tearing and eyed her antagonist.

'I don't think you let your clothes trouble you much, Sidonia, you're so constantly taking them off. I understand from this letter that you did so in the cloakroom at Miss Valery's—last Monday, I think. Am I right?'

Sidonia was silent, then she burst into tears. 'Bores don't undress, anyhow,' she sobbed angrily.

'Oh, indeed they do, they constantly undress in public, they like to be thought unusual. They think that people admire their daring, whereas really people laugh at them behind their backs, as no doubt they do at you, my poor child.'

Sidonia hurled herself on to the floor, where she rolled in a paroxysm of weeping. 'I don't do it to be queer and daring,' she wailed; 'I do it because my clothes feel all wrong!'

'Then *Don't*,' advised Frances gravely. 'Miss Valery will give you private lessons; you will dance alone in future.'

Sidonia sat up. 'No, no, *please*!' she wept. 'I don't want to dance alone, always.'

'But why not? You often dance all alone here.'

'Yes, I know, but it's not so right, somehow.'

'Not so right? What do you mean?'

Sidonia tried to stifle her sobs, she stuttered in her effort to speak calmly. 'I d-don't know what I mean, but we never d-did it, we always danced all together.' She paused. 'It was under some big dark trees—no—I can't remember, Frances.'

She fell to weeping bitterly again; but now the sobs came from her heart.

'Come here,' said Frances gently enough. 'One can grow out of being a bore if one tries.'

'It's all so queer,' choked Sidonia, 'but I don't know how. I think the devil gets me at times.'

'My darling,' said Lady Shore, almost weeping in sympathy, 'I'm quite sure the devil doesn't get my little girl.'

'But he does, I do be tellin' you,' Sidonia insisted, remembering the Irish housemaid. 'And Kathleen said he'd got a tail and two horns, perfectly awful horns! And Kathleen said that hell was a lake of burning bubbling fire where the wicked burn for ever and ever while the saints and angels watch them. Oh, I'm frightened!' wailed Sidonia, clinging to her mother, 'I'm frightened—perhaps bores go to hell!'

'Not while they're still young,' Frances reassured her, 'there's time for you yet if you'll only try hard.'

'I'm glad Kathleen's gone,' murmured Lady Shore. 'Whoever heard such rubbish!'

2

'Well, of all the queer fish!' remarked Frances thoughtfully, when Sidonia had disappeared upstairs. 'Did you hear what she said about dancing together under some big, dark trees?'

Lady Shore nodded mournfully, mopping her eyes. 'I think she remembers something.'

'I dare say, but what?'

'*Ah!*' said Lady Shore mysteriously, in the voice of one who knows.

'Now, Prudence, don't be childish, don't put on that voice; you don't know any more than I do.'

'I often wonder——' Lady Shore began. then she caught her friend's smile and stopped.

'Well, anyhow, let's hope I've done some good,' said Frances with assumed cheerfulness.

'You snubbed her so terribly,' whimpered Lady Shore. 'I kept wondering if Godfrey was listening.'

'Well, and if he was I'm quite sure he approved. Sir Godfrey was a man of good sense—sometimes.'

'Indeed he was not,' retorted his widow hotly; 'he was far too clever for that.'

3

After all, it was Frances who pleaded Sidonia's cause with Miss Valery. Frances went to see her a few days later, and was not very long in discerning the chink in her armour.

'I don't understand it myself, Miss Valery, it's almost as though Sidonia remembered something, something free and fearless and—pagan.'

Miss Valery started.

'I've thought that too, in fact I've felt convinced of it.'

'Then you think——you believe——?'

Miss Valery hesitated, but in the end the temptation proved too strong.

'It might be reincarnation, I suppose?' she said, with a laugh that was meant to sound sceptical.

'I wonder.' Frances' voice was thoughtful, she appeared to ponder the point.

'It would certainly explain a great many things,' said Miss Valery reflectively.

'Your appearance, for instance,' suggested Frances, with the wiliness of the serpent.

'No, really? Do you think that I look Greek, then?'

Frances hesitated, but only for a moment. 'Oh, but absolutely.'

Miss Valery blushed, and Frances pressed her advantage.

'You *feel* Greek to me somehow.' She let her eyes rest on Miss Valery's hair. 'It's everything about you,' she said mendaciously.

'It's very strange. I suppose such a thing might be?' Miss Valery's voice was eager now, her expression almost pleading.

Frances thought: 'Poor old thing, I am being a bit thick, but I want her to keep Sidonia, and after all if it makes her happy to think she looks Greek——'

Aloud she said: 'It's because there may be something in the reincarnation business that I hadn't the heart to oppose Sidonia about her dancing in class. The child seemed so certain that it was the right thing, that she ought to dance with the others. She said that they used to do it that way under some large, dark trees.'

'Ilex trees,' murmured Miss Valery reminiscently.

'Probably. You would know more about that than I would. Anyhow, that's what she said.'

Miss Valery emerged from a fleeting dream, and returned to Fulham with an effort.

'I'm so silly,' she explained, pressing her forehead; 'I'm so stupid about things sometimes. But I must consider my school, mustn't I? You do think I ought to be practical, don't you?' She looked up at Frances with a vague, Greek smile.

'It's very hard to be practical, Miss Reide, one's so apt to drift back a little.'

'I can understand that,' Frances told her soothingly. 'I expect that's Sidonia's trouble.' To herself she thought: 'I'm becoming an awful liar. I was not at all truthful to Sidonia when I interpreted that letter, and of course this poor woman doesn't look at all Greek. I hope the end will justify the means.'

Miss Valery was considering; Frances guessed that much from the far-away look in her eyes. Her fillet had slipped a little askew, and Frances felt suddenly sorry. But she sat on her conscience.

'I don't think,' she said softly, 'that Sidonia would get on at all well alone, not if she has this curious instinct about big, dark trees and things.'

Miss Valery looked at her appealingly. 'But there aren't any big, dark trees now, not here,' she said in a voice that struggled to be practical.

'Ah, no,' agreed Frances, 'there aren't any trees, but dancing with the children reminds her of them.'

'But,' objected Miss Valery, 'one would think—one might have thought——' She paused and flushed a little.

'Yes?' queried Frances, screwing in her eyeglass.

'Well—that I would have reminded her of them, too.'

'But you do, you do!' Frances hastened to assure her. 'I don't see how you could fail to remind her. But Sidonia seems to need the whole thing complete, that is with the exception of the trees, of course. Given you *and* the pupils she can picture the trees.' Her voice grew grave: 'I believe—I've got a feeling, that those trees may be more important than we know.'

Miss Valery nodded. 'It's not that I mind the nudity myself,' she said firmly.

'No, of course not; how absurd to imagine that you would!'

'But parents are so different,' Miss Valery went on; 'and as for uncles!'

'Oh, uncles!' agreed Frances in a voice of disdain. 'One hardly likes to think of them in connection with ancient

Greece! I suppose they must always have existed, even then, but if so they must have been quite different.'

'Everything was different,' said Miss Valery with a sigh.

'No, not you,' thought Frances, 'you could never have been different.' Aloud she said: 'Well, I've come here to plead Sidonia's cause, to ask you to take her back. Sidonia's not an ordinary child, and I know she's a little difficult; but if you will only try her again I can promise that she'll be more obedient.'

Miss Valery's defences gave way all at once. She flung out impetuous arms. 'I'll do it!' she exclaimed to no one in particular, unless to the Niké of Samothrace, upon whom her gaze rested triumphantly.

Frances got up. 'That's top-hole!' she remarked. 'Now I can relieve the child's mind.'

On the way home she felt a little doubtful. 'I do hope I have done the right thing,' she thought. 'It's a bit of a risk with Sidonia. The little devil shall keep her clothes on though, if I have to pin them to her skin!'

4

'But will you try to be really good?' inquired Frances of Sidonia that evening. 'Hang it all, child, I've done my best for you; don't go and make a fool of me!'

Sidonia considered this last remark for some seconds before replying; then she held out a grubby hand, which Frances shook very gravely.

'I like you, Frances,' Sidonia remarked.

'Good!' said Frances. 'Then it's a bargain?'

'I promise I'll *try*,' said Sidonia.

CHAPTER FIVE

I

SIDONIA did 'try' for nearly three years. The result was very disappointing. She had kept on her clothes, and had been quite docile anent the limbering exercises. She had led the dances in several performances, to the sound of applause from delighted onlookers. Indeed, for a time it seemed as though Frances had succeeded beyond her dreams.

Miss Valery was in the seventh heaven. What a pupil! What grace, what finish! Sidonia would take all London by storm, all England, perhaps all Europe! Sidonia would establish once and for all the claim of the divine antique. No more contortions on malformed toes, no more calves crudely bulging with muscle. No more anything except Miss Valery, her school of Greek dancing and her wonderful pupil. A few years now, and out would prance Sidonia to reform and educate the public.

And then, towards the end of the third year, something happened to Sidonia. Something very subtle and intangible at first, which, however, grew and grew. Miss Valery refused to believe her eyes, refused to believe her senses. Sidonia was working as well as ever, better; and yet—and yet—gradually the quality of her dancing was changing; it was growing distinctly British. Very painstakingly, stolidly even, she went through her steps and poses. She put on her wreath and her cashmere tunic, and proceeded to dance like any other child brought up in a Kensington square.

'No, no!' wailed Miss Valery. 'That was heavy, Sidonia. Prance lightly, dear. Prance as though you liked it!'

Sidonia the obedient had ceased to like it, nevertheless she pranced. Thump, thump, thump went Sidonia's feet.

And Miss Valery groaned aloud.

She sent for a harp and a man to play it. That might awaken a memory, she thought. Sidonia looked coldly upon the harp.

'I can't get my rhythm without the piano,' she declared, promptly going out of step.

'But you said—oh! Sidonia, don't you remember——?' Sidonia shook her head.

'Yes, you did, Sidonia, you said you'd like a harp.' Sidonia smiled rather vaguely.

'Oh yes, I remember; I was only a little girl then, though.'

'Absurd! You're only eleven now.'

'But it does make a difference,' said Sidonia.

Miss Valery said: 'You've broken my heart.'

And Sidonia felt genuinely sorry.

2

Frances took it very philosophically. 'You're like a young elephant,' she remarked one day, after having seen Sidonia dance.

Lady Shore said: 'What? She can't dance any more. Dear, dear!' Then forgot all about it.

The dancing lessons were soon abandoned, to Sidonia's immense relief. No one was any the worse for the episode, always excepting Miss Valery.

For close on eight months Sidonia lay low.

'After all, she's a very ordinary child,' thought Frances, with a tinge of regret. The old Sidonia had interested her to quite an unusual extent. The Sidonia that she now beheld was beautiful, it is true, but not vital. She was quiet and extraordinarily well behaved; rather dull, or so Frances thought.

Lady Shore said: 'Isn't it a comfort, Frances, Sidonia's settling down. I used to feel very anxious about her, she was really too highly strung.'

Sidonia was very attentive at lessons. The governess gave excellent reports. Indeed, the peace that now reigned in the house was almost celestial in nature. Sidonia was placid; she did her sums, she went for her walks in the park. She ate well, slept well, never complained, and seldom said anything amusing. Yet Frances was not quite easy in her mind.

'I don't like the vacuum feeling about her. I wonder what will get in next,' she thought; 'she's so empty just now, it can't last.'

3

'Good heavens!' exclaimed Lady Shore a week later, 'who's that playing the piano?'

She was sitting in her study with Professor Wilson, discussing his preface to her book.

Professor Wilson stared over his glasses. His expression was mildly surprised. 'Those researches regarding the mummy,' he said, 'should have very special attention.'

'Yes, but who's that playing the piano upstairs?' persisted Lady Shore, looking startled.

The Professor shook his head gently. 'And the photographs taken at the actual tomb must be carefully reproduced. I hope you will see to this, Lady Shore, I consider them most important. Though I cannot help doubting the identity of the mummy. Sir Godfrey knew that I always had my doubts.'

'There is not a soul in this house who can play,' said Lady Shore, turning a trifle pale. 'None of us here can play the piano.'

For some reason the sounds that now reached her ears filled her with strange alarm. For once the enthralling lure of the past failed completely to hold her, she could not concentrate on the Professor, could not concentrate on her book even. The identity of the mummy seemed suddenly less important than that of the mysterious musician. All she knew was that someone was playing a piano, which no one knew how to play.

'If you'll excuse me, I'll just go and see,' she said, hastening from the room.

At the drawing-room door she stood transfixed, speech-

39

less in her amazement. Perched on the piano stool sat Sidonia, eyes closed, apparently rapt. Her small, thin hands worked over the keys with astonishing ease and agility. She was playing a swift but demure little tune, somewhat reminiscent of Mozart. She opened her eyes and gazed at her mother.

'Oh, listen!' she exclaimed, 'just listen to me. Isn't it lovely? I'll play it again.'

She did so. Her foot groped and found the loud pedal. 'That's expression!' she said happily.

Lady Shore gasped. 'My darling child! But—but—where did you learn to play?'

'Nowhere, it just came this afternoon. Isn't it splendid? I love it!'

Lady Shore stared at her daughter in silence.

Presently she said: 'You hated the piano, you used to say so at your dancing.'

'I love it!' Sidonia repeated ecstatically.

Lady Shore felt suddenly very uncomfortable. She knew that had she been Ptah, the cat, the fur on her tail would have bristled. None of Sidonia's previous crazes had made her feel at all like this. She could not explain to herself why it was that the child at the piano frightened her. She turned, and quickly leaving the room, went down to Professor Wilson. She longed intensely for all the dear, familiar things —mummies and kas and sarcophagi.

'That was my daughter Sidonia,' she explained; 'I didn't know that she could play.'

4

From the moment of discovering her musical ability Sidonia played incessantly. Lady Shore got used to the new idea, and her fright gave place to partial resignation. From the Queen Anne drawing-room over her head came constant distracting sounds. They were liable to break out at all hours of the day, and to vary considerably in character. Sometimes it would be Tosti's ' Good-bye', picked out with one stumbling finger; but at other times the music flowed full and free, possessing a curious charm. Lady Shore, struggling with the intricacies of the past, tried not to listen as she wrote:

'Says Professor Budge in his introduction to *The Book of the Dead*: "He has conversed with Set, and visited Mendes the sacred Acacia Tree, Elephantine——" '

Sidonia struck a resounding chord. Lady Shore groaned.

'Oh dear, where was I? "Elephantine, the seat of the Goddess Sati, Qem-ur, Busiris, the temple of——" '

What on earth was Sidonia playing now? Something familiar? No—she took off her glasses and rubbed them fiercely. A languid time conducive to repose stole softly into the study. But Lady Shore did not find it reposeful; sighing, she sat back in her chair. The music trailed off, then faltered, then stopped. There ensued a series of fearful bangs; Sidonia must surely be striking the keys with her fists, it sounded like that. Lady Shore got up and hurried to the telephone; her movements were unnaturally flustered.

'Western 811,' she called sharply. 'No, *not* Kensington. Western, *Western* 811!'

A pause, and then—

'Hallo, is that you, Frances? Can you come round here? No, now at once. Oh, thank you, my dear; yes, do.'

Lady Shore turned and went up to the drawing-room. 'I won't have that noise, Sidonia!'

Sidonia was sitting hunched up on the stool. Her face was dark with anger.

'Take that!' she said furiously, striking again, while the piano vibrated painfully. Then she suddenly burst into dismal sobs. 'I can't find it! I can't make it come!'

'Dear, dear, this is dreadful!' complained Lady Shore.

'Yes, isn't it?' sobbed Sidonia.

Frances came quietly into the room.

'What's up?' she demanded, with some curiosity.

'I don't know. Sidonia's hitting the piano. She's angry, I don't know why.'

Frances said:

'Is it the music, Sidonia?'

Sidonia nodded vigorously.

41

'I nearly get it and then it goes. I can't make it right. It makes me feel funny. I feel like my monkey when his sawdust came out!'

'She means,' suggested Frances, 'that she doesn't know enough. She's got no knowledge of harmony.'

Sidonia wept more quietly now.

'I can't, can't, can't find something I want!'

'No, of course you can't,' soothed Frances kindly. 'You don't know the way to find it.' She turned with a smile to Lady Shore: 'You leave us, Prudence; I'll come down in a minute or two.'

And Lady Shore hastened to make her escape. She felt that the Present was closing in around her.

5

'I should chuck nearly everything else for her music, I really think it's worth while,' said Frances later on in the study. 'I'd let her go in for the piano seriously, as well as counterpoint and harmony.'

Lady Shore bit thoughtfully at a long-suffering thumbnail. In many a crisis that nail had consoled her; she thought it consoled her now.

'If you think so, dear,' she said a little doubtfully. 'But I can't forget the Greek dancing!'

'You *must* forget it,' said Frances, 'and begin all over again.'

'To Sidonia's beginnings there is no end!' murmured Lady Shore between nibbles.

'Shall I see about the lessons, or will you?' asked Frances.

'Oh, would you?'

'Yes, I'll go to-morrow and make inquiries. Would you like her to go to the Royal Academy?'

Lady Shore shook her head. 'No, I think better not. Remember what happened at Miss Valery's.'

'Yes, of course, but she won't want to play the piano naked.'

'Who can tell?' said Lady Shore resignedly.

Frances got up and stood staring at the floor. Her brow was heavy with thought. 'We've got to moor Sidonia, you know.'

'But how?' inquired Lady Shore.

'By finding the one right thing for her to do. There must be a right thing somewhere.'

Lady Shore nodded without conviction. 'She's so unlike Godfrey and me,' she sighed. 'She doesn't take the slightest interest in Egypt, and Egypt is very settling.'

'I doubt if you'll ever settle Sidonia, Prudence; that is, short of embalming her.'

'Please, don't be flippant!' said Lady Shore huffily.

'Flippant? Good heavens! I'm deadly serious. Sidonia would make the most alluring little mummy.'

'I hope she'll make a good citizen first.'

Frances looked suddenly rather grave. 'Yes, I hope so too,' she said quietly.

CHAPTER SIX

I

M R. WILLOWBY-SMITH was engaged for the piano; Mr. Lovell for harmony and counterpoint. They were both immensely impressed by Sidonia, that is for the first six months, after which it became apparent that something, they could never make out what, was obviously lacking in the child.

Sidonia seemed quite incapable, for instance, of advancing beyond the rudiments of harmony. She either could not or would not see why certain effects were unpermissible.

'But I like it that way,' she was wont to remark. 'I like my chord better than yours.'

In vain did Mr. Lovell explain patiently. Sidonia still clung to her chord. With the piano it was very much the same. Her technique remained quite fluent but faulty; her reading was a negligible quantity.

'When I look at those black blobs and O's and things it all goes out of my head,' she complained.

'Never mind your head,' said Mr. Smith tartly. 'You read what other people had in theirs.'

'I can't feel it like that,' Sidonia protested. 'I can only feel what's inside *me*.'

The hours of practice were usually spent in a series of improvisations.

'Sidonia, your scales!' Lady Shore would warn on her way downstairs to the study.

But having arrived at the scale of G, Sidonia would drift away again. And so it went on for a year. At the end of this period she suddenly remarked: 'I don't think I'll learn the piano any more, it doesn't seem to go with me.'

Frances was studying *The Times* at the moment, in search of a cook for Lady Shore, but she looked up quickly.

'What's that you say?'

'I don't think I'll learn——'

Frances threw down the paper and walked over to Sidonia, who was innocently playing with Horus. She caught the child's shoulder and swung her round. 'Wrong, Sidonia! You'd better guess again. You will go on learning the piano, my child.'

'I shan't!'

'Yes, you will!'

'No, I won't!'

'And I tell you you *will*!'

It came to Frances in her desperation that this moment was great with portent. If Sidonia gave up her piano now, if they allowed her to give it up, then the future would stretch out a dreary vista of countless failures to fulfil. The piano had suddenly become an emblem, a mystical symbol, a thing of psychic import.

'You will!' she repeated, glaring through her eyeglass.

'All right,' said Sidonia, suddenly acquiescent, 'but you're awfully silly to make me.'

2

As time went on they began to wonder if they had been silly to make her, for even Frances had to admit that Sidonia did not improve. She now played well, but only by ear, and only to amuse herself. It was often a very charming performance, for the girl had a sympathetic touch and a sense of rhythm and feeling. But at fifteen Sidonia had failed completely to master the more laborious intricacies of music, and moreover her incurably restless mind had stretched out another feeler. She suddenly bought some modelling wax and proceeded to model the head of a child. The effort was crude but arresting, the tousled head of a little girl wearing a wreath of leaves. The lips were curved in an innocent smile suggestive of laughter not very far off. The wide, square

45

brow and half-closed eyes looked almost uncannily wise. She showed her effort to Frances one day.

'It's me, as I used to feel,' she announced.

Frances, who had not taken the new craze very seriously, gazed at the head in silence. The spirit of Sidonia's earliest youth stared back at her from the wax, and yet for the life of her she could not praise; her heart was heavy with misgivings.

'Well?' said Sidonia eagerly. 'Don't you like it?'

'Yes, it's very nice indeed,' replied Frances.

3

At fifteen Sidonia was tall and slim. Her face was still childish, but now at times its expression was very grave. Her wide, green eyes were more questioning than ever, her mouth a little pathetic. Yet withal there was a defiance about her, she seemed almost to be defying herself. She had made few friends of her own age, though she naturally knew the other children in the square.

'Oh, yes, I know them,' she would say if questioned. 'Only they're not my friends.'

She appeared to feel that immense importance attached to the privilege of friendship. On the whole Sidonia was a lonely soul, except for her mother and Frances. She would sometimes talk this over with Frances, gravely, painstakingly even.

'I know I've not got friends, real friends. It's lonely not having a special friend.'

Frances had one day stretched out her hand: 'There's me, Sidonia, if you'll have me.'

But Sidonia had slowly shaken her head. 'No, you're mother's; you can't be mine too.'

'I can try.'

'No, I won't have half anything, Frances; I want all of a thing, every tiny scrap.'

And Frances had sighed, perplexed.

As one of the natural complications of her age, Sidonia became intensely shy; 'people' began to frighten her.

She dreaded the long afternoon once a month when Lady Shore was 'At Home'. Tongue-tied and miserably conscious of herself, she sat awkwardly upright, or passed plates of cake, or spilt cups of tea in an agony of embarrassment. Lady Shore herself was far from enjoying these uncomfortable social functions; but her generation, and, moreover, The Square imposed them upon her as a duty.

'I don't see why you should,' Sidonia argued. 'You always look bored and unhappy.'

'My dear, there are obligations in life.'

'Are there?' said Sidonia vaguely.

She became very idle, inclined to lose interest in most of her daily pursuits. She played when she felt like it, modelled when she felt like it, and when she felt like it (but this was seldom) she did her lessons, yet for the most part her days were passed in doing nothing at all.

'She's growing too fast,' said Lady Shore anxiously.

'I don't think so,' Frances reassured her. 'I think, on the contrary, that she's having a rest, a kind of hibernating period. One day soon she'll jump up like a giant refreshed. I wonder what will happen then?'

Upstairs in the schoolroom Sidonia was modelling with languid, uninterested fingers. Presently she pushed away the wax and sat staring out of the window. Her mouth drooped dolefully at the corners, her eyes were wet with self-pity.

'Oh, I'm so sorry for Sidonia!' she murmured. 'She's such an adorable, talented creature, and so unspeakably sad.'

These moods of ecstatic melancholy thrilled her from head to foot. She literally plunged into them head-foremost, grasping for a sorrow that she had never felt, whose nature she did not understand. For the moment, her violent fits of rage had almost completely left her. She seldom if ever now flew into a passion; she usually felt too depressed. She confided her state of mind to Frances one day in Kensington Gardens. It was April, and the trees either side of the Broad Walk were pushing out little, happy green thoughts along the whole length of their branches. Some matinal babies in

47

shiny perambulators grabbed at invisible motes in the air or kicked at their rugs with the will to grow.

'Aren't they pathetic?' said Sidonia.

Frances put in her eyeglass and looked.

'Jolly little beggars, I think.'

'Oh, Frances, how can you, when they've got to get old! It's dreadful to be a baby!'

'God bless you, child, they don't feel that way.'

'That's because they don't know, poor darlings!'

Frances turned to examine Sidonia; her lips twitched a little at the corners.

'You had frightful colic when you were an infant; I expect the memory of it haunts you.'

'Oh, it's not that,' said Sidonia loftily, 'it's the hopelessness of beginnings. I think sometimes I hate the sun. I'm like something that's crawled up out of a grave.'

'Don't be so morbid, Sidonia.'

'I can feel the mould clinging round my eyelids.'

'Then use your eyewash,' said Frances.

Sidonia ignored this tactless remark.

'I dream the most extraordinary things.'

'What sort of extraordinary things?'

'Oh, people I've known and don't know any more; passionate, yearning people.'

'They sound distinctly bad form to me,' said Frances with some decision.

'But, Frances, listen! I'm dreadfully sad. I'm all weighed down with things somehow—with the awful splendour and glory of living!'

'Have you been reading Swinburne?' inquired Frances suspiciously.

Sidonia nodded.

'Ah, I thought as much. He's given you mental indigestion.'

'Oh, you!' exclaimed Sidonia, trying not to laugh. 'You don't understand; you'd never understand. I believe it's the fault of that eyeglass.'

'Maybe; you see, I'm an eye to the good, that helps me to see through Sidonia.'

'And what do you see when you've seen through me?' Sidonia inquired with deep interest.

'Everything and nothing, if you want to know. A kind of kaleidoscopic muddle.'

Sidonia felt suddenly in need of love. She sidled up closer and took Frances' hand. 'I do love you, Frances, though you're not my special friend. Do tell me all you think about me.'

'You old hypocrite!' said Frances. 'This is cupboard love. What it is you want at the moment?'

Sidonia stared tragically out into space. 'Sympathy, please,' she whispered.

'You'll find the liver pills in the right-hand corner of the bathroom cupboard. I should take a dose,' advised Frances.

CHAPTER SEVEN

I

By the time the trees in the Broad Walk were dropping their leaves Sidonia had begun to recover. She no longer found the babies quite so pathetic, in fact they rather bored her. It may have been the two months of sea air in Devonshire that had brought a faint colour back to her cheeks and restored to her a faint sense of humour. Or it may have been merely that her hibernating period was drawing quickly to a close. This latter was certainly Frances' opinion, as she watched her with increasing interest.

Whatever the reason, there could be no doubt that Sidonia was stirring again. The whole household, including Lady Shore, was uncomfortably aware of the fact.

The British Museum was the latest goal of Sidonia's spiritual cravings. No matter what the weather, the protesting Blake was dragged forth to this storehouse of learning.

'I'm fair creaking with rheumatism,' grumbled Blake. 'Nasty, cold vault of a place.'

But Sidonia, all smiles and cajoleries, persisted nevertheless.

'Does she study the mummies?' inquired Lady Shore, a faint note of hope in her voice.

'Bless you, no, me-lady! She never goes near them, it's them freezing things that she's after.'

'The freezing things?'

'Yes, immodest I calls them.'

Lady Shore had a sudden inspiration. 'Do you mean the Parthenon Frieze?'

'That's it me-lady,' said Blake primly. 'The Parthenon Frieze; it's horrid!'

Lady Shore sighed and pushed back her hair; she had hoped that it might have been mummies. She was beginning to fret over the gulf that lay between her and her only child. If Sidonia could have been like many other girls, showing no marked interest in anything in particular, Lady Shore would have felt far less aggrieved, less resentful on Sir Godfrey's behalf. She sighed again and turned to Blake.

'It's antique, not immodest,' she said patiently.

'A body's a body, excuse me, me-lady, whether it's ancient or modern, and ancient or modern, clothes is clothes, and no clothes is no clothes to my way of thinking.'

'But what does Miss Sidonia do when she gets to the Parthenon Frieze?'

'She just stands there staring and talking to herself about its being wonderful and such-like, and then she goes flying all round the room and standing in front of them others. Awful some of them is, me-lady, not fit for her eyes to rest on. And yesterday she talked to a man who was drawing a naked figure, discussed it with him, she did indeed, and he listening quite attentive. And on the way home she bought a sketch book and said she was going to draw, too. She scarcely gives me time to eat me Bath bun and drink up me glass of milk. I do think you might speak to Miss Sidonia, me-lady, she's like someone what's lost their wits.'

In the meantime Sidonia, now thoroughly alight, was working with enthusiastic fury. All day long and every day her hands were sticky with wax. She could scarcely be induced to come down to meals, and when she did so her attention wandered, her food was swallowed in gulps. Mere lessons naturally went by the board; the governess complained and Lady Shore wept. She who so seldom permitted herself tears wept helplessly on Frances' shoulder.

'My child is mad, quite mad!' she choked. 'What would her poor father say?'

'You might forbid her,' suggested Frances feebly.

'Forbid her?' cried Lady Shore, tearfully shrill. 'And what good would that do, I'd like to know?'

'Probably none,' said Frances.

2

There were times now when Sidonia experienced true joy, the infinite joy of creation. At others her soul was bathed in a peace whose depths she could not fathom. She was still too young to analyse these things, to understand their significance; but now, when she held the soft wax in her hands, pliant, responsive, almost living, she thought, she said to herself: 'This is what I've been needing; this thing is somehow *me*.' Her face grew more animated, fuller, clearer. She sang as she dashed about the house, always eager to get back to work. Models she had none, so she press-ganged the servants, the housemaid, Blake—even Ptah, the cat, came in for his share of the burden. She dragged her board down to the stately drawing-room and made Frances sit in the evenings. She left lumps of wax on the Queen Anne tables, and once on the study divan. Lady Shore sat down on this latter outrage, and went to a bargain sale at Barker's before it had been discovered.

'Oh, if I could only understand you, Sidonia!' she complained despondently.

'Well,' said Sidonia, 'it's like a kind of memory, the memory of something wonderful you've dreamt about, but can't quite get back when you wake.'

'But do you mean it? Are you in earnest?'

'How can you ask me such a thing as that, Mother? Can't you see that I mean it?'

Lady Shore felt abashed. 'It's certainly a nice quiet talent,' she said, suddenly remembering the piano.

Sidonia frowned.

'Then it oughtn't to be. A statue ought to strike you all of a heap; come alive at you, like Galatea. It ought to make you gasp for breath, or go wild with pleasure and shout.'

'I never heard that Pygmalion shouted,' murmured Lady Shore apprehensively.

'I expect he did, though,' Sidonia told her. 'I expect he shouted and danced for joy; that's how you feel when you're not too muzzy with trying to get things back.'

Lady Shore stared helplessly at her child in an effort to understand. She thought of Sir Godfrey, so placid, so frail, a trifle devitalized even. She thought of herself, of her own past youth, with its quiet, well-ordered days; of her married life, with its charming ideal and its one all-absorbing interest. No, she could not comprehend Sidonia as the outcome of so discreet a mating. She almost began to doubt her own virtue, in view of present events.

'My dear——' she began, then stopped abruptly, not quite knowing what to say.

A protest of some sort was clearly needed, but was difficult to formulate. Indeed, there was little room just now in her mind for Sidonia's vagaries. Unless she was forced to meet them face to face, she most earnestly wished to forget them. Professor Wilson was being very tiresome anent the identity of Sir Godfrey's pet mummy. The book, which had taken her so long to finish, was now being held up by his preface. In vain did Lady Shore explain that Sir Godfrey had never been wrong; in vain did she bring out mountains of notes in that great Egyptologist's handwriting. Professor Wilson only smiled kindly and clung to his own opinion. She wished him to write the preface to her book, he and Godfrey had been such old friends—still—to choose this occasion to air his doubts—ah, no! It was too disloyal. This question of the mummy might lead to a quarrel, might end in a rupture, a most distressing thought. After all, there might be no preface to her book, and she felt that it needed a preface. She, the most unsuspicious of creatures, had almost begun to wonder lately whether Professor Wilson was jealous. He might very well be jealous of Godfrey, who had, after all, discovered the mummy. Her mind was straying away to this trouble, when she realized that Sidonia was speaking again.

'You see, it's got a kind of a high-light, and I'll need that when I have lessons.'

'What's got a high-light?' inquired Lady Shore, riveting her attention with an effort.

'Why, the attic upstairs. I must have it, Mother, before I can really learn modelling.'

Through the worry and distraction of Lady Shore's brain one thing leapt into distinctness; Sidonia had started yet another idea and was off once again with the bit between her teeth.

'You want lessons in modelling, you say?' she faltered.

'And in painting and drawing,' said Sidonia.

'But since when have you felt that you want to be an artist?'

Sidonia considered for a moment.

'Well, always really, at the back of my head, only it's just coming out.'

Lady Shore flushed with sudden irritation, an unusual sensation for her.

'If you were not my own child, Sidonia, I should lose all patience with you. I sometimes think you must be mad, flying from one thing to another as you do; I said so to Frances the other day.'

Sidonia laughed.

'I may be mad, Frances says genius is always rather mad.'

'And does Frances say that you are a genius?'

'No,' said Sidonia, 'but I am.'

This statement took Lady Shore aback, it sounded so very conclusive.

'That's why I'm morbid,' Sidonia went on happily, 'genius is always despondent.'

'Rubbish!' retorted Lady Shore. 'Your father was the happiest man on earth, and he was certainly a genius.'

'That must be where it comes from then,' said Sidonia, 'I've inherited my genius from him.'

Lady Shore frowned.

'And this is just a whim, like all the rest of your crazes!'

'No, Mother, it's not, this is desperately serious. I mean to do simply *enormous* statues, things that they'll have to put very high up so as to make them look right.'

'But look at your dancing,' began Lady Shore, 'look at your music, your harmony——'

Sidonia smiled her delightful smile, showing her small white teeth.

'Nothings, just nothings, they didn't count; this is the thing that's *me*.'

'You've said that every time, Sidonia.'

'Then I must have been making mistakes. It's dreadfully difficult to explain—father would probably have understood, because he was a genius too.'

Lady Shore felt her vagueness coming on; she gripped at the nearest tangible straw.

'The attic is full of boxes, my dear, and the boxes are full of your father's papers.' She was thankful she had remembered that, it obviously settled the question. 'And so,' she concluded, gaining self-assurance, 'you can't have it for a studio, can you?'

At that moment Horus began to scream. His screams sounded rather unusual.

'Oh, dear!' cried Lady Shore, springing to her feet. 'I believe he's caught up in his swing again.'

The parrot was literally brawling by now. 'Help! Help! You old fool!' he yelled.

'I'm coming, ducky,' called back Lady Shore. 'Be good for a moment. I'm coming!'

She hurried away to release the bird, and Sidonia began to laugh. She felt suddenly very far from depressed; she scented a coming battle. 'I will have that attic,' she said aloud. 'I will have that attic, if the devil's in the way!'

A defiant, combative spirit possessed her; she longed to defy someone openly. Her mother was not a worthy antagonist, too meek, too easily flustered. She seized her hat and coat and tore along the square in search of the more fulfilling Frances.

3

Frances sat at the large writing-table in the little front room in Young Street. A cigarette hung between her lips, the smoke drifted under her eyeglass. She let the glass drop and rubbed her eye; then she stretched and laid down her pen. Turning in her chair, she surveyed the room with a little grunt of contentment. On the wide, low sill of the leaded-paned window stood bowls of comfortable-looking earth that would presently give forth hyacinths and jonquils. A log-fire crackled in the grate. The room smelt of burning ship's logs, leather furniture, beeswax and cigarette smoke. Nearly everything in it was much too large, including a huge, red leather arm-chair, which looked as though it had been transported from the smoking-room of a Piccadilly club. The portrait of an ancestor in full regimentals hung over the mantelpiece. He might have been Frances in fancy dress, a fact of which she was secretly proud. In spite of the smallness of the room and the massive nature of the furniture, the place had an atmosphere of comfort that was somehow more masculine than feminine. Frances had managed to express herself in this tiny house in Young Street.

She sat down contentedly in the huge arm-chair and stretched out her feet to the fire. She felt warm and rather deliciously tired, her eyelids drooped and she dozed.

'Rot! I must see Miss Reide, I tell you. Of course she's at home to me.'

Frances sat up and opened her eyes. The commotion in the hall continued.

'She's not at home, miss.'

'You're new, you don't know. Frances!' came a loud, impatient voice.

'Come in, come in! Don't stand there shouting.'

Sidonia blew in like a whirlwind.

'And now,' began Frances, 'what's it all about?'

'The attic!' panted Sidonia.

Frances surveyed the turbulent figure as it stood in a patch of late winter sunshine. The thick, auburn hair glowed like copper in the light; the face was flushed, with parted lips; the strange, green eyes gleamed angrily. Tall and straight as a young birch tree, Sidonia stood and confronted her.

'Yes,' thought Frances, 'you're very lovely.' Aloud she said, 'What attic?'

'I intend to have it whatever any of you say. I intend to do

56

my work there.' Sidonia's voice was distinctly provocative. 'I intend to have it!' she repeated.

'There are quite a lot of attics in London, Sidonia, several million of them, I believe. Which particular one may this be?'

'Our attic at home. Why shouldn't I have it?'

'I'm sure I don't know,' said Frances.

'You'll say that I mayn't.'

'I haven't said so.'

'No, but you will; I feel it.'

'Have you come round here and roused me from sleep hoping that I'll say that you *can't* have the attic?'

Sidonia hesitated uncomfortably for a moment. This was precisely what she had done.

'I've come round to tell you that I *mean* to have the attic.'

'Well, that's that!' said Frances, and yawned.

Things were not going in quite the right way. Frances was palpably bored.

'You none of you know how to treat a genius. I sometimes think I'd like to hang myself!' cried Sidonia tragically, watching the effect.

'It's a nasty, gurgly kind of death; I don't think I'd choose it,' said Frances, smiling.

'Who cares a damn for Egyptology!' Sidonia burst out furiously. 'Who cares for beastly, old, mouldy notes when they've got the Parthenon Frieze! Who cares for rotten old Rameses when they've got the Apoxyomenos! Who cares for mummies when they've got the Steles! Who cares for kas when they've got Ilyssus! Who cares——'

'Oh, stop, do stop!' cried Frances. 'I care for nothing at all at the moment except to know what all this fuss is about.'

Sidonia stamped her foot angrily.

'Mother's just said that I can't have the attic for a studio, because father's papers are up there; and I want to have lessons in modelling, I tell you, I must have lessons in modelling.'

'So that's it, is it? Sit down, Sidonia, and let us try to keep calm.'

Sidonia obeyed with a lowering brow.

'Now,' said Frances, 'we can talk. You're in one of those

mental cyclones of yours, and this time it blows towards sculpture. A little while ago it was playing the piano, and before that it was Greek dancing. Before that again—oh, I can't remember, there have been so many of them. At the moment, however, it's modelling, you say. How long do you think that will last?'

She looked at Sidonia with a questioning smile, but the smile died away on her lips. Sidonia's eyes were full of tears which overflowed and ran down. The girl was sitting in a desolate heap, huddled up in the corner of the chair. Nothing remained of the lust for battle that had brought her hot-foot to Frances. Something in the dreariness of the figure made Frances' heart contract sharply. These tears were quite different from any other tears she had ever seen Sidonia shed. Whatever their source, they were falling slowly, like the difficult tears of the old. Frances became uncomfortably aware that this trouble was not of the complacent kind in which Sidonia had been indulging recently. She moved rather nervously and cleared her throat. If Sidonia would only have wept aloud; but she did not, she just sat there staring into space, while the tears welled up silently and fell. Neither of them spoke for a minute or two, then Frances said:

'I am your friend, though you can't have all of me, Sidonia.'

Sidonia groped for the proffered hand and held it tightly in hers. She said:

'You see, I'm different somehow—it's beastly, but there it is. I'm always pretending I like myself, that's just to hear myself say it. I hate myself, only I can't get away—I can't get away from myself. I always mean to go on with things, but I can't go on when they've gone. The things get away, but I'm stuck here—Frances, I swear I'm telling the truth—I'm stuck here, but they go.' She paused, peering anxiously at Frances through her tears. 'You do believe me, don't you?'

Frances nodded.

'But to-morrow, Sidonia, you'll probably feel quite different again.'

Something very like fear came into Sidonia's eyes. 'Don't say that!' she cried shrilly, 'it scares me.'

CHAPTER EIGHT

I

Sɪᴅᴏɴɪᴀ got her attic in the end, as she usually did get what she wanted, by the force of sheer self-assertion. Rather than hear that monotonous request, repeated at ever-shortening intervals; rather than face that discontented brow, those angry, reproachful eyes; rather, indeed, than live in the same house with a foiled but still combative Sidonia, Lady Shore had moved her Godfrey's papers to the big wine cellar, which was fortunately dry.

'After all,' she explained apologetically to Frances, 'I used to go upstairs; well, now I go down. I don't suppose it makes much difference.'

And Sidonia worked. Quietly, methodically, she settled into her stride. The first fine frenzy for modelling left her, but now no hiatus ensued; the fire died down to a steady glow of strong, well-balanced industry. She was like a creature who after many storms had sailed into deep, calm water. Lady Shore had, of course, provided masters, as she always provided in the end. It would have been far simpler had Sidonia attended classes, but to this Lady Shore would not consent, and Sidonia, well satisfied for the moment, at all events, did not press the matter.

Unfamiliar figures came and went in the house; seedy-looking youths, pretty, frowsy girls, an occasional octogenarian. Sidonia's taste in models was distinctly catholic, so catholic indeed that on one occasion Lady Shore had screamed softly, suspecting a burglar, when she saw what was going upstairs. On the whole, however, she had no cause for complaint. High overhead, in her attic eyrie, Sidonia was living her own life very fully, but for the moment without ostentation. Humbleness of spirit she had not attained, but the self-satisfaction which she now experienced was too vast and too deep to find ready expression.

She had said, and had meant every word at the time, that she hated herself, her fickleness, her strangeness. She had thought herself strange that day not long ago when she had sat talking to Frances. How frightened she had been. Yes, actually frightened; she remembered this now with surprise. But all that had passed, and if she was strange, she had nothing to fear from her beautiful, soul-satisfying strangeness. Her strangeness made her feel calm, assured, even a little aloof. It became a delightful condition of mind. 'The Above and Beyonds', she christened this state, a name that undoubtedly expressed it very well.

Her modelling was remarkable, everyone said so, including Sidonia herself. But she said it so gently, so tenderly even, that no one took exception, unless it were Frances.

'Pride cometh before a fall!' cautioned Frances.

And Sidonia answered very simply: 'Yes, but this isn't pride.'

2

A year slipped by, and another year. Lady Shore began a new book.

'It's so peaceful, I think I could work again.'

'Sidonia's seventeen,' said Frances.

Lady Shore looked puzzled.

'So she is, my dear. I shall write my hand-book on scarabs.'

'Some people would think Sidonia quite lovely.'

'Yes, of course. Have you seen my spectacles?'

'Here they are. We don't know many men, do we, Prudence?'

Lady Shore was trying hard to breathe a scratch off her glasses. 'There's Professor Wilson,' she murmured abstractedly.

'I said men, not ichthyosauri!' snapped Frances.

'But why do we want to know men, my dear?'

'There's safety in numbers,' Frances remarked thoughtfully; 'the thing to be dreaded and feared is one man. One man is usually the wrong one.'

Lady Shore put down her glasses.

'Oh, dear!' she complained, 'I know, you want to discuss something tiresome.'

'Sidonia's seventeen,' repeated Frances stubbornly. 'Sidonia's no longer a child.'

Lady Shore looked frightened.

'You don't think—you can't mean—oh, no! Not Professor Wilson?'

Frances lit a cigarette.

'Honest, Prudence, you're not safe to be at large in this twentieth century! No, I do not mean Professor Wilson; I don't mean anyone at present; but the day may come soon when Sidonia will look about her, and then there'd be safety in numbers.'

Lady Shore stared at her friend rather blankly; her eyes seemed unusually weak. Presently she said: 'Is it marriage, you mean?'

'Well, I don't mean free love!' retorted Frances.

Lady Shore considered. She gloomed for a while, then suddenly brightened up.

'The Gilberts, they've got a nice boy, I believe.'

'Yes, he's twelve,' said Frances dryly.

'Oh, no! He must surely be quite sixteen.'

'He's in Etons,' murmured Frances.

'Dear me, so he is! No, that won't do. Now let me think. What about Lady Poulsen?'

'Yes, there's Joe Poulsen, he's twenty-three, but he's only one,' objected Frances.

'Still, he's a beginning,' Lady Shore reminded her.

3

They invited Joe Poulsen to dinner forthwith. He came; a well-groomed, good-looking young man, a facsimile of every other well-groomed young man that Sidonia had ever seen. He spoke; his voice was pleasantly modulated. His voice and his words were the voice and the words of every other youth who had been in his set at Oxford. Sidonia had no experience of youths, yet she divined that this was so. During dinner the young people were distinctly constrained. In his thoughts he blamed Sidonia, and in hers she blamed him. His conversation seemed to her somewhat limited.

'I say, do you play tennis? Do you go to many dances? My mother's going to give a little hop soon, you must come. Have you been to that new show at Daly's? It's awfully jolly, the clothes are awfully pretty, and it's got some ripping tunes. Do you play golf? No? I say, what a sell! I'd like to have played you one day.'

His rather weak mouth smiled continually at her. His eyes were controlled, but admiring. He thought her somewhat heavy in hand, but nevertheless very beautiful. Sidonia, who at seventeen had quite lost her shyness, surveyed Joe Poulsen with critical eyes. She found him good-looking, but dull. She did not play tennis or go to dances. Musical comedies she frankly loathed, and in golf she took less than no interest. To his well-meant but vapid questions she could find no helpful answers. She heard herself murmuring, 'No,' 'No,' and 'No.' It sounded ungracious, almost rude. It was strange that he never once made a bull's-eye—that all his shots flew so wide of the mark. She tried to give him a lead once or twice, but he seemed incapable of following. After dinner matters did not improve.

'Play for us, darling,' suggested Lady Shore, nervously aware of atmospheric flatness.

Sidonia obeyed, only too glad to escape from the boredom that was stealing over her. She felt that she was playing rather extra well, conscious of countless little pleasant melodies that went drifting through her brain and out by her fingers. But before her last chord had completely died away she could hear young Poulsen's voice.

'Thanks most awfully,' he was murmuring. And then, because she would not even smile at him, 'Simply ripping!'

She asked him: 'Are you fond of music?'

'Rather!' he lied glibly.

Sidonia yawned and glanced at the clock.

62

Presently Lady Shore beckoned to Frances, who followed her into the back drawing-room.

'I thought they might get on better if we left them for a little,' whispered Lady Shore, trying to look crafty.

'I say that's a ripping dress you've got on!' began Joe Poulsen as soon as they were alone. 'It goes so awfully well with your hair.'

They were sitting side by side on the chesterfield. Sidonia was wondering rather uncomfortably how they had managed to get there. Her strong and yet delicate profile was towards him, and he noticed the charming, blunt tip to her nose and the gracious line of her lips.

'You've got wonderful hair!' he murmured, thinking of her lips, and of how unusually delicate was their colour, how different their texture from those of his sister.

She turned and looked at him, smiling a little.

'I must be older than he is,' she thought. 'I feel like a great-aunt or something.'

His own hair was fair and straight. His eyes were brown, very round, very stupid. They were looking stupid now and a little sheepish.

'I do wish you danced,' he said rather desperately, touching her sleeve with his finger.

Out of sudden compassion she humbled herself.

'I must learn; it's so stupid of me not to!'

'Oh, I say!' he protested. 'Don't call yourself stupid! You're dreadfully clever, aren't you?'

To his infinite surprise Sidonia nodded gravely.

'I'm a sculptor,' she told him. 'I shall be great some day.'

He stared.

'Good Lord!' he murmured.

She surveyed him calmly.

'You'd make a good model, I like the line of your throat.'

His hand went up quickly to his faultless bow.

'I say!' he laughed, looking uneasy.

'And your jaw's rather jolly when your face is in repose; you've got a good bony construction.'

'Oh, hell! This is awful!' he thought. Aloud he said: 'Yes

63

—thanks awfully—I'm afraid I'm rather a duffer about art. I say, it must be getting abominably late.'

'Yes, I think it is,' agreed Sidonia.

They were sitting in silence when Lady Shore came back, and their faces lit up with relief at her entrance.

'I'm afraid I must be going,' said Joe Poulsen, jumping up with ill-concealed alacrity.

He departed, and Sidonia gave an enormous yawn.

'I'm for my bed,' she announced.

Lady Shore and Frances looked at each other. Then Lady Shore smiled contentedly. Sidonia's quick steps could be heard on the stairs; she was literally running up to bed.

'We must get more and more,' announced Frances. 'Go out into the highways and by-ways and compel them to come in.'

But Lady Shore was not listening. She was bathed in a flood of immense relief. After all, no need to think of marriage for Sidonia, not for several years in any case. Sidonia was not at all what Frances imagined. Sidonia quite obviously did not like men. Sidonia was wedded to her art.

She told these glad tidings to Frances.

4

Frances remained entirely unconvinced. Sidonia did not look like someone wedded to their art. Yet neither did she seem to suggest the wedded state in its purely physical sense. Her mind was too explorative, her beauty too unusual, almost a little strange, or so it seemed to Frances. There was something flame-like in the quality of her face, and at the same time cold and aloof. That was it, the girl was like some queer, unnatural fire, that gave out brilliance but no heat.

'I pity the poor devil who tries to warm his hands at that glow!' she thought; 'and yet one never knows——'

She seemed to be for ever pondering Sidonia, these days, for ever trying to solve the enigma. 'I never thought that the infant I used to snub could have got firm hold of me like this,' she mused. 'It's like ivy with me for the long-suffering oak; I'm not sure I enjoy the feeling.'

But whether Frances enjoyed it or not, Sidonia had certainly begun to cling. Clinging is perhaps too tame a word; what Sidonia was doing was to shoot out roots, and firmly, triumphantly grow. She had suddenly realized Frances Reide one day in the attic studio: her queer, flat, Oriental eyes, her skin smooth and colourless as vellum, the gentlemanly tinge of grey hair on her temples, the hard-bitten, whimsical mouth.

'What on earth are you staring at?' Frances had inquired.

'At you. I've just found you. You're awfully jolly!'

'Well, it's taken you a long time to find that out.'

'I know, that's the fun of it; it's really rather thrilling.'

And Frances had laughed uneasily.

She laughed a little now, considering Sidonia in conjunction with Sidonia's mother; in conjunction with her own staid, comfortable house; with the enormous red leather chair that suggested the smoking-room of a Piccadilly club, the chair that was gradually becoming Sidonia's.

Sidonia had discovered the red leather chair soon after discovering Frances.

'Ripping!' she had said contentedly one day, curling up in the comfortable depths.

Frances had agreed.

'Yes, my favourite chair.'

'No, mine,' Sidonia had announced.

There had been no really turbulent scenes since the ownership of the attic had been settled.

'My work has given me perfect poise,' was the way Sidonia explained it.

And, indeed, as far as the work was concerned they had really nothing to complain of. However, as Sidonia was careful to point out, inspirational work was the sort of end that required a variety of means.

'You rest me, Frances, and stimulate me too; you're good for my work. You don't mind, do you, if I come round to see you pretty often?'

And Frances, who had hitherto pictured her home as a

kind of Englishman's castle, found herself giving a pleased consent to Sidonia's impromptu visits.

There was another aspect of the case, however, that was more difficult to deal with. Sidonia's visits were all very well, interfering as they did with no one but Frances. It was quite a different thing when Sidonia began to demand her frequent presence in the studio. It would be:

'Come up and look at my new group, Frances.'

'Not now, your mother wants me.'

'Oh, rot! She's forgotten your very existence; she's deep in Thutmosis II!'

Or:

'Let's make tea in the attic this afternoon, just you and me, and we'll talk.'

'Heavens, child, we've talked for the last ten years!'

'No, we haven't, we've only just found each other.'

'There's nothing whatever in me to find. I'm forty-five and a dragon.'

'Well, I'm not Saint George, so don't be afraid. You're a very well-tailored dragon.'

'Sidonia, you know it's your mother's day at home. I must go and pass round the cake.'

'Good Lord! How funny! You passing round cake!'

And it seemed rather funny, somehow.

It was all so unexpected, so startling even. Frances was startled at herself.

'Am I fifteen years old,' was her fierce mental comment, 'to enjoy tea and hot buttered toast in an attic?'

'You're young, young, young!' Sidonia was fond of saying, squatting in a limp, adoring heap at Frances' knee.

'No, I'm old, old, old!' Frances would assure her, with a mixture of amusement not untinged with desperation. Sidonia's roots were very tough indeed.

'Well, but nobody knows your real age, Frances; they say you've always looked the same.'

'But you know, I've told you; and I don't look the same, I was rather plump at your age.'

'Then I like you as you are, tall and beautifully thin, with your darling, flat Chink eyes.'

'I'm as blind as a bat; perhaps you like this too?' said Frances, screwing in her eyeglass.

'Of course I like it, you vain old thing; you only did that because you knew I liked it.'

'Do come down, Sidonia, and help me with the tea.'

'Not much! I detest a Zoo.'

'It's not a Zoo, you impertinent child.'

'Yes, it is; feed the old bears with buns!'

'But they're not all old bears. Frank Littleton's coming. Don't you want to know any young men?'

'Not the kind that you've snared into poor mother's Zoo. I don't want to know young men, anyhow.'

'Damn it all!' exclaimed Frances, suddenly angry, 'you must and you shall know young men.'

'Oh, you lamb! Do you really want me off hand?'

Frances lit a cigarette in silence.

No, assuredly it would not do; Sidonia ought to get married. Well, not married, perhaps, she was too young for that, but engaged. An engagement was steadying. And because she was conscious of a little empty feeling at the thought of Sidonia engaged, being Frances, she stubbornly redoubled her efforts to bring an engagement about.

Of course, there was no necessity for Sidonia to marry if she didn't want to; at twenty-one she would come into money, a thousand a year, perhaps more. Enough in all conscience, or so Frances thought, for the average woman to live on. She herself had more than double that income, but that had no bearing on the case. She had never been able to regard herself in the light of an average woman. It was no good, she simply could not judge them (the other female millions) from a purely feminine standpoint. Women, she considered, were far safer without money. God intended them to marry and have nice little babies. She herself had never married; but then that was different. Why? Oh! well, because it was.

She thought it very tender, very beautiful even, to see a woman moving with a kind of clumsy shyness, a woman heavy with new life. Once in Rome she had stood in the Piazza di Spagna to watch a peasant girl who was suckling

67

her child. The great, generous breast, so startlingly white beside the baby's brown face, had seemed a lovely and arresting thing, finely, fiercely unashamed. The girl had looked up and smiled.

'Mio Bimbo!' she had explained, with the gentle patronage of one who feels slightly aloof, and her eyes had dwelt kindly but pityingly on Frances.

Frances had nodded and walked on quickly. She had felt that she wanted to pray.

Pictures, quiet pictures vaguely tinged with sadness, hidden away in the deeps of Frances, drifting across her mind all unbidden, bringing a smile that was somehow not quite a smile to her hard-bitten, whimsical mouth. Pictures of things seen and half forgotten—sometimes of things imagined. Pictures of rooms looking out on old gardens; pictures of gardens folded up in twilight; pictures of evenings beside a pleasant log-fire; pictures of nights filled with soft, contented breathing; pictures of a woman with a child at her breast. Frances would smile and wonder where they came from, these pictures that belonged to somewhere and someone that had nothing to do with Frances Reide. Would wonder at the strength of the diaphanous things to stir in her a feeling of longing, a sudden discontent with the little house in Young Street, a sudden rather fierce resentment against life, a vague, uncomprehending pity for herself, a desire to lift up her voice in protest and ask, 'Why? Why? *Why?*'

But Frances was not a dreamer, nor was she introspective, by choice at all events. So when the pictures came she would plunge into accounts, or go round to Lady Shore, or struggle for a westward-bound bus outside Barker's. Or if it chanced to be the middle of the night, switch on the bedside lamp and read Sax Rohmer.

CHAPTER NINE

I

NOT so easy to entice willing swains for Sidonia to the cloister of the Queen Anne square. Young men did not linger very long in Kensington, they seemed to prefer the Colonies. But Frances, nothing daunted, sallied forth to the chase, and succeeded tolerably well. It was then that old friends, neglected for years, friends who had eligible sons, were retrieved and beguiled with countless invitations into past intimacy. It was then that mere acquaintances, also having sons, found themselves becoming friends before they could turn round. It was then that the little house in Young Street bulged with tea-parties; that Lady Shore, bewildered, patient, vague as ever, was pressed into service and found herself a hostess giving countless luncheons, dinners, and even theatre parties.

'Oh, dear! Oh, dear! What *is* it all about?' she inquired now almost daily.

'Sidonia,' answered Frances, with a tightening of the lips.

'But, my dear, she's still so young; she isn't even out yet.'

'Well, she'll not come out at all unless we get her going. You can't force her to "come out" when the time comes if she won't.'

'Oh, she will—girls always do, I did,' said Lady Shore.

'Yes, you're you, but she's Sidonia.'

'But surely——'

'There's no surely. That's the trouble; with Sidonia there'll never be a surely.'

'Isn't this "coming out"? Do you think I should present her?' Lady Shore looked rather frightened, it was all a great disturbance.

'I was going to speak of that. She refuses point-blank.'

'But why?'

'I don't know, Prudence, I only know she does.'

Lady Shore sighed with relief.

'Then there's nothing we can do. I always told you, Frances, she was wedded to her art.'

The object of all this, now nearly eighteen, behaved in a way that was truly diabolic. She was bored and superior, speaking very little; she was gloomy and depressed, escaping into corners; she was pert and self-assertive; flirtatious or repelling; in fact, she ran successfully through the gamut of her moods, and throughout glared at Frances with a furious resentment. Well-meaning, kind young men felt snubbed and therefore angry; at home they told their mothers that the Shore girl might be pretty, but dull, distinctly dull, and just a little odd. 'You know, a bit too brainy, stand-offish, such a bore!'

Frances cajoled, implored.

'Sidonia, do be civil.'

'I won't! It's all your fault. I want my work and you.'

'What nonsense!' exclaimed Frances.

'Frances, why persist? You must surely see by now that it's no earthly.'

'I see that you're a hopelessly opinionated youngster.'

'Why? Because I like you better than pimply young men?'

'Don't talk like such a fool!'

'But I do, so why not say it? I like you ten times better.'

They were sitting in the studio. The afternoon sunshine slanted in through the skylight and lit gaily upon Frances. She moved away into the shadow, Sidonia, watching her, smiled; then she stared at the half-finished bust of Frances, where it stood in the middle of the room. Frances followed the direction of her eyes.

'Is that thing like me?'

Sidonia nodded.

'The image of you. Are you glad you look like that?'

Frances flushed a little in the kindly shadow; she had just been thinking that the face was arresting.

'Work and you, you and work,' Sidonia went on dreamily.

'It's queer, Frances, that I've known you in a way all my life, —you used to snub me outrageously once.'

'I do now,' said Frances quickly.

'Not really; you try to, but you don't succeed. You're too fond of me now to snub me.'

'Not I! I'm as critical as ever, my child.'

'I'm not your child,' snapped Sidonia.

'No, I know, but you might be, I'm old enough.'

'Oh, do drop this eternal talk about age! If you were a man I'd marry you, Frances. I'd fall in love with you if you were a man, so you see I don't find you too old.'

'Frances!' came a rather apologetic voice from the foot of the attic stairs.

Sidonia sprang quickly in front of the door.

'There's mother. You're not to go!'

Frances stood up.

'What on earth do you mean? Of course I must go. Let me pass.'

They stood for a moment confronting each other, then Sidonia bent suddenly forward.

'Kiss me before you go, Frances.'

Frances laughed.

'Why should I kiss you?'

'Because I feel that I want you to.'

Frances said quietly:

'Look here, Sidonia; I'm only Frances, the same old Frances that you've known nearly all your life. I'm not new or alluring, I do assure you. Now let me pass, there's a nice child.'

Sidonia flung away from the door.

'I ask you to kiss me and you won't!' she said furiously. 'Oh, you! You're all Mother's! Mother this, Mother that! God! I'm sick of it! Don't I count at all?' She was childish now, stamping her foot. 'What does Mother need? Just a mummy, that's all; but I need someone real, I need *you*! Why can't I have you? Aren't I younger than Mother. Aren't I attractive? Don't I interest you enough? Frances'— she began to speak softly now—'Frances, look at me! Don't you love me? Frances, *won't* you be my friend? All, *all* my

71

friend? I don't want to marry anyone, I tell you; I just want to work and have you, all of you. Frances, mother would never miss you. Listen, I'm not being beastly about mother, but please, please try to love me a little; I need you much more than she does.' She laid her hand caressingly on Frances' arm. 'Frances, why won't you love me?'

Frances disengaged her arm very gently and left the studio.

CHAPTER TEN

I

Iᴛ was on the occasion of Sidonia's nineteenth birthday
that Lady Shore realized for the first time that all was not
well with Prudence Shore. Perhaps she had felt this dimly
for months; thinking back, she was almost certain that she
had; but on 10th August, Sidonia's birthday, the uncomfortable sensation came well to the fore. A nebulous sensation
as yet, without a name, but, nevertheless, most disturbing.

She had opened her eyes with the birthday feeling—so upsetting to one of her temperament—the feeling of total in-
adequacy to rise to the spirit of the day. Not that she did not
feel maternal, she did, that was the trouble. She wanted so
desperately to look the right thing, to say the right thing, to
behave like a mother. But the more she worried the vaguer
she grew; it had always been like that.

It was not alone the birthday feeling that was troubling
her to-day, however; she had grown used to that, had borne
it resignedly from the moment Sidonia had made her first
appearance. It was something more intimately connected
with herself, not detachable as Sidonia had been; a feeling
that something had changed in life, something that mattered
very much.

They had come to Brendon for the summer this year, to
the quiet 'Stag-Hunter's Rest'. Lady Shore loved the garden
with its sloping lawn, and the river that ran at the foot of the
lawn, making little contented sounds. She loved the simple,
homely rooms, and the moor that seemed to be bending
down in friendship towards the house. She had taken the
three best bedrooms in the inn, and a pleasant, low-ceilinged
parlour. They had brought Ptah the Second in his warmly-
lined hamper (Ptah the First was no more); Horus had come

in his travelling cage, and Frances was spending the holiday with them, as she did from time to time.

'And so,' said Lady Shore, thinking aloud as she dressed, 'we're all here, all happy, all well, thank God; therefore, what is the matter with me?'

She hurried down to breakfast with Sidonia's present, a handsome pigskin dressing-case. The case was heavy with silver fittings, it made her arm ache to carry it. She was late, it seemed, for Sidonia and Frances were already seated at the table. Oh, dear! How unfortunate to be late to-day, she had meant to be in time! She stood rather awkwardly in the doorway, a little lop-sided because of the case. Her hair had been dressed not ten minutes ago, and yet she could feel that lock tickling her cheek. Oh, dear! How vexatious that short bit was, she had wanted so much to look tidy.

She said, 'Many happy returns, my darling,' on a note that was over-festive.

'Thank you, Mummy,' came Sidonia's cool young voice. Hadn't she noticed the parcel?

'Here, give me that thing!' commanded Frances. 'It's much too heavy for you.'

'It's my present, Sidonia,' explained Lady Shore, relinquishing her burden with relief.

Sidonia devoured a spoonful of Devonshire cream, then she took the parcel from Frances. She tore off the paper.

'Oh, Mother, how ripping! I love pigskin. Come here and be thanked.'

Lady Shore thrust out an obedient cheek, which Sidonia brushed somewhere in the region of the ear.

'Why can't I fold her in my arms?' thought Lady Shore desperately, but the bare idea made her feel shy.

She looked at her tall and slender child, with the curling, auburn hair. The green eyes looked calmly back at her, not unkindly, but oh, so calmly. Sidonia began to feed busily again—more Devonshire cream, more jam. She ate cream and jam in alternate spoonfuls, not troubling to spread them on bread. She was wearing riding breeches and gaiters, and a loose, white linen coat.

'Are you riding to-day?' inquired Lady Shore.

'Um-m,' Sidonia murmured, mouth full.

Frances was also dressed for riding. She looked her best in such clothes. She was no mean horsewoman, although of late years, in fact until this summer, she had ridden very little.

'I thought we'd go right out over the moor, and take some lunch in our pockets,' she explained. 'Why don't you meet us somewhere for tea? Get the man here to drive you in the runabout.'

There was a just perceptible moment of silence, then Lady Shore shook her head.

'Oh, no, that would tie you down as to time. I might be late, my watch is always wrong, besides I must work to-day.'

'Well, if you don't feel like it,' said Frances doubtfully. 'Have you got your stylo ink?'

'Yes, I found it in my underclothes drawer, after all.'

'And your blotting paper?'

Lady Shore nodded.

'But I wish we'd brought those reference books with us; not that they're very much use——'

She stifled a sigh. This morning somehow her handbook on scarabs seemed rather dull. She had worked on it now for eighteen months, and yet it remained unfinished.

Frances put in her tortoise-shell eyeglass and looked at her friend more closely. Horus, transferred to his handsome brass cage, broke into a volley of shrieks. Lady Shore got up patiently and gave him some toast, which he hurled to the bottom of the cage.

'Give us a kiss, old girl!' he lisped hoarsely. 'Come on, give us a kiss!'

She stood there staring at the turbulent parrot with her kind, short-sighted eyes. He ducked his head and she tickled his neck.

'Pretty poll,' she murmured.

Her black serge skirt was sagging away from the safety pin at her belt; some short, grey strands of hair in her neck had escaped from their celluloid clasp. Frances got up and hiked at the belt, then she fingered the straying locks. Without turning round Lady Shore found a hairpin and raked them into the slide.

75

Sidonia sat back with a sigh of repletion; she stretched out her long, thin legs.

'Finished?' inquired Frances.

Sidonia nodded.

'Then come on, we ought to get ready.'

They left the room, and Lady Shore continued to tickle the parrot. Presently she heard the horses coming round, and she went out and stood by the door. Sidonia and Frances came downstairs; they were laughing, arm in arm.

'Now, Prudence, please be good,' cautioned Frances, 'and don't frowst indoors all day. Why not take your work out on to the lawn? It's such a heavenly morning.'

Lady Shore stretched out a friendly hand.

'I'll be all right, don't worry about me; you two go off and enjoy yourselves.'

She watched them mount and ride away in the direction of the moor. Sidonia's young back was held very straight; she had only just learnt to ride, taught by Frances. Frances slouched easily over her horse; she was smoking a cigarette. She had the careless, flexible seat of one who has ridden much to hounds; the deceptive seat, that looks almost too careless and is yet so very secure.

2

Lady Shore turned and went into the parlour, where the maid was clearing the table. When the servant had gone she spread out her books and put on her spectacles. She found her place and began to write; she wrote quickly for twenty minutes and then quite suddenly put down her pen with a little jerky movement. She wanted to think, she was full of thoughts, they were interrupting her writing. She thought:

'Godfrey's scarabs, little bits of stone, they've got no particular meaning——' No, no, that wasn't at all what she meant, of course they were full of meaning. Then she thought: 'There is no time—past—present—we said that once. And yet I don't know; Sidonia, so tall—how long her legs looked in breeches. It's nice that those two should be such good friends, I used to worry in case they shouldn't be,

Frances seemed so severe. Natural enough when one comes to think of it, Sidonia must be very companionable—a mother's not a good judge of those things, she still seems a child to me. Frances, what a remarkable woman! Evergreen, that's Frances. I think she's grown younger lately too, that's being so much with Sidonia. Nice for Sidonia to have such a friend, such a staunch dependable creature. Sidonia's not dependable—oh, I don't know, she's very young yet to judge. They seemed like two girls coming down arm in arm. Frances is evergreen. Sidonia knows how to bring Frances out—Sidonia's very amusing. It's good for Frances to ride again—I haven't ridden for years, not since Egypt. Never could ride, as a matter of fact, Godfrey used to make fun——'

She got up and wandered over to the window. What a wonderful day it was. White clouds skimming over blue expanses and their shadows skimming under them over the moor! Away up there, somewhere on the moorland, Sidonia and Frances would be riding by now. They had been right to go, it was such lovely weather, and one ought to have open air. Frances had wanted her to meet them for tea and she had refused, that was silly; she had said that she wanted to work to-day, and yet now she wasn't working. Had Frances really wanted her?

'Of course she wanted me,' she thought quickly, 'she wouldn't have asked me otherwise. I ought to have planned a birthday treat, a picnic or something. Oh, dear, how like me, I always think of things too late. They went off very happily together; I'm glad they decided to ride.'

Ptah strolled languidly into the room and, sitting down, scratched his ear and moaned. Lady Shore stared at him absently while he continued to scratch. Presently his moans made him seem more real.

'I wonder if Ptah is itching?' she thought. 'I hope he hasn't got ticks! Perhaps it's canker. I must get a vet., he's looking a little peaky. Wish I could make up my mind about that doubtful scarab, I don't like the feel—that crack —I don't know. Yes, I'm glad they decided to ride, why shouldn't they spend a day on the moor? They spend a lot of time on the moor——' And then a new thought that struck like a hammer: 'I'm desperately lonely, that's what's been the matter—I'm missing something that used to be wrapped round me, something warm and protective. I don't seem to be wrapped up any more—I'm missing—I'm missing—it's Frances.'

She stared in blank amazement at Ptah, pushing him slightly with her foot.

'Well,' she said, 'what do you think of that?'

But Ptah continued to scratch his sore ear with a horrid kind of enjoyment.

'I'm spoilt,' she told him, 'that's it, I've been spoilt; but I do feel horribly lonely.'

She sat down again and took up her pen. She tried to think about scarabs; but somehow she thought of Sidonia instead, of the large possessive Sidonia. Then some instinct she did not analyse made her force her mind back over nineteen years. She rested her aching head on her hand, while her lips moved in soft repetition.

'Sidonia, my little baby!' she murmured. 'Sidonia, my little baby!'

3

At half-past four they came hurrying home. In time for tea, that was dear of Frances! Lady Shore heard Sidonia's voice in the hall, high, imperative, a little shrill with hunger.

'Food! In the name of the Prophet, food! I'm literally famished, aren't you, Frances?'

More cream, more jam, in which Frances joined this time, and thick chunks of home-made bread.

Lady Shore looked up with her usual smile. 'Had a good time?' she inquired.

Yes, they had had a heavenly day, it had been quite perfect on the moor. What a pity she hadn't joined them for tea, it was too fine to stop indoors. Frances fished for the eternal cigarette and proceeded to blow smoke rings. She blew them very neatly in and out of each other, it was rather a talent of hers.

'Well,' she said presently, 'we must go and change. Ough! I'm stiff; it's old age coming on.'

CHAPTER ELEVEN

I

O F course the weather was very depressing, especially after Brendon. That autumn they paid the inevitable toll for a fine July and August. By the end of October fogs had set in, it was also unbearably chilly. Still, Frances could hardly conceive that the weather accounted for Sidonia's melancholy, and not only her melancholy, but her lowering brow, her gusty fits of bad temper. Sidonia was obviously quite well, she looked the picture of health, she had even filled out a little in the face, the result of Devonshire cream. But day by day and week by week her brooding brow grew darker, her mouth drooped a little more glumly at the corners, her eyes looked a little more restless. Moreover, she evinced a deep interest in Theosophy, and began to borrow books on the subject.

'What on earth's the matter, Sidonia?' inquired Frances.

Sidonia was reading. She hurled away her book.

'I'm *bored*!' she announced explosively.

Frances was silent.

'Well, why can't you speak?' snapped Sidonia, frowning at her.

Frances put in her eyeglass and stared.

'Don't do that! It gets on my nerves.'

Frances dropped the eyeglass obediently, and whistled softly to Horus.

'Of all the intolerable tunes!' groaned Sidonia. 'What fool thought of "Pop goes the weasel"?'

'I wonder?' said Frances, continuing to whistle, while Horus swayed gently and joined in.

'If that parrot does that I'll go stark, staring mad.'

'Poor bird, why shouldn't he feel happy?'

79

'Happy!' said Sidonia with bitter emphasis. 'Happy! That's a tall order!'

'I wonder if all that Devonshire cream——'

'What about it?'

'Oh, nothing—it's bilious stuff——'

'If you think I look bilious, why not say so at once?' Sidonia went over to the glass.

'No, you don't *look* bilious, no need for alarm, but you sound——'

'Now, Frances, don't bring in those liver pills; I'm sick of that hoary old chestnut.'

'It's a pity you're too old to spank,' remarked Frances.

'Oh, really; I suppose you'd like to spank me.'

'Like to! I'd simply adore the job.'

'I dare say, you're so unimaginative.'

'Not at all. I'm revelling now in my mind; my fingers are positively tingling.'

'Can't you see beyond mere, gross physical things?'

'Not without my eyeglass, I'm afraid,' said Frances.

'Then put in your eyeglass.'

'May I? Thank you, my dear.'

'And now, look at me,' Sidonia commanded. 'Well, I'm waiting. What do you see?'

'I see a beautiful, pale-faced girl, with masses of auburn hair. Her eyes are green and positively huge, her lips are like—wait a minute—coral! I see a tall, very handsome man with a heavy, drooping moustache. He is bending towards her, now he stoops——'

'Shut up!' said Sidonia crossly.

'Don't interrupt, you're spoiling conditions. Where did I get to? Oh yes, he stoops and ardently kisses her hand. Now I see masses of snow-white flowers—wait, it's clearing—they're orange blossoms!'

Sidonia shrugged her shoulders.

'You are funny, aren't you?'

'Oh, no, not at all. I'm trying to be psychic, not just grossly physical, you know.'

'Of all the deplorably boring things a misplaced sense of humour is the worst.'

'I don't agree with you,' said Frances firmly; 'a misplaced sense of tragedy is far more trying.'

'You're merely idiotic this morning,' snapped Sidonia, flouncing out of the room.

Everyone felt the strained atmosphere, it reached even Lady Shore. She confided her trouble to Blake one day.

'The house feels as though a wet blanket had fallen, a kind of suffocating feeling.'

'Suffocating rubbish, me-lady!' said Blake. 'Miss Sidonia's in one of them moods.'

'In one of them moods?' queried Lady Shore, absent-mindedly adopting Blake's grammar.

'Yes, me-lady, them devilish moods! One of the British Museum kind that gave me the rheumatism.'

'Oh, I remember, the Parthenon Frieze. But she's got her work now, she is modelling.'

'Maybe,' said Blake, 'and again maybe not. Leastways, she's hatching on something. She's broody like, all ruffled up and sweaty.'

'*Sweaty*, Blake?'

'Well, maybe not sweaty, but kind of queer. I've seen it in hens lots of times. There's many a lesson to be learnt from hens for them as 'as eyes to see. I've watched them old roosters many's the time, chasing round after the females.'

'My hair-net, please,' said Lady Shore nervously; 'no, not that one, Blake, it's torn.'

2

The volcano erupted again ten days later; this time it was up in the attic.

'What *is* my life?' said Sidonia suddenly. 'I ask you, what *is* my life?'

Frances was deep in a new Sax Rohmer; she adored detective stories.

'Yes, what is your life?' she inquired mechanically. They were just garotting the hero.

'Ah!' breathed Sidonia, 'exactly. What?' Her voice was grimly triumphant.

'Well, what?' Frances turned down her page with a sigh.

'No wonder you ask!' said Sidonia.

She slapped a large, squelchy chunk of clay on to the bust she was modelling. With a vicious thumb she pressed in the cheeks, making the face cadaverous; then she pulled round the stand with its back to Frances.

'Don't watch me, *please*,' she grumbled.

'Good Lord! I'm not watching.'

'Then read your book—— No, don't go, I want you here.'

The villain was escaping via a telegraph wire when Sidonia broke out again.

'You asked me about my life.'

'I did not, it was you, my dear, who asked me.'

'Well, what does it matter? It's all the same.'

'Oh, all right, but I didn't start it.'

'What is my life?'

'Yes, for Heaven's sake! What?'

'A desert!' said Sidonia tragically.

Frances surveyed her in some alarm. 'Are you sure you're quite well?' she inquired.

'Physically, yes, but spiritually, no. My spirit is starved to death.'

'But why? I wish I could understand.'

'You none of you understand.'

'Oh, come, don't be morbid, we're not so bad.'

'You're too gross, it would never reach you.'

'What would never reach me?'

'My spiritual vibrations, they're much too tenuous to reach you.'

'Now, Sidonia, that's theosophical rot! You've been reading all that stuff in books.'

'Well, what if I have? I like those books, they help me to understand.'

'Well, as long as you don't ask me to read them——'

'No fear!' said Sidonia grandly.

She worked in silence for half an hour, then she called Frances over to look.

'My God! What is it?' Frances breathed.

The hideous face leered back at her from its eager, stretching neck.

'What do you think of that for work?'

'I think it's awful!'

'It's me; that's the way I really am, that's my soul.'

'What rubbish!' said Frances.

'In Art,' Sidonia went on sternly, 'one should try to show souls, not bodies.'

'If they all look like that I'm glad they've got bodies, it seems to help them a little.'

'What I've tried to portray is the way my soul feels.'

'In that case I'd go and say my prayers.'

'We live prayers, we've no need to say them.'

Frances considered, then she said, 'Sidonia, let's ride every day in the Row.'

'Why?'

'I don't know, it might be amusing.'

'Oh, no, I hate riding except in the country. That thing I've just done's jolly clever!'

'I suppose so, but why does your soul look like that?'

Sidonia surveyed her in silence for a moment. 'Because I'm stifling it,' she said slowly.

And then without warning of any kind she burst into noisy sobs. Frances was too much appalled to speak. This was a dreadful happening—Sidonia modelling devilish things and talking about her soul, Sidonia in floods of hysterical tears while her soul gasped for breathing space! And all so sudden. Eight weeks ago she had seemed as happy as the day. Could anyone have seemed more thoroughly happy than Sidonia galloping on Exmoor? Her mind flew back to the time long ago when Sidonia had wept with rage over her dancing; and later, when she had beaten the piano for not responding to her mood. And here it was again —or something very like it—only being more mature it was more alarming.

'Oh, do let's take up our riding again,' said Frances, finding her voice at last; 'I know it would do us both good.'

Sidonia shook her head in between sobs, then she looked up, tears and all.

'That thing I've just done isn't really good, it's rotten. I know it's rotten!' and seizing a hammer she smashed in the face, leaving a pulp of clay.

Frances put a firm arm around her, holding her close for a moment.

'Look here, Sidonia, let's have this out. I must know what's the matter.'

Sidonia still continued to sob, now she wept on Frances' coat.

'Let's sit down on the divan,' suggested Frances, 'you can cry more comfortably there.'

After a little Sidonia spoke.

'It's my work, it's all going wrong. If you knew the big thing that struggles inside me and can't get out into the clay.'

'You can't express all the things you feel?'

'Yes, that's it—no, it's not quite that either. I don't feel enough to open the door for the thing that's inside me to get out—my talent, my genius—whatever it is. The thing can't live because I'm not living.'

'But you're very much alive, you're the most vital creature in all the world, I should think.'

'No, Frances, I'm not; this isn't real life, it's just home and three meals a day. Oh!' she burst out, pushing Frances from her, 'it's three meals a day and *you*!'

'What on earth——'

'Don't argue. It's you, chiefly you, all cuffs and collars and neat sarcasm and "be a nice child, Sidonia!" and "Now I must go down and help your mother." As though I didn't need help! It's a hot bath twice a day prepared by Blake, and clean linen sheets and embroidered towels, and roast beef on Sundays with Yorkshire pudding, and those damnable chimes of St. Mary Abbott's, and upholstered people all going to church with enormous morocco prayer books, and you in a black tie because it's Sunday, and shoes with patent leather toe-caps and a ladylike toque that makes you look awful, in case they should think you're eccentric, and your everlasting "I'm nearly fifty, my dear"—well, you are, that's the trouble, Frances. You're nearly fifty and I'm nineteen, and I won't be squeezed into your prim pattern. I don't feel prim and I won't be! You and Mother, Mother and mummies, there's nothing to choose between you. I want to get out and meet flesh and blood people who aren't ashamed to feel. I want to get out and see life as it is, not a Queen Anne spectre of life——' She paused to take breath.

'You dislike us, then?' said Frances, and her voice sounded queerly constrained.

'No, I don't, that's the frightening part of it all; I long, simply long to hate you. But you've always been there, you and Mother and mummies, and lately, Frances, just you. And I like hot baths and clean linen sheets and Blake to bring in the soap. I even like beef when it's underdone,' she finished, smiling a little.

'But it won't do, Sidonia?'

'No, no, it won't do. I'll never be a really great artist at this rate.'

'Then, what?'

'I don't know, I haven't thought yet, I've only been sure just lately.'

'How long is it since you've been sure it won't do?'

'Only after we came home from Brendon. I knew the moment I started work that I couldn't go on any longer.'

Frances stared hard at the ruined bust, her long, dark eyes enigmatical.

'We must think,' she said gravely.

Sidonia seized her hand impulsively.

'Frances, why aren't you different?'

Frances was silent. Presently she said:

'There's the Royal College of Art, of course—it used to be rather a stodgy sort of place, but Jensen has altered all that, I believe. He's a wonderful teacher. Curiously enough, someone was talking about it only the other day, who was it?—oh, well, never mind. They say pupils come to him from all over the world. Do you think you'd like to go there?'

Sidonia considered.

'I'd meet other workers, people who may be going to be great——'

'You would, and all under fifty, I imagine.'

'I'd rub shoulders a bit with real life if I went, at least I'd meet flesh and blood people. What I need, Frances, is the

85

stimulus of brains, other brains, you know, the adventurous sort, the kind that aren't afraid of taking mighty big risks. I'd meet those kind of people there.'

'Perhaps. I believe they drink milk at eleven.'

'I shouldn't mind that.'

'No, I suppose not. In any case, they may not have two baths a day.'

'Oh, what *does* that matter!'

'It doesn't, I agree, it may make them all the more vital.'

'I'll go,' said Sidonia, 'I'll go after Christmas. Why didn't I think of it before?'

'There's a Travelling Scholarship you might take, it would give you something to work for.'

'I'll take it!'

'Don't be too sure, my dear, it's not so easy to get.'

Sidonia laughed.

'They won't stop me if I really make up my mind.'

'Very well then, that's that!' said Frances.

She got up.

'I'm going home now, I've got some letters to answer.'

'Frances!'

'Yes?'

'You're not angry with me?'

'Good heavens, no, of course not.'

3

Frances walked slowly across the square to her white front door in Young Street. Still slowly she slipped in her latch-key and turned back the brass Yale lock. The pleasant log-fire that she loved on the hearth; the room with its smell of beeswax and leather, cigarette smoke and flowers; over the mantelpiece Uncle Charles Reide, very calm, very like herself; and Sidonia's enormous red leather chair pulled pleasantly close to the fire. A comfortable room, a sober room, a room that looked every day of fifty. She laughed; what else could anyone do in this queer, topsy-turvy world? Presently she lit a Russian cigarette, and ringing the bell, ordered tea.

CHAPTER TWELVE

I

SIDONIA stood in the doorway and surveyed the large, square, ugly studio with bright, imperious eyes. Above her head on a neat white board appeared the words: 'Women's Life.'

The room was entirely devoid of charm, that is, to the uninitiated. Grey walls much stained and finger-marked, much scarred and pierced by nail holes. Innumerable heaps of dirty, grey rags, stiffened with last term's clay, and here and there a strip of pink flannelette, faded and discoloured until it toned with the rest. Grey-painted turntables supporting grey skeletons composed of compo piping; sub-human these, with their twists and loops and grotesquely spread wire fingers. In the middle of the room a platform on which the model would pose. On shelves and floor and hanging from the walls a collection of amputated human members, whose plaster had also become somewhat grey filmed over by the fine, insidious mildew that seemed to be the spirit of the place.

Clay, clay, clay! It was everywhere, nothing and no one could escape it. Its breath rose up from the galvanized troughs in the adjoining room; large oozing troughs from which it was taken and pounded with iron bars, then kneaded into neat little loaves and rolls by the brawny Jenkins and his mate. These rather uncanny loaves and rolls were reposing now on a shelf; a kind of spectral bakery this, smelling of earth instead of dough.

Some fourteen women stood about the studio or squatted on wooden boxes. They had put on clean cotton overalls, for this was the beginning of the term; but already the inevitable stains had appeared on hands and overalls and shoes. The women varied considerably in age, this much Sidonia took in at a glance; for the rest, old or young, fat or thin, short or tall, most of them were exceedingly plain. The craze for bobbing was as yet unborn, and many were the curls and knobs and knots and artistic Liberty hairpins. On the whole, however, the effect was not good; there was something too hurried about it.

Sidonia touched her own pleasing waves with a feeling of satisfaction. Her hair had always refused to grow long (by long, she meant down to her knees), and as she objected to half-way things, she had not allowed it to grow at all. It framed her face in a thick, soft curve that ended just below her ears. A little unusual, short hair at twenty, but Sidonia cared nothing for that.

'As an artist I must be allowed my whims,' she had often explained to Frances.

And since Sidonia's whims became whirlwinds when opposed her explanation had been ruefully accepted. She was thinking now as she stood in the doorway how more than right she had been. These women with their frowsy, hasty heads, how often did they wash their hair? Not often, she decided; and then she remembered what manner of women they were.

Life, real life! Or a bit of it, at all events. Real flesh and blood, purposeful people. If they didn't wash their heads—well, no wonder they didn't, they were too busy living, she supposed. And perhaps after all they did wash their heads—it was only a trifle, anyhow. They seemed to have pale, intense kind of faces; she could not see very well from the door, but it stood to reason that they would have such faces, she wished them to look like that. And their voices? No, their voices were not really shrill—only rather challenging and eager. The whole place was redolent of something big and fine to which all these women contributed.

She longed to stretch out her arms to them, to embrace them and call them her sisters. To cry out in loud and compelling tones:

88

'Here I am, Sidonia, who has come among you; teach me the meaning of work, of life!'

But someone was talking about Albert biscuits; a sentence drifted to her where she stood.

'Oh, no, not Alberts! Couldn't you get Pat-a-cakes? They're ever so much nicer than Alberts.'

How simple! Not dull, no, of course not—just simple, the simplicity of true Bohemia. Did people eat 'Pat-a-cakes' and 'Alberts' in Bohemia? Well, obviously they must do. She took a step forward, smiling her welcome. Why didn't they all smile back? One or two students glanced round, it is true, but nobody smiled or moved.

'Who's the kid?' whispered someone a little too loudly.

'Don't know. I say, look at her hair.'

Sidonia stood still, her progress suddenly checked. She was not really feeling dashed, she decided; but things were not happening quite as she had pictured them.

'Now then, which of you has torn my cage?' came a voice whose depth astonished Sidonia.

A white-haired woman strode into the studio from a door at the other end. She was tall and carried her shoulders well back like a General on parade. But unlike a General, a dominating bust preceded her every stride. Over this breast-work she glared at the room, waiting for someone to speak.

'No use your all smiling,' came the deep voice again, 'my cage has been torn, I tell you.'

'It's just where you put it, Crossby,' said someone.

'No, it's not.'

'Well, we haven't touched it.'

'Jenkins, come here!' bawled Miss Crossby more loudly, jutting out her masterful chin.

From the room of the oozing, galvanized troughs came Jenkins, very dirty, but serene. His torn list slippers were stiff with clay and so were the hairs on his arms. He looked at Miss Crossby with the patient eyes of one who is just too big to fit in, stooping a little as he did so.

'My cage is all torn to bits again,' said Miss Crossby, pointing accusingly.

'Well, maybe you tore it by accident, miss. Them cages is very fragile.'

'Should I send for you if I'd torn it myself? Good gracious, man, where's your sense?'

'Well, I didn't tear it, miss,' said Jenkins, peeling some clay from his fingers.

'It's your place to see that my things aren't touched.'

Jenkins spat on his hands thoughtfully.

'Look here, miss, don't worry yourself this way, we can soon put a patch over that little rent. Here's a cage, you can use this one to-day if Miss Flemming don't object.'

Miss Flemming was just about to object, but apparently thought better of it.

'Anything for peace,' she said, shrugging her shoulders, 'this fussing gets on my nerves.'

From somewhere out of space the model arrived.

'She's late!' said Miss Crossby truculently. 'I can't abide unpunctual people. My father was a regular Napoleonic man. "Time is money" was his motto.'

The model drew her coat more tightly around her and glanced in the direction of the hot pipes.

'Good morning,' she said. 'This room strikes cold, I can feel it right through me clothes.'

'Positively muggy to-day,' said Miss Crossby.

'It's raining cats and dogs!' replied the model, shivering.

She retired behind a canvas erection that served as her dressing-room, and Sidonia, suddenly tired of waiting decided to tackle Jenkins.

'Can you tell me——' she began, but Miss Crossby interrupted.

'You want Miss Lotter,' she announced decidedly. 'Here she comes, she's late too.'

Sidonia supposed that she must want Miss Lotter, as nobody looked surprised; but as Miss Lotter came hurrying forward it was difficult to imagine that anyone could want her, had ever wanted her, would ever want her.

Miss Lotter had very straight, dusty-looking hair of no particular colour. Her teeth protruded disconcertingly over her pale underlip. Her nose might have been a redeeming feature, had she not been continually blowing it; Sidonia was to learn as time went on that she suffered from chronic colds. But the most remarkable thing about her was her tallness, her thinness and the slope of her shoulders; they seemed to toboggan down to her waist under her brown cashmere blouse.

'I *am* so sorry,' she began nervously, 'to have kept you waiting like this. I've been helping Professor Jensen this morning, there's so much to do at the beginning of a term. The cloakroom's over there; if you'll follow me I'll show you, and then you can get to work.'

2

In the narrow passage that served as a cloakroom Sidonia caught her breath, for now with the smell of hot pipes and clay there mingled a far more personal odour, the odour of women's clothes. The mackintosh smell; the tweed coat smell; the hat smell, rather brilliantiny; the woollen smell from mufflers and shetlands; the smell of old fur tippets; the Properts smell of sensible footgear; the Meltonian smell of less sensible; the smell of galoshes and wet umbrellas; the black, stinging smell of sand shoes. And more vague—yet there—lurking somewhere in the background, the smell of brush and comb and ginger snaps.

'All the pegs are very full this morning,' said Miss Lotter, voicing the obvious.

Sidonia looked round her in silence for a moment, then she took off her hat and coat. Some fastidious instinct of which she felt ashamed prompted her to lay them on a chair. She turned to Miss Lotter.

'All right, I'm ready.'

'Have you got a penny?' asked Miss Lotter.

'Yes.'

Sidonia felt rather bewildered.

'Then you'd better put it on a glass.'

Sidonia followed the direction of her glance. Along the

sill of the one low window stood a row of glasses upside down with pennies laid on their bottoms.

'For your milk,' Miss Lotter explained.

'But I don't drink milk,' said Sidonia sharply, thinking of Pat-a-cakes and Alberts.

'What, not at lunch?'

'Oh, no, I hate it!'

'I expect you'll need it,' persisted Miss Lotter; 'it's very stuffy in there.'

Sidonia shook her head; she would *not* drink milk.

'Oh, well,' sighed Miss Lotter, 'you know best.'

They turned and together went into the studio. The model was apparently having a rigor in close proximity to the hot pipes. Over her shoulders was thrown a long woollen cloak, from which her bare knees protruded. She was making small, protesting sounds, indicative of bodily discomfort.

'It's terribly cold in here,' she began, in her underfed, Cockney voice.

Sidonia looked at her with distaste. The skin of her face was chapped and rough and one of her lips was cracked.

'I must have the place kept warmer than this,' she went on with tiresome persistence.

Miss Lotter looked worried; she glanced at the thermometer.

'It's seventy-two in here now.'

'Don't feel like it to me, I'm that terribly cold; me body's a mass of goose-flesh.'

Miss Lotter ignored this last remark.

'There's your turn-table in that corner,' she told Sidonia.

'But I shan't see well right away over there. I must push it a little nearer.'

'You won't be working from the model to-day, you'll begin with the antique, Miss Shore.'

'Not working from the model?' said Sidonia incredulously, scarcely believing her ears.

'Oh no, Professor Jensen wants you to copy the head of Julius Cæsar; he always begins with the antique.'

Sidonia flushed.

'There's some mistake. I've worked from life for a year.'

'But not under the Professor,' corrected Miss Lotter with her difficult, dental smile.

Sidonia hated her large, white teeth and her nervous yet superior manner.

'I shall certainly not copy Julius Cæsar,' she said coldly. 'I came here to work from life.'

Then something happened that surprised Sidonia. Miss Lotter's face changed completely. It became inspired, fanatical even, and at the same time austere. She stared down from her unusual height as though she disliked what she saw. When she spoke her voice was trembling a little. She plaited and unplaited her fingers.

'We don't argue with Professor Jensen; you'll find that it's not done here. What he says goes. We obey him, Miss Shore, because we both love and respect him.' She paused and swallowed something down in her throat. 'Love and respect him,' she repeated. 'When you know him you'll understand, I expect. He will make you understand.'

Sidonia stared, then she shrugged her shoulders. What a ridiculous creature!

'Very well, Miss Lotter,' she said with dignity, 'I'll speak to Jensen myself.'

3

A queer little gnome with a crooked back, that was Sidonia's first impression. A gnome in incredibly shabby clothes, brown shoes and thick worsted socks. He had come in quietly to pose the model and had quietly left again. Later in the morning, when she saw him better, she decided that he looked like Saint Paul. But this latter description did not please her either, though his curly grey hair and short square beard gave him a scriptural appearance. Saint Paul, she felt, must have looked rather fierce, an eagle-nosed, black-eyed man; whereas this man's features were rugged and his eyes were intensely blue.

'Blue as an ice crevasse,' thought Sidonia, 'disconcertingly bright and piercing.'

They were eyes that seemed to look through and beyond

while missing no trifling detail. They set him apart from other men, successfully defying comparison. That was the way with Einar Jensen, you never quite knew what he looked like.

'Oh, Jensen?' you said. 'What is Jensen like? I don't know—he's—well, he's like Jensen.'

He came and stood by her side and smiled; his smile was wide like a schoolboy's.

'Good morning, mademoiselle. Does it go well?'

She told him quite firmly that it did not.

'I want to work from the life.'

Still smiling, he shook his head very slightly.

'But I came here for that,' Sidonia persisted.

'A week or two and we see,' he said in his rather husky voice.

She thought: 'Why don't I answer him back? A little, untidy man!'

But she stood there finding nothing to say; his eyes had passed through and beyond her. As he turned to go he looked over his shoulder.

'Acorn—oak,' he remarked briefly.

A trick of his, this pruning out of words, he expected you to fill in the gaps. He was always very busy yet never seemed hurried, except in his speech; he economized time in words.

Sidonia worked on in gloomy silence. Nobody noticed her. Once, when she found herself in need of more clay, she was told to go and fetch it herself. The students all knew each other, it seemed, she was the only new one. They chattered incessantly or stalked about measuring the model with callipers. The model was chary of holding the pose for more than twenty minutes. A delicate girl, she decided beforehand that every new pose would be straining. Miss Crossby grumbled.

'Can't get along—could stop in that position myself for ever!'

During the model's frequent rests they discussed their family affairs.

'Mother's got bronchitis.'

'Oh dear, I'm sorry. Illness is such a worry.'

'Yes, I know, and her heart's never been very strong. My sister's come home to nurse her.'

'Have you seen the new thing at Wyndham's yet?'

'Not yet, I'm going with my brother. Thank heaven, he's got a good job at last, they've taken him on at Parr's Bank.'

'That must be a great relief to you.'

'Well, it certainly helps the financial situation.'

'I bought that serge costume we saw at Ponting's, it really is sweetly pretty!'

'Yes, I thought it suited you, such a lovely blue. I can't afford any new gewgaws just now, the children cost so much at school.'

'It's too awful at my place, the landlady's kids are all whooping and being sick.'

'Oh, I wanted to ask you about those rooms. Are they dear?'

'No, cheap and dirty.'

Sidonia stuck on Julius Cæsar's ear with a vicious, exasperated dab. Someone had started a new topic now, they began discussing their favourite food.

'I do adore strawberries and cream, don't you?'

'They're not up to ices, especially Fuller's.'

'Do you like their Walnut or their Angel Cake best?'

'The Angel.'

'Now I like the Walnut.'

'Have you ever eaten Risotto?'

'What's that?'

'An Italian dish made with rice. It's simply scrumptious; they make it at Dino's, I'll take you there one evening.'

'Let's all get together and give a revel; chocolate and cream and cinnamon buns.'

'What will you bring? I'll bring the buns.'

'All right, let's; I'll scare up some chocolate.'

Chocolate and cream and Julius Cæsar's ear, cinnamon buns and ices. Mother's bronchitis and Julius Cæsar's nose, with a match stuck in to mark the measurements! The model hopping in and out of her pose and Crossby's eternal protests.

And then poor Miss Lotter's streaming cold. Her nose seemed inexhaustible, a veritable widow's cruse.

At half-past twelve Sidonia sat down and nibbled her lunch alone. After lunch she returned to Julius Cæsar, with a heartfelt, personal hatred. At four o'clock she joined Frances in the street; it had been arranged that Frances should meet her.

'Well?' inquired Frances.

But Sidonia was silent, so Frances held her peace.

CHAPTER THIRTEEN

I

At the end of a week Sidonia had decided to go immediately to Paris. At the end of a month she was quite convinced that no one could teach but Jensen. After ten days of grinding at the antique he had set her to work from life. Not until then did Sidonia discover the thing that made Jensen great.

Jensen as a teacher gave nothing of himself, the giving all came from his pupils. Gently, almost silently, he seemed to galvanize the personality in others. It might be a poor, rather feeble thing, or it might be akin to genius; but worthy or unworthy, it belonged to the student.

'Make—*you*,' he told Sidonia, 'your feeling, your thought in clay. None of us see model alike, make me understand how *you* see her.'

He would pad round the room with his slow, shuffling gait, sometimes stopping in front of a student's work and saying nothing at all; sometimes pointing out the faults, in his quick, jerky sentences.

'Big—fat—keep under size, only butchers slice off.'

Or:

'Surface too smooth—whitened sepulchre—not run before walk—good proverb!'

Sometimes he seized a lump of clay and worked on the thing himself.

'Like this—so—like this—not afraid—get it quick— make clay come alive in your fingers!'

Then he would shake his head.

'Not you now any more—little bit of me, that spoils it.'

And his eyes. Blue and bright as an ice crevasse, so aloof,

yet so terribly personal. You tried to think only the thoughts that would please him when he looked at you with those eyes. He was poor, you knew that; as a sculptor he had failed. 'Can't express,' he once told Sidonia. But the thing that he knew he could not express seemed to cry out to you for expression.

'But not me, not me!' he was always saying. 'Yourself, it all inside you.'

He was such a patient man in spite of his abruptness; he was infinitely patient with Crossby, for instance; Crossby who did little finicking work, quite unlike her aggressive personality.

'You—big,' he would say, with an illustrative gesture; 'big body, big voice—make spirit big too. Not prick at clay as if your tool a pin; no, give strong strokes, more generous —be generous.'

Crossby would jut out her chin and glare at him over her mighty bosom. But her voice was never loud with temper in his presence, she took it out afterwards on her fellow-students. Miss Lotter was another source of worry to Jensen; so good, so painstaking a pupil. She always did exactly and precisely what he told her, and when she had done it the result was nil. She had worked with him now for nearly five years, making but little progress. Nobody knew why she persisted, unless it was because she worshipped Jensen. She adored him and she bored him.

'Can I help you, Professor? Shall I go through those letters? I could stay on a bit this evening.'

'Shall *I* speak to Jenkins about that new clay?'

'Were your pipes hot enough this morning?'

'Shall I tell them at the shop that they forgot to send your paper? Oh, indeed, it's no trouble, not at all out of my way.'

He endured it just because he was so very patient. Because she was plain, no longer young, and quite devoid of talent. Patient and pitiful—that was Einar Jensen.

In three months' time Sidonia knew her fellow-students as well as she was ever to know them. She had joined in one revel of chocolate and cinnamon buns, had introduced a few of them to Frances after work hours, and had been to tea with Miss Lotter.

Miss Lotter lived in a dreary little studio somewhere in the wilds of West Kensington, a studio from which she had managed to crush out any vestiges of character that the place might once have had. Sidonia learnt her history. Miss Lotter was an orphan, the daughter of a dentist in Shrewsbury. Miss Lotter had pointed to her teeth with a smile, and had said that they were not a good advertisement. She had a little money which she eked out with commissions; an occasional medal for some slight commemoration, posthumous bas-reliefs, done from faded photographs. No, it was not a good trade, she admitted; your materials cost too much. Why had she chosen sculpture? She didn't know, exactly. She loved beauty, perhaps that was why—she wanted to create it.

How she tried to like Sidonia! Rather heroic really—her eyes would almost water in her efforts to be affable.

'Jensen thinks the world of you.'

'Does he?'

'Oh, yes, you know it. He always spends more time with your work than with ours.' And then, supremest effort, 'But he's right, you have got genius. You've got the thing he loves, a kind of dash about what you do.' No news this to Sidonia, she knew what Jensen felt, she could see it in his face when he stood before her work. He would nod his head and sometimes, very rarely, he would praise.

'Oak beginning out of acorn.' Or: 'Yes, good! It's full of something——' Then thoughtfully, 'I wonder, full of some-thing—is it you?'

Before another six months elapsed she was working in his studio. It had come about quite naturally. He had said to her one day:

'You care work on Saturdays and Sundays in my studio? I

not always there, but sometimes; still, you work just the same.'

She had accepted with alacrity. Work! She did nothing else. She was like a thing wound up. Frances watched her with misgiving.

'Don't exhaust it all, Sidonia. Don't be greedy with your art.'

'But, Frances, it's so wonderful to feel you're really getting there, to feel nothing can stop you. I am greedy, that's just it.'

They would often work in silence, she and Jensen, in his studio. Sometimes she would pause to watch his crooked back. One day he caught her at it.

'Crooked!' he said.

She nodded.

'Dropped as little baby—too big for my sister—she herself only a child.'

Sometimes they talked for hours, breaking through his habit of silence. He told her about Denmark, about his childhood there. They had all been very poor.

'But I'm glad,' he said. 'It better, it makes you understand.'

Sidonia dropped her tool.

'Is that what's wrong with me?'

'You do not understand?'

'No.'

'You speak right—you do not.'

He surveyed her very gravely.

'You learn about it some day, you learn some great, big lesson—I often wonder how. At least, perhaps you learn, some people never do.'

'Do you know why I came here, mon maître?'

'To study with me—Jensen.'

'Not at all; to learn about it, to learn about real life.'

'And you found?'

'I found Miss Crossby and Miss Lotter and the others.'

'Ah, yes. They teach you nothing?'

She shook her head and laughed.

'And yet,' said Jensen slowly, 'they are life——'

She looked at him incredulously.

'Miss Crossby and Miss Lotter?'

'What else?'

'Oh, I don't know. I pictured something different; more vital, daring people—rather wicked if you like.'

'Wicked people—but so dull! Duller than poor Miss Lotter. Even fewer sins than virtues, mademoiselle.'

'Still, I'd like to see a few.'

'You will, but they will bore. Always the same you find, dressed up in different clothes; in the end one sin, just only one sin—Self.'

'Do you think I'm selfish?'

'Yes, mademoiselle, at present. To me it seems so strange that your work what it is. Where do you get genius, all shut up as you are?'

She frowned.

'I don't know. What must I do to get out of myself?'

'You read *Grimm's Fairy Tales*?'

'Long ago.'

'Read again; read the story of the man who had not learnt to shiver and shake.'

'What about it?'

'You will see. You must learn to shiver and shake.'

'And then?'

'Then you will be complete, it will consecrate your work.'

They discussed a thousand things, Theosophy among them. Jensen had studied deeply on such subjects, it seemed.

'You see, my wife bed-ridden. Where she go to when she die? All day long she knits me socks, nothing else she can do.'

Sidonia had a vision of bed-ridden Mrs. Jensen, producing woollen tortures for her husband's long-suffering feet.

'Don't you find them rather rough?' she asked, looking at his socks.

'They tickle,' he said gravely, 'but silk so expensive. Can I tell her not to knit when it all she has to do?'

'No, of course not,' said Sidonia, feeling sorry.

'Then there's me,' he went on. 'I can feel, but not in clay. My work a disappointment, poor work, inferior; no life, only technique—that's why I teach so well. Rodin made little

Rodins, I make you all yourselves. Then because I cannot do, I can have larger patience. I have patience with Miss Lotter, she good but very stupid—that however, not her fault——' They were silent for a moment, then he smiled apologetically. 'And my back, so very crooked! I like strong, beautiful people; I like not see my back—it also aches. What will happen when I die? Shall my back grow straight, you think? That is what I ask the books—that, and other things.'

'Then you believe in an after life?'

'Oh, yes, but I am certain.'

'Why, mon maître?'

'I cannot tell you; myself has told myself.'

CHAPTER FOURTEEN

I

During that year Sidonia grew more considerate; perhaps it was Einar Jensen. It was difficult to be so much with the man without imbibing something of his spirit.

'They all so interesting—people,' he would say, 'and somewhere, deep in, so sorrowful.'

Sidonia tried to see through his eyes, but with only partial success. Like everything else that she did her kindness was inclined to be somewhat violent. Lady Shore and Frances were the first to feel the effects of her change of heart.

'I shall go through your filing cabinets, Mother, they're in a disgraceful condition.'

It was so unexpected that Lady Shore was completely taken off her guard.

'Oh, no, my dear, that would never do; they're full of important papers!'

'I think I'll arrange them another way. I don't like that method of yours.'

'Please don't, Sidonia, I'll never find a thing!'

But Sidonia went through the filing cabinets, and left them arranged according to her own ideas.

'I'll get your cigarettes for you, Frances, I'm going quite near the shop.'

'Will you? Thanks. Five hundred of my usual Russians. Tell him to put them on the bill.'

'Those Russians are awfully bad for your throat. By the way, how is your cough?'

Sidonia came back with five hundred cigarettes, but not the usual Russians.

'I've brought you these; they've got little pads, cotton wool to catch the nicotine.'

'Not a mouthpiece, Sidonia, don't say they've got a mouth-piece!'

'Yes, that kind are so much healthier.'

'Oh, damn! And it's Saturday afternoon and I've just run out of my own!'

'Don't be stubborn, you've got to smoke these to please me.'

'But I hate a mouthpiece!' groaned Frances.

The studio gave her yet wider scope, there were so many people to help. She noticed that Crossby's work looked dry as she passed it one Sunday morning. 'I'll just go and damp it down a bit,' she said, with an eye on Jensen.

How she came to deluge the thing as she did Sidonia never knew. She was thinking of Jensen, she remembered afterwards, and of what impression she was making. When Crossby removed the wrappings on Monday she uttered a howl of despair. An arm and shoulder plopped on to the floor in a pool of slimy mud.

Sidonia had borne it rather well, she had not even answered back. All she had said was: 'Sorry. I tried to be kind. Don't bellow like a mad bull, Crossby.'

But Miss Lotter came in for the most attention, because she was obviously jealous, and, moreover, she had projecting teeth, and not a vestige of talent to excuse them.

'Do come into Jensen's studio to-morrow morning, I know he'll be glad to see you. You can sit and talk to us while we work; talking never disturbs him.'

Miss Lotter stiffened and blew her nose, which always gave trouble at such moments.

'Thank you. I wonder if I know my way? Perhaps you will take me, Miss Shore.'

'Oh, now you're cross,' said Sidonia sadly. 'I only meant to be nice.'

'Before you came I took care of all his papers!' Miss Lotter's voice sounded shrill.

'Well, that job's still going,' smiled Sidonia pleasantly. 'I'm much too busy to sort them.'

The next day she arrived with a box of chocolates, specially bought for Miss Lotter. As Miss Lotter bit them they stuck to her front teeth. She had to wipe them off with her handkerchief.

Sometimes Sidonia would bring theatre tickets.

'I've got you two stalls for the Garrick, Miss Lotter. I know you hate standing at the pit door for hours, it's so awfully bad for your colds.'

And Miss Lotter would accept in bitterness of spirit, because she could never resist stalls.

Jensen, seeing all, while appearing to see nothing, said to Sidonia one day:

'How do you understand kindness to others?'

'I don't know exactly, how do you?'

'Difficult—terribly hard explain—sometimes in saying nothing.'

Sidonia looked surprised.

'Then how are they to know?'

'That just it, they must never know.'

Sidonia pondered these things in her mind; she found it more difficult to ponder in her heart. Yet, in spite of this, she began to see dimly that other people mattered a lot to themselves, quite apart from their relation to her. She was stiff and awkward enough in her methods, tactless and self-assertive. She worried most where she wished to help, hurt where she wished to heal. Perhaps only Jensen discerned in all this a tentative flicker of spirit. He would sometimes sit staring at her thoughtfully, smiling a little to himself. They were excellent companions, though he treated her as though she were a child. But she could not resent this treatment at his hands, all the world was a child to Jensen.

He patted her shoulder gently one day.

'You make so glad,' he said.

Sidonia looked round.

'Why?' she asked, surprised.

'Because you wake up; also your work—getting soul in—goes well.'

'Oh, mon maître, are you really pleased with my work?'

He smiled and nodded slowly.

'I have waited long. Only two with great talent in years—you and another. You think heart not break over them sometimes, Lotter and Crossby and the rest? They pay money; what I give in exchange? Only talk—no good—bring out nothing. You try taking Travelling Scholarship next year, then you work—get great. You have your diploma under usual time—that not hard to arrange through me—then in five, ten years I come and see your work. I say, "Fine teacher, Einar Jensen." I say, "Never mind if he can't do himself—was able to make this one do." Ah, yes, mademoiselle, I look forward to that. The other I had—she died.'

She held out her hand.

'If only I can, if only I don't disappoint you!'

'Not disappoint Jensen,' he said very gravely. 'Remember, he count on you.' Then he laughed. 'No, don't remember him at all, just remember his excellent teaching.'

Sidonia's eyes filled with unexpected tears.

'It's your faith in me,' she told him unsteadily.

He said: 'Big mountains—a little real faith and no mountains any more. My faith in you that kind, remember. When you go away, take it with you.'

2

At the end of her second year at the school Sidonia won the Travelling Scholarship. No one was surprised, least of all Sidonia, but Jensen was pathetic in his joy. He said very little, but his eyes were continually smiling.

'You like my art child—proud father, Jensen. You go—work hard—come back—great things—world more beautiful after.'

Beyond these few mutilated remarks he did not discuss her success. Miss Lotter wrote her congratulations in a cold little formal letter.

Sidonia would go to Italy in November, beginning her tour with Florence.

'We'll have a heavenly time!' she told Frances. 'We'll love every minute of it!'

Frances, who was dusting Lady Shore's books, looked round with a startled eye.

'*We?*'

'Yes, of course you're coming too, Frances; I can't speak a word of Italian.'

3

That evening Sidonia went to bed early. Lady Shore and Frances did not.

'But if I go who'll look after you, Prudence? And yet Sidonia—alone——'

'And in Italy, too,' murmured Lady Shore, 'where the men are so very un-English!'

'And Sidonia's rather remarkable looking——'

'I know. They admire fair hair.'

'Still, at twenty-two she ought to be able——'

Lady Shore sat up abruptly.

'They might marry her for her money!' she exclaimed. 'I *won't* have a foreign son-in-law. I've borne a great deal, *but I won't bear that!*'

'No, of course not,' soothed Frances sympathetically.

'I shall get along all right,' continued Lady Shore. 'I've had to do without you to some extent lately. Whenever Sidonia's in the house she expects you to dance attendance. It's natural enough, I'm a dull old woman, I'm too vague to be a mother. You two have always been very good friends since Sidonia began to grow up.'

Frances glanced at her in surprise; this did not sound quite like Prudence.

'I've missed you, of course,' Lady Shore went on, 'but at my age those things happen.'

'Don't be so absurd, I'm nearly as old.'

'No, Frances, not in your mind. My mind's as old as ancient Egypt—I've begun to realize that lately.'

'Damn!' exclaimed Frances with sudden impatience. 'You two just tear me in half. If I stay Sidonia may elope with a dago, and if I go you'll probably get lost!'

They laughed. Lady Shore took Frances' hand and began to pat it lightly.

'I used to say there was no time, Frances; a consoling thought, but not true. Time has found me out, he always does; I'm very old for my age. I ought to be going abroad with my daughter—looking forward to it, I suppose—but the thought leaves me absolutely paralysed. I could no more stay Sidonia's course than fly to the top of Saint Paul's. Still, I have my duty towards the child; she ought not to go alone, and as I'm incapable of giving her myself I must give her my friend, that's all.'

They sat in silence for quite a long time; neither of them felt very happy. Presently Frances got up.

'All right, I'll go to Italy with her.'

CHAPTER FIFTEEN

I

SIDONIA stood on the Ponte Vecchio and gazed down at the Arno. Up in the mountains there had been a fall of snow, and the water was intensely green. Sidonia's eyes were also very green, not unlike the river they stared at, but misted over, as though half hidden behind a curtain of dreams. Presently she lifted her eyes from the water and looked intently at the mountains, which stood in an exquisite clear-cut line, deep blue against the sky. Her hair blew back from her slightly flushed cheeks, the fur at her throat had fallen open. People paused to stare, struck by her beauty and by the expression of contemplation on her face.

Frances stood patiently waiting behind her, with the collar of her coat turned up. Her hands were thrust deeply into her pockets, for the wind, blowing straight down on Florence from the snow, was bitterly, cruelly cold.

The traffic on the bridge proceeded noisily: 'E-e-e yup!' And the cracking of whips. Crack, crack, crack! The clatter of hoofs and the jangle of bells from passing market carts. A beggar stood still and pulled up his sleeve, exposing a withered arm. He explained to Frances, in voluble Florentine, that God was particularly fond of His poor. Frances shook her head, but Sidonia turned round.

'Give him something,' she ordered briefly. And then, apparently forgetting the man, she continued to gaze at the view.

'It's nearly lunch-time, Sidonia.'

If Sidonia heard she gave no sign; she appeared to be smiling at her thoughts.

Presently Frances began again:

'Well, I'm going, anyhow, I'm frozen to death. Do come, you'll get influenza or something; look at your fur all undone!'

Sidonia turned and followed reluctantly; she was walking more slowly than usual, dawdling along in the bitter wind of which she was apparently unconscious. The ancient buildings either side of the bridge seemed to attract her irresistibly. Her eyes dwelt with love on their low-hung tiled roofs and heavy projecting beams.

'It's queer,' she remarked, 'but it all seems familiar. It seems like a very old friend.'

They continued their walk to the Hotel Albion, where they had taken rooms. Sidonia was very silent, with slightly drooped head, apparently lost in thought. She had been in this strange, introspective mood ever since their arrival on the previous day; and Frances, who had never seen her quite like this before, began to feel rather worried. Had Sidonia overworked? Was she tired, perhaps? But she did not look at all tired. Frances, glancing at her now, thought how splendidly vital she looked. Vital, yes, but a little subdued.

'She reminds me of an arc-light with a shade thrown over it,' she thought, still puzzled and anxious.

She was somewhat relieved at luncheon, however, by Sidonia's huge appetite.

'I simple adore this food!' she announced, heaping up a plateful of spaghetti.

Luncheon finished at last, they went upstairs to their little sitting-room. The windows looked over the river to the Borgo San Jacopo. Sidonia stood for some time at the window, then she sighed and stretched her arms.

'What's the programme for this afternoon?' inquired Frances.

Sidonia turned round, looking vague.

'I don't know—don't let's have any programme, let's just wander about the streets.'

The suggestion did not appeal to Frances, but she gave in nevertheless. No doubt this queer mood of Sidonia's would pass, and then she would get to work.

They wandered about the streets until dusk. It was market day, Florence was crowded. In the Piazza Signoria they found themselves jammed in a huge, gesticulating, heaving throng, who jostled and swore and laughed. Farmers in heavy, red homespun coats with yellow fur collars turned up to their noses; women with loudly-protesting chickens tucked away under their arms; business men, vainly trying to pass, pushing and thrusting with their shoulders; children scrambling in and out or dodging in front of the slowly-moving horses. 'E-e-e yup!' Crack! Crack! 'E-e-e yup! E-e-e yup!' from the impatient drivers.

The dusk, when it fell, was a thing of beauty, calm and very translucent. It came to Florence from the outlying hills, from the still more distant mountains. A tinge of after-glow lingered round it, like a smile on a thoughtful face. It cast its spell over people and buildings; mellowing, blending, welding together, melting them into its lovely whole, making them part of itself. The huge crowd still rocked from side to side, but its laughter seemed to have grown softer. It was slowly dispersing down the darkening streets, wandering in groups of twos and threes into the neighbouring Trattorie. Farmers and their wives climbed into ancient carts with crates of fowls tucked away under their seats. 'Avanti!' Crack! Crack! 'Avanti! E-e-e yup!' There was more room now, you could hear hoofs striking sharply on the stones. The fiaccherai waved their shabby whips. 'Vettura, Signore? Vettura?' The spell of the dusk had lifted. Dogs, long imprisoned in the crowd, barked their freedom. A child began to wail. Some girls, arm in arm, strolled across the Piazza, bare-headed. The Piazza was gradually finding itself again, stretching its arms in relief. A star came out over the Palazzo Vecchio. It looked like a point of very bright steel pricking the evening sky. Some clouds, still faintly tinged with pink, sailed slowly behind the open arches of the tower.

'E-e-e yup!' And the crack of whips growing fainter, as the little vetture drove off with their fares. Street lamps—now one, now two, now three; then, suddenly, all alight. The dusk had quietly sidled away, and night had come down on Florence.

That evening Sidonia said thoughtfully:

'Frances, I've found a new friend.'

Frances looked startled.

'Already, Sidonia?'

'Yes, it was love at first sight.'

'Well, who is it?' inquired Frances, trying to speak brightly, but feeling a little resentful.

'You'll never guess.'

'I'm not going to try. Where and when did you meet them?'

'In the Piazza Signoria.'

'This afternoon?'

Sidonia nodded.

'Are they male or female?' asked Frances.

Sidonia considered.

'She's old, very old; I expect she's really older than she seems. There's something a little dour about her, a little gloomy and fierce. She makes me think of the queerest things, battle and sudden death. Yet she's tender, too, she's terribly tender, her tenderness makes you afraid. And, above all, Frances, she's the symbol of home; of home that's been fought for and died for.'

Frances said:

'Darling, you sound quite mad. Supposing you try to explain. Who is this creature? I don't think I like her.'

'Florence!' said Sidonia gravely.

3

Florence! Of course, an entrancing city—still, one must be moderate in all things.

'But Sidonia's never been moderate in her life,' Frances argued with herself as the days slipped by.

But this reflection could not alter the fact that Sidonia was doing no work. In vain did Frances remind her of the scholarship, she merely shrugged her shoulders and smiled.

There was quite a new quality, too, in her smile, a kind of lazy indifference.

'We've been here three weeks and seen nothing at all.'

'There's plenty of time,' said Sidonia.

Not like her these words, 'There's plenty of time.' Yet now they were for ever on her lips.

'You've not even unpacked your note-books,' grumbled Frances, 'and we've not seen a thing of interest.'

'What on earth do you mean—we've seen nothing of interest?'

'Well, no galleries, no museums. You've scarcely looked at the Perseus even, though we walk through the Piazza every day!'

'I know him by heart, and, moreover, I don't like him.'

'You don't like him?'

'No, I don't. Benvenuto may have been a good enough jeweller, but he's too ornate as a sculptor.'

'I don't agree; still, let's go to San Lorenzo. You must see the Medici chapel.'

'Very well,' said Sidonia, but without enthusiasm, 'we'll go this afternoon if you like.'

'I don't understand you,' Frances exclaimed crossly. 'Here you are, a student of sculpture, and all you do is to dawdle round the streets in a kind of ridiculous trance. Up the Borgo San Lorenzo, down the Borgo San Lorenzo, admiring a lot of red blankets!'

'Yes, but think of the shops where the blankets live, they're almost under the pavement.'

'Well, what does that matter?'

'It matters a lot. That's exactly how I remember them; and then there's that darling Giovanni delle Bande Nere, sitting on his big stone perch. How can you say I'm not interested in sculpture? I stand in front of him for hours!'

'You bewilder me, Sidonia, I'm getting rather worried. You'll be asked to give an account of your work. Are you going to tell them that you used your scholarship to walk up and down the streets of Florence?'

Sidonia yawned.

'Don't fuss so, Frances, there's really plenty of time.'

'There is *not* time, my dear, only about four months left. We can't stop in Florence for ever.'

'Why not?'

'Oh, well, if you won't be serious——'

'But I am,' Sidonia assured her.

4

They went to San Lorenzo that afternoon. Sidonia was languid but patient.

'It almost seems a shame to go in out of the sun,' she remarked regretfully, as they entered.

'Got your note-book?' asked Frances, looking at her sharply.

'Oh, bother! It's at home. How stupid!'

She showed some interest in the Michael Angelos, especially in the tomb of the Magnifico. But her interest struck Frances as being historical rather than artistic in nature.

'He was indeed splendid!' murmured Sidonia.

Frances hastened to agree.

'Michael Angelo? Yes, a wonderful sculptor.'

'I wasn't thinking of him,' she was told, 'I was thinking just then of Lorenzo.'

The next day they visited the Bargello in the morning.

'What a building!' exclaimed Sidonia. 'Look at those splendid blocks of stone, the strength, the virility of them!'

Once inside, her enthusiasm appeared to wane, though this time she had brought her note-book. She engaged a voluble Tuscan guide, and could not understand a word he said. Frances translated as best she could, but Sidonia's attention wandered.

'Don't talk so much, Frances. It doesn't really matter, it's amusing to watch his face.'

'But——the Donatellos, the Verrocchios, Sidonia——'

'Yes, I know; well, here they all are!'

'They're superb!' said Frances in the voice of schoolmarm.

But Sidonia had turned away. Presently she said:

'It's curious, Frances, but they seem to me rather cold.'
Frances could scarcely believe her ears.
'Cold? You, a sculptor, consider them cold?'
'In Florence, yes,' said Sidonia.
The Della Robbias called forth more enthusiasm.
'Ah, colour at last!' she exclaimed.
She spent quite a long time examining the plaques,
especially the fruit round their borders.
'I can't help feeling,' she told Frances gravely, 'that
colour counts a great deal. I don't paint, more's the pity;
still, no good denying that colour makes all the difference.'
'What about form?'
'Oh, form's all right. It's quite satisfying in England, but
out here, somehow, one wants colour or sound. Sound is only
colour made articulate.'
Frances grunted.
'You shall have your colour; let's go on to the San Marco
convent.'
They went. Fra Angelico interested Sidonia, but not so
much as Savonarola. She was quite enthusiastic over his hair-
shirt.
'I like vital people,' she asserted.
'But I thought a hair-shirt was specially invented to reduce
vitality,' remarked Frances.
'Not at all. It requires enormous vitality to be able to
sustain it,' Sidonia told her.
Frances thought:
'Good Lord! This is awful! She's simply wasting their
money. They'll probably stop her next instalment. Has she
forgotten Jensen?' Aloud she said: 'Well, I don't like
extremes, in hair-shirts or anything else. Can't people say
their prayers without itching all over?'
'That depends on the temperament, Frances.'
But Frances was feeling argumentative, a fact which she
regretted the next moment.
'There are more ways than one of wearing a hair-shirt,
one need not always wear it physically.'
'Don't I know it!' exclaimed Sidonia with sudden passion.
'I'm perpetually wearing mine!'

'Wearing yours?'

'Yes, mine. Oh, you don't understand. I'm my own hair-shirt!' she finished fiercely.

They drove home together in gloomy silence, Sidonia refusing to speak. Even the Palazzo Vecchio failed to evoke her usual screams of delight.

'What perfect proportion!' suggested Frances, anxious to dissipate the gloom.

But Sidonia, chin sunk in the collar of her coat, did not even turn her eyes.

5

They spent a truly miserably evening, Frances not knowing why. Everything she said seemed to irritate. Finally she gave it up.

'Let's go to bed,' she suggested desperately. 'My feet are aching, aren't yours?'

'No, it's my heart. You go to bed; I'm not sleepy, I'll come along presently.'

And with this anti-soporific remark Frances had perforce to be content.

6

The next morning the atmosphere had cleared again; presumably Sidonia had slept well. There was nothing suggestive of the hair-shirt about her as she strolled into Frances' room. Her face was serenely calm and untroubled, her big, green eyes were luminous. But her first words after saying 'Good morning' were far from reassuring.

'Let's slack to-day, I feel beautifully lazy. We might go for a drive or something.'

'We *might*,' said Frances, sitting up in bed, 'only I don't think we will.'

'Why not?'

'Now look here, Sidonia, this can't go on. It's getting badly on my nerves. There's Rome to do and Venice and Naples, and we haven't begun Florence yet.'

'But there's plenty of time, why worry your head?'

Frances shot off one word.

'Jensen!'

If she expected Sidonia to flinch she was bitterly disappointed. All she got was:

'Jensen likes everyone to be themselves. I shall get going presently.'

People—Frances wondered if people would help, she knew a good few in Florence. So far she had not looked anyone up, perhaps she had better begin. But the people must be of the energetic kind, likely to shame Sidonia.

'I know!' she thought, with sudden inspiration, 'I'll write to Liza Ferrari.'

She had known the Ferraris for many years. Liza had once been a drawing-room singer of very marked talent and charm. When Ferrari had married her they had been quite poor. They had met in Paris when he was a student at the Conservatoire. Now they were said to be very rich through the death of an uncle of Ferrari's, but in spite of this they were mighty workers. Both of them still taught singing, presumably for the love of the thing, since money could be no object. Their villa had become the meeting-place of all the intellectuals in Florence. They themselves were quite the most interesting and original couple that Frances had ever known.

'I shan't explain them at all,' she thought, 'I'll just let them break on Sidonia.'

CHAPTER SIXTEEN

I

THROUGH the Barriera di Bellosguardo and up the steep, winding road. White walls on either side of the road, topped by olive orchards. The leaves of the olives silver-green in the rainy midday sun; a pale sun, bright and cool as water; it reminded you of moonlight. Along the road an occasional shrine painted on the side of the wall. Uncomplaining Madonnas with storm-scarred faces, clasping eternally smiling Infants, Infants who never cried. Sometimes a bunch of withered flowers left by a passer-by. Sometimes no flowers—nothing at all but the Baby's eternal, questioning smile, and His mother's enduring face. Here and there at a turn in the road a glimpse of Florence below. A small city heavy with bells and towers, bowed down under its domes. To-day a city of sunlit mist, lying in the curve of the sheltering hills like a child in the crook of an arm.

The horse strained and paused; he stumbled a little on the steep, rough surface of the road.

'Have we got much farther to go?' inquired Sidonia.

'No, here we are,' Frances told her.

The carriage stopped before the wooden gates of the Villa Sant' Antonio. It was seldom called by its name, however; it was known as the Villa Ferrari. As they pushed the gates open and walked into the garden they were greeted by a torrent of noise. Ten dogs of various breeds and sizes, from a large Maremma sheep-dog to a Yorkshire terrier, circled around them barking. The barking varied according to the dog, from deep baying to short, shrill yaps; moreover, it was rather difficult to know what sentiments inspired it.

From somewhere behind the Villa itself came more barking, distinctly angry; it sounded as though a pack of hounds were anxious to break from their kennel.

'Good Lord!' said Sidonia, not feeling brave, 'I hope the rest of them won't come to welcome us.'

A kid, tethered to the side of the path by a very smart collar and chain, called loudly for its mother in a peevish voice, growing more hysterical each moment. The clucking of fowls, the screams of a macaw, the not very distant crying of a baby; and more faintly, proceeding from the villa it seemed, a curious inharmonious sound that was yet suggestive of music.

'I think you said sound was colour made articulate!' remarked Frances, smiling slightly.

'Then this must be a kaleidoscope,' Sidonia admitted.

The villa was long and low and pink, with a very beautiful loggia. On every side stretched a terraced garden with groups of pointing cyprus. Near the house grew an ancient ilex tree of quite astonishing proportions.

They rang. The bell contributed its voice to the general pandemonium, a clamorous bell that seemed bent on suggesting that you must have pulled too hard. The sound of music was quite plain now, and still plainer when the door was opened. A piano, a violin, another piano and people singing in chorus—three different melodies played and sung at once, producing anything but melody.

'Will you please wait a moment?' said the servant, 'Signor Ferrari teaches.'

They waited in a wide, stone-vaulted hall among pots of arum lilies. At the end of this hall stood wrought-iron gates, through which they could see a room beyond. From this quarter came the loudest sounds, a lusty chorus and piano, though the violin being played upstairs seemed quite capable of holding its own.

Frances walked over to the wrought-iron gates.

'Umberto!' she called, peering in.

'Macché!' came a cheerful welcoming voice, as the music stopped abruptly.

A man sprang up from the grand piano and hurried

towards the gates. He was not very tall and inclined to be stout; dark skinned for a European. His eyes were large and red-brown in colour, fine eyes under heavy brows. His snow-white hair was cut *en brosse*, it gave him a fierce appearance, which, however, was contradicted by the gentle lines of his mouth. He was dressed from head to foot in white, even his pumps were of white doeskin. On nearly every finger of his beautiful hands he wore large emerald rings.

'Frances, how jolly to see you again!'

His English was very perfect; except for a trick of rolling his r's, it might have been his native tongue. As a matter of fact, he prided himself on having no native tongue; half Turkish, half Italian, and brought up in France, he spoke a variety of languages.

Frances introduced him to Sidonia; he surveyed her with grave approval. Sidonia looked back with less approval; she thought him distinctly strange. And, indeed, Ferrari did look strange until you got used to him; like everything else in the Villa Sant'Antonio, he wanted a lot of getting used to. After a time you thought him quite usual, white clothes, emerald rings and all; you could not conceive of him dressed otherwise, and moreover you grew to like it.

'Have you seen Liza?' he inquired rather eagerly; he was always eager about Liza.

They explained that they had only just arrived.

'Wait a minute, I'll call her,' he said.

But he did not call, he literally bellowed; the sound was astonishingly powerful.

'Liza, come down! Here's Frances and her friend.'

'Come up, come up!' came a voice.

They turned to ascend in the direction of the voice, which kept on giving instructions.

'I'm in the day nursery, fourth door on the right, mind the two steps down on the landing!'

The nursery was an outsize room, it had at least five large windows. It seemed to be looking everywhere at once and greedily collecting all the sunshine. On a brick hearth burnt a huge log-fire, counteracted, however, by the five open windows. In front of the fire sat Liza Ferrari with a naked, sun-tanned baby on her lap. She was deeply engrossed in tickling its stomach with a teasing, maternal finger.

She tucked the infant under her arm and got up to welcome her guests. Like her husband, she was dressed entirely in white; but in her case the fact that she wore flowing garments made her look slightly sacerdotal. Her silver-blonde hair was loosely knotted in her neck. She was tall and full-breasted, pale and blue-eyed, with unexpectedly red lips. As you looked at Liza you knew she was not beautiful, and you wondered why you thought that she was. When she smiled you understood the illusion, for the smile redeemed her whole face. Her voice was quiet and she spoke very slowly, in striking contrast to her husband, who literally gabbled in his moments of excitement, which were frequent. Her mother had been a Roman, her father English, and in consequence she was bilingual. She combined the majestic soul of ancient Rome with the generous soul of the Eton playing fields. Her parents' union had been an unalloyed success. The consequence of it was Liza.

She turned to Frances.

'Sit down, my dear. Miss Shore, take that comfortable chair. You don't mind my baby, I hope? He's teething, he may begin to cry at any minute.'

As though he had understood her words, the baby puckered up his face, then he caught sight of Frances' eye-glass and yelled, kicking strongly the while. Ferrari took his protesting son, and began to prance round the room.

'Gira gira il mondo,
Gira gira tondo,'

he sang in his huge bass voice.

In the midst of the overwhelming hubbub, howling infant and booming father, Liza remained inexpressibly calm, talking to Frances and Sidonia.

Sidonia thought:

'She's like Ceres the Mother, she ought to have a sheaf of corn. I believe if she went out and smiled at the garden things would begin to bloom.'

A mighty gong, in keeping with all the other noises, vibrated through the house. A nurse was summoned to take the baby, and they went downstairs to *colazione*.

2

The dining-hall was even bigger than the nursery, a truly palatial apartment, in the middle of which stood a long refectory table, large enough to seat a school of monks. The table was very simply appointed, roses were its only costly feature. They stood in a low bowl of beaten copper, a mass of deep-red blooms. Around the table were eighteen oak chairs of the strong, rush-bottomed variety. They appeared to belong to the several stages of human development and growth. There were adult chairs, semi-adult chairs and baby chairs on kind, long legs. Sidonia, who had thought that the infant upstairs was the only offspring, looked surprised. The next moment she understood, however, for the children began to come in. They filed past, in a neat, well-groomed procession, smelling slightly of coal-tar soap. By way of introduction their mother called their names. It was like the roll-call of an army.

'Maurice! Geppe! William! Flavia! Jane! Pietrino! Giacinto! Olivia!'

Eight in all, not counting the baby, Ascanio, who appeared in his nurse's arms. The eldest, Maurice, was just fourteen; the youngest, six months old.

'I have them so easily,' Liza explained, 'much more easily than some of our ewes. I go up in the morning and I'm down in the evening. In the meantime I've borne a child.'

A governess marshalled the children to their seats, the nurse took her place with the baby on her knee. Four of the pupils were staying to lunch, two young men and a couple of girls. There was some confusion over the seats. Jane, aged three, wished to sit by her mother. But the places either side were for Frances and Sidonia, and next to Sidonia sat Ferrari.

'If I don't come up here we shan't hear each other speak,' he explained in his penetrating voice.

It reminded Sidonia a little of Crossby. She thought she must have heard him wherever he sat, and however great the disturbance. Jane began to cry. It was not an English cry in spite of her English name. It was purely Latin, a kind of throaty blare, hoarse with temper and abandon.

'Io voglio! Io voglio! Io voglio!' she screamed, clinging to Sidonia's chair. Disengaged at last, she subsided on the floor in a furious, crumpled heap.

In the end they were settled, including six dogs, who reposed on rugs in a corner. The food was served by two men in white duck, wearing white cotton gloves. One of the gloves had a rent in the finger, but the nail that protruded was clean. Had it not been, its owner would almost certainly have been sent to attend to the offending member.

'I can't endure dirt,' Liza was always saying, 'I hate it inside or out.'

Several neat maids stood behind the children's chairs, doubtless to avert disasters. Their faces wore the anxious, vigilant expression associated with fielding at a cricket match. The dishes were all vegetarian, but delicious nevertheless. There was also an endless variety of them, over which the children disputed.

'We never eat corpses,' Liza told Sidonia, 'poor, decomposing beasts!'

'I like this food better,' Sidonia said politely.

'You would if you knew what happens to meat when it's left too long in the sun.'

Sidonia tried hard to curb her imagination; she was eating spaghetti at that moment!

Everyone said exactly what they liked with astonishingly naïve abandon. And everyone ate exactly what they liked, exactly how and when they liked it. The children all grabbed and talked and grabbed; they spoke English and Italian equally.

'Dai mi dell'uva.'

'Pig! You've had enough grapes.'

'No, I haven't; ancora dell-uva!'

'There's a fat white worm in my fig,' remarked Geppe, holding up a maggot for inspection.

'Be careful, don't kill it!' exclaimed his father anxiously. 'Go and put it out in the garden.'

'Papà, papà, I've got one too!' shrieked Jane in triumph. 'Mine's much bigger than Geppe's.'

'Give it to me,' commanded Ferrari, 'we'll let it walk about on the roses.'

Sidonia wondered what they did with fleas; she could not resist asking.

'I open the window and they hop,' he said gravely, not at all amused at her question.

The two male pupils began to get excited.

'Ma nò!'

'Ma sì!'

'Ma *nò* ti dico!'

Sidonia could not hear what else they said, if indeed there was anything else. They seemed to be crossly bumping up and down on a kind of verbal see-saw.

'Ma nò!'

'Ma sì!'

'Ma *nò*!'

'Ma *sì*!' They were quarrelling like naughty children.

Liza rang a minute silver bell, which produced a temporary silence.

'I have to call Time occasionally,' she explained, 'it's so bad for the voice to get angry.'

Flavia, aged five, had been quiet so far, engrossed in filling her stomach. Now she looked up with a bright expression, taking advantage of the lull.

'Our cats got married this morning,' she piped, 'they'll have a lot of little cats to-morrow.'

Her mother smiled placidly:

'Not to-morrow, dear, in nine weeks; God is never in a hurry.'

A very fat sheep strolled into the room through one of the open French windows. It wore a red collar with silver studs, and its fleece had obviously been combed. It stared at the table with stupid eyes, then, turning, stamped its foot at the dogs. Hitherto they had been very good, but now there was general post—barking, scuffling, charging, butting. A game of the purest pretence.

'Enough!' boomed Ferrari in a cheerful, warning voice.

'Povera pecorella!' murmured Liza sympathetically.

Finally, the pecorella beat a retreat by way of the garden window. But the dogs were roused; they desired to play and accordingly started to do so, under the table and round the table, bumping into the chairs.

'You don't mind our beasts, do you?' inquired Liza. 'We each have a dog.' And then, as though wishing to be strictly truthful, 'The servants each have one too.'

3

At the end of luncheon Ferrari said abruptly:

'Miss Shore, let me look at your throat.'

The request was so sudden that Sidonia felt startled. Did he think that she looked ill or something? He took her arm and led her to the window.

'Open your mouth. Wider, please.'

Everyone went on laughing and talking, no one evinced surprise.

'Now wider—say "ah"! Yes, just as I thought; you should have a magnificent organ. It's a bad time to try it directly after food; still, if you don't mind. Leave us alone for ten minutes,' he ordered, pushing Sidonia into the hall and towards the wrought-iron gates. Once through the gates he turned and stared at her. 'I knew it from your face, I could see it.'

'But I'm a sculptor,' she told him weakly.

'Cold! cold!' he murmured, shaking his head.

Curious that he should say that, she thought; she had felt it herself just lately. He went over to the piano.

'Now then, a scale,' he commanded, giving her the note. 'Say "ah", and go right up the scale, stopping when you feel you must.'

'But my voice isn't trained, I've never tried to sing.'

'All the better. Now, we'll begin.'

She opened her mouth and let it come, a full, strong, satisfying sound, and finally lit on E in alt, like a bird that drops on to a bough. She was conscious of a new excitement as the notes bubbled up in her throat, a thrill that was almost akin to joy at the sounds she herself was producing.

'Liza!' roared Ferrari. 'Liza, come here! Oh, hell, where are you, Liza?'

She came, not hurrying at all, it seemed, in spite of his excitement. Her quiet eyes dwelt on the two by the piano, and she smiled at them, comprehending.

Ferrari turned impetuously to Sidonia.

'Do it again,' he ordered.

Sidonia, nothing loth, did it again.

'What about that?' inquired Ferrari. 'Don't say I can't see a voice in a throat. What about that, my Liza?'

Liza nodded.

'Yes,' she said, in her quiet, slow tones, 'a wonderful voice, but quite untrained; it needs training. Didn't you know that you had such a voice?'

Sidonia shook her head.

'I'm a sculptor,' she heard herself telling Liza. 'I'm out here on a Travelling Scholarship.'

'You don't look like a sculptor,' said Liza thoughtfully, 'you look much more like a singer.'

Ferrari was walking up and down with excitement.

'You shall take her first, my Liza. You shall place the voice, and when that's done you'll hand her on to me, and I'll teach her.'

'But I can't——' began Sidonia.

Liza looked at her and smiled.

'But you *must*, with a voice like that,' she said gently.

'You don't understand. I'm not free, I'm bound, I'm here to study sculpture.'

'Well, don't let us worry; come on Wednesday at eleven, and then I'll give you your first lesson. After that you can go home and think it all out. Where there's a will there's a way.'

They joined the others in the pleasant salon.

'Has she got a good voice?' inquired Frances indifferently.

Ferrari expatiated on Sidonia's voice, while Sidonia sat brooding uncomfortably. When Liza interrupted to talk about her children she was conscious of distinct relief. Liza had wonderful children, it seemed, they nearly all showed some talent; but she talked quite naturally and gently about it, as though it were a matter of course. There was Maurice; they had heard him playing that morning? He would make a very fine violinist. And Pietrino, aged ten, who could read scores at sight, he wanted to conduct an opera. She went over them one by one on her fingers.

'In case I lose count,' she explained. 'I only hope I may have nine more. I'm a blissfully easy breeder.'

CHAPTER SEVENTEEN

I

WHEN the day arrived for Sidonia's first singing lesson Frances refused to accompany her.

'No, I'm not coming,' she said briefly, and would give no other explanation.

Sidonia found the Villa Ferrari in its usual good-tempered uproar, but Liza took her to the top of the house, where she had her own little studio.

'We shan't be disturbed in here, Miss Shore. It's better so at the beginning.'

They went through a number of exercises. Liza was quietly enthusiastic; Sidonia had a wonderful voice, a fine dramatic soprano. In the end, Sidonia did not quite know how it happened, she found herself arranging to take four lessons a week; Liza would not hear of less than that. She telephoned down to Florence for a piano to be taken to Sidonia's sitting-room.

'I've told them that they must deliver it at once. They know me, you ought to get it to-day; whatever we do, we mustn't lose time.'

Sidonia refused to stay to lunch, making some vague excuse. She thought:

'If I can't be alone to think this thing out I know I'll go raving mad!'

Her vettura was waiting, and she told the man to drive to the Boboli Gardens. All the way down from Bellosguardo her mind kept hammering out one name: 'Jensen, Jensen, Jensen.'

Jensen had not written, but then he never wrote. When his pupils went forth to try their wings he preferred to leave them quite free. She had sent him two picture-postcards, she remembered, but that had been on her first arrival. Since that she had not cared to write to him, not knowing exactly what to say.

Einar Jensen—such far-seeing eyes, such coarse woollen socks, and such faith! A man had no business with faith like that, it was cruel to himself and to others. His sort of faith was an outrage, she decided; he talked about leaving everyone free, and then chained them down with his faith.

After all, what was faith but a huge self-delusion? You wanted a thing very much indeed, and then you proceeded to grow your faith because that made you feel that you would get it. Faith was selfish too, excessively selfish. What Jensen wanted was not her success so much as his own by proxy. But he dressed it up, people always did, it sounded more picturesque to call it faith. Einar Jensen—coarse woollen socks that his bed-ridden wife lay knitting. Einar Jensen, how crooked he was—dropped as a little baby. How rough this road was that led down to Florence! Why didn't they roll in the stones? What a beautiful city, a frightening city; it had snared her—she could not get away. Jensen loved beauty, but he was in London helping Miss Lotter and Crossby. Working without any faith, this time, patiently. Why was he so patient? He had worked hard for her too, to get that diploma granted under the usual time. Well, that was for himself; he had wanted a star pupil, he had chosen to call it faith, that was all. There was nothing really genuine anywhere.

The vettura stopped at the Boboli Gardens. She got out and paid off the man. It was long past luncheon time, she didn't want luncheon. She was glad to find the gardens practically deserted. She began to wander aimlessly about among the ilex trees. Ilex, the symbol of immortality—Jensen, who longed so intensely to go on, who believed in his immortal soul. Faith again; but she wished she had it, even if it were a delusion. Christianity, theosophy and all the rest, they could not give her this boon of faith, she sought in vain in their books. Books, what were books? You could not find faith ready-made in printer's ink, it had to be in you, an integral part of your make-up, as it was with Jensen. And yet, even he had doubts, it seemed——— 'What will happen when I die? Shall my back grow straight, you think?' How he hated his crooked back!

She suddenly disliked the ilex trees, and walked to another part of the gardens. Why *should* Jensen be immortal? God! What an awful thought, to live for ever and ever! She must write to Jensen. What should she say? Should she tell him she had given up sculpture?

'But I've not given it up,' she said, speaking aloud. 'It's only that I'm not feeling like it at the moment!' The sound of her own voice reassured her a little; she was probably making herself miserable for nothing. Not likely that she would have worked for three years, only to give it all up in the end. She needed a rest, or at all events a change; she had worked too hard, that was it. If she didn't use her scholarship no harm would be done, provided she sent back the money. How lucky that Jensen was so understanding, so anxious that everyone should be themselves; it was one of his greatest qualities.

'But I wish his back wasn't so crooked,' she thought.

2

She left the gardens and walked slowly home. It was nearly three o'clock. Frances would probably be worried to death; she might even be waiting in the hall. But Frances was not waiting in the hall. Oh well, no doubt she thought that Sidonia had stayed at the villa for luncheon. She hurried upstairs to their sitting-room. Frances was placidly reading.

'Your piano's arrived,' she remarked, looking up.

'Already?'

'Yes.'

'Was there anything to pay?'

'I don't know, you'd better ask the porter.'

No word of inquiry as to where she had been, not even a sign of interest. A few months ago this must have hurt her; she had been so devoted to Frances. She was still devoted but in a different way; the glamour of Frances had died. Now it was just: 'That darling old thing who makes you feel you can't do without her.' At the moment, however, she omitted the 'darling'.

'I've had no luncheon,' she said crossly.

'Why?' inquired Frances. 'Are you fasting or something?'

'Of course not. I've been walking in the Boboli Gardens.'

'What an unseasonable occupation.'

'Yes, I do feel rather cold.' She waited, but no reply was forthcoming. 'I said I felt cold,' she repeated.

'Well, why not have a hot bath?'

Sidonia ignored this practical suggestion; she went to the piano and began to play. She had played so little lately that her fingers felt stiff. She banged down the lid and jumped up.

'Oh, I know what you're thinking about me, Frances!'

'For your sake I hope you don't.'

'As bad as that?'

'Yes, quite as bad. I think you're behaving like a cad!'

Sidonia flushed angrily.

'Be careful—*please*!'

'I don't intend to be careful.'

'I'm not a child. Frances.'

'No, that's the trouble, you've arrived at years of discretion.'

'May I ask if all this is because I've had a singing lesson?'

'That's only a part of the whole.'

'Well, is it because I don't feel like studying—studying sculpture, I mean?'

Frances quietly closed her book.

'It's because you've taken money that you had no right to, and not only that——'

Sidonia interrupted.

'But I'm going to send the money back at once.'

'And not only that,' repeated Frances slowly, 'you've deprived another student of winning the scholarship; you've stolen someone else's opportunity.'

This aspect of the case had not occurred to Sidonia; it

was certainly disconcerting. She began to pace up and down the room.

'If I tell you that I can't help myself——'

Frances frowned.

'Then it's time you learnt how; you're not a child, as you say.'

Sidonia stopped pacing, she stood very still. Her eyes looked bright and startled.

'Frances, I think it's going to happen again.'

'Do you? I think it's happened.'

They were silent for a time, then Sidonia said softly:

'You despise me rather, don't you?'

Frances threw away a half-smoked cigarette.

'Yes, frankly, I think I do. Your infant manias, drawing, poetry, painting, religion, were all very well. Then came your dancing and piano playing; even then you were only a child. But your sculpture is different, it's more mature, and consequently more significant. What you do to your sculpture you do to yourself, it's become so much part of you. For over three years now you've worked at modelling, worked as though you were possessed at times; yet now, in three weeks, you propose to give it up and study something quite different. You go to lunch with my friends, the Ferraris; Ferrari tries your voice. He always tries everyone's voice that goes there—he tried mine once, years ago. Then Liza insists on giving you a lesson, that's because she's mad about teaching. I assure you she sees a prospective pupil in every beggar she meets. You may have a fine voice, I don't know, I can't see that it matters much either way. I only wanted you to meet the Ferraris because I knew they were workers. I thought: "If Sidonia meets those kind of people they may shame her into doing her job." And what's the result? Four men and a piano that's much too big for the room! I can only suppose that you mean to take lessons, otherwise why the piano? And all this in the middle of a Travelling Scholarship that you've stolen from someone else. Good heavens! You throw away things and people as though they were so many old boots! Have you no sense of duty? No stability? I was almost going to say, no pity?'

132

'Pity? For whom?'

'I was thinking of Jensen; you don't show much pity for him, do you?'

'Or for myself either I think you might add.'

'Yes, I might, but I don't intend to. You've always got pity to spare for yourself. You're so busy pitying Sidonia Shore that you can't see an inch beyond her.'

'I don't know why I let you speak to me like this,' said Sidonia, amazed at her own forbearance.

'Don't you? Well, then, I'll tell you; I know quite well. You'd infinitely rather I talked about *you*, no matter how, than not at all. What you'd hate would be for me to ignore you.'

'Then why don't you ignore me?'

'Because I can't,' said Frances thoughtfully. 'No one will ever be able to ignore you.'

Sidonia seized her hand.

'Be patient with me, Frances. Darling, do try to understand. I think it's this place, I think it's bewitched me. If you'd studied as much theosophy as I have you'd know that that sort of thing can happen. It's a kind of pre-natal lure.'

'What perfect rot! It may strike you as interesting to have nine lives like a cat, but in my opinion it's preferable to concentrate on living one life honestly.' Frances got up. 'I must write to your mother, she'll have to be told what has happened.'

'Very well,' said Sidonia, 'I'll write to Jensen and send him a cheque. I don't know where to return the money, I shall ask him to do it for me.'

Frances stared at her incredulously for a moment, then she left the room.

3

Sidonia sat down and seized her pen; she must write to Jensen at once. She felt hard and not a little resentful. Frances had misunderstood her. She began:

'CHER MAÎTRE,

'I enclose a cheque for the Scholarship money received

133

so far. I am quite unable to work, I find; a pity, but there it is. I can't keep the money and not do the work. Will you send it to the proper quarter for me? Of course, I have not given up my sculpture, this is only a temporary lull. Later on, perhaps in a year or sooner, I expect I shall take it up again. This loss of interest in my work does not surprise me, it has happened to me over other things before, and feeling as I do, it is absolutely useless for me to force my inclination.'

She paused and nibbled the top of her pen. She had a sudden vision of Einar Jensen—little and grey and crooked. Oh, damn it all! What *was* the use! Better be brutal and have done with it. But she wrote:

'Oh, mon maître, when I think of you I can scarcely bear what has happened! You, who had such great faith in me. Why did you have such faith? I wasn't worthy of it; no one living could be worthy of faith like yours. What will you say when you get this letter? No, that doesn't matter, it's what will you think? You were such a friend to me, don't stop being my friend. A truly terrible thing has happened; my love for sculpture seems to have gone. I look at the splendid statues out here, and I don't seem to understand them; I've lost my appreciation. When I tell you that I find ours a cold, lifeless art you will realize the greatness of my disaster. It has all come so quickly, with such awful suddenness, that I scarcely realize what has happened. But I want to be perfectly frank with you, I feel I must keep nothing back. I am going to study singing in Florence, I had my first lesson this morning; and now I know that I simply must sing, the urge is too great to crush down. I have always longed to express myself, and in singing I may find expression. Write to me quickly and say that you forgive, say that you understand.'

In ten days' time she got his reply. He wrote English better than he spoke it.

'CHÈRE ENFANT,
    'I do not understand, but that is my fault, not yours. I see

134

only darkly, we all of us do, therefore ridiculous to judge. You must be yourself, wherever it may lead, that is all that anyone can be. Everyone acts according to his lights, according to the spirit that is in him. Perhaps in time spirit grows so pure that it makes mistakes no longer. In any case, mon enfant, every path leads somewhere, there is no *cul de sac* in life. But you, you will not be a sculptor any more, that I feel in myself. You had a very beautiful gift, it gave me great joy to see it. If it has left you you are not to blame, perhaps there was fault with my teaching. You know I must always be your friend. Come and see me sometimes when you get back to England.'

4

Lady Shore wrote a somewhat involved epistle in reply to Frances' letter. She said that she had had very bad lumbago, that Sidonia would always be difficult to manage, that Horus was down with a moult and asthma, that Blake and the cook disliked each other and in consequence the housemaid had left, that Professor Budge had asked her to tea in his room at the British Museum, that Ptah was showing peculiar propensities considering his limitations, and when on the third page she returned to Sidonia it was only to say what Frances knew already, namely that since Sidonia had money of her own she would obviously study whatever she pleased, however and wherever she chose.

5

For nearly three weeks Frances held aloof, in spite of Sidonia's wooing. In the end, however, she bowed to the inevitable; what was the good of quarrelling with Sidonia? And then it was Christmas, a bad time for quarrels. Sidonia was thoroughly launched on her lessons. She had shown Jensen's letter to Frances.

'He's a wonderful man, don't you think so, Frances? You see he bears no resentment.'

On the whole Sidonia seemed happy and peaceful, a peace not altogether shared, however, by the other inmates of the hotel.

'Do, do, do! Ré, ré, ré! Mi, mi, mi!' sang Sidonia, varied by other vocal gymnastics all with abominable tunes. There were also a great many 'Ahs' and 'Ous' to be heard at all hours of the day.

Her voice was so big that you could not escape it, it chased you wherever you went. People stood still on the Lung' Arno to listen.

'Che bella voce!' they murmured.

The occasion when she arrived home with her first song was almost epoch-making.

'Caro mio ben!' she sang delightedly, and yet again, 'Caro mio ben!'

But she found it difficult to learn the song, she was not a quick musical student. Reading had always been her stumbling-block, and she found it so now more than ever. But Liza was not at all down-hearted; she assured Sidonia that opera singers were often rather stupid about learning their rôles. They had to employ a long-suffering man to din their parts into them note by note. Sidonia might have to do the same. After all, what mattered most was the voice, and Sidonia had plenty of that.

CHAPTER EIGHTEEN

I

EASTER came early but warm that year, and with it came Lady Shore. She had suddenly decided to visit Frances, and incidentally Florence and Sidonia. She arrived without Blake, to save expense, a quite unnecessary economy. It took her a week to recover from the journey, and another to get used to the food.

'It's all so greasy!' she complained distastefully. 'I must be growing very insular.'

Frances thought that she was looking older and not at all well. She evinced certain new timidities too, she was nervous of going out alone.

'They all talk so fast that it bewilders me,' she said. 'I never could learn Italian.'

She had brought with her a Baedeker and what appeared to be a kind of conversation handbook. Frances found the latter in her bag one day. It was called *The Little Help-Mate in Italy*. She opened *The Little Help-Mate* at random and read with some surprise: 'I will wear my green coat and my nankeen pantaloons.' 'Kindly bring me my black cashmere boots and the new crinoline from my wardrobe.' And further: 'I trust that the train will not be late. At what time does the packet leave Naples?'

Frances looked up at Lady Shore.

'Have you studied this book?' she inquired.

'Not yet, I found it among Godfrey's papers; I thought it might come in useful.'

'Well, I think I'd let it alone,' said Frances, 'it seems to me rather decadent.'

They took Lady Shore to tea with the Ferraris, but were

careful to prepare her for what she might find. What she did find was Giacinto, aged six, stark naked, except for a large pink bow on his head. He was playing with a dog in the music-room, and he shook hands with them gravely.

'It's so warm,' explained Liza, 'and I love them to feel free.'

It gave Lady Shore an unpleasant shock, her mind flew back to the dressing-room at Miss Valery's dancing class. Of course, Sidonia was older now; still—the force of example——

The other children began to appear, they all seemed scantily clad. As far as Lady Shore could make out they were not wearing more than one garment a-piece.

'Aren't you afraid they'll catch cold?' she inquired, but Liza shook her head.

'Oh, no, I believe in sunshine and air. We all take sun-baths later on.'

'Not *all* of you surely?' murmured Lady Shore in a confidential undertone.

'Oh yes, we do, and the pupils as well; it's wonderfully good for the voice.'

A silence descended on the group after this, but Liza continued to smile. Presently she said:

'My husband and I always try to live very close to Nature. For one thing we find that it keeps us well, for another that it keeps us kind.'

She suggested that Sidonia should sing for them.

'Your mother must hear your voice, my dear.'

Sidonia, nothing loth, sang her limited repertoire, while Lady Shore listened astonished. The volume of sound which her daughter produced made her feel a little breathless; she remembered that Horus was suffering from asthma in addition to a most prolific moult.

'I hope Blake won't forget to put those drops in his water,' she thought, growing suddenly anxious.

Giacinto sidled over and slipped his hand into hers.

'Don't you think my bow nice?' he whispered.

Lady Shore nodded untruthfully.

'I like it too,' said Giacinto in her ear. 'My hair gets so

greasy we have to tie it up. When it's hot it gets greasy like Papà's nose—it's terribly greasy now.' He lifted her hand to the top of his head. 'You feel, it will make your hands shiny.' And then more loudly: 'You can rub it if you want; I like you, I'll let you rub it.'

Ferrari came in, dressed in white as usual; his rings looked extremely large. They were also painful, as Lady Shore found, when he gave her his cordial handshake. He talked about Sidonia, she should have a great future, she had compass and a beautiful quality of tone. She had looks, too; he thought her a lovely creature, the perfect type for Isolde. Several pupils had followed in his wake, bringing with them a blast of high spirits. They began to invent new games for the children; one young man crawled on the floor.

'I'm a bear! I'm a bear!' he kept shouting in Italian. 'Catch me! Gr—r—r—r; I'm a bear!'

Liza sat watching this noisy performance with a lap-dog curled on her knee.

'I must always have Santuzza or a baby on my lap, otherwise I feel lonely,' she said.

2

That evening, Lady Shore complained of a headache and retired to bed with a hot-water bottle. Frances was giving her aspirin, when Lady Shore looked up with the pellet in her hand.

'My dear—of course they're old friends of yours—but really they shocked me terribly.'

Frances laughed.

'They're a law unto themselves, Prudence; they're the kindest-hearted people in the world.'

'But supposing—oh, no, I'm being ridiculous! How old is Sidonia, nearly twenty-three?—still, Madame Ferrari distinctly said that they *all* took sun-baths later on.' She sat up in bed looking suddenly frightened. 'It's just occurred to me that they'd take them together. I'm sure it's like mixed bathing!' Frances was silent, and Lady Shore went on: 'I mistrust this living so close to Nature, Nature's most unexpected. Look at Ptah, such a charming cat, and yet now——' She broke off abruptly.

'But, darling, the Ferraris aren't cats, they're very advanced human beings.'

'They may be too advanced; if you go too far you're apt to slip off the other end.'

'Well, I really wouldn't worry, I'm sure Sidonia's safe.'

Lady Shore swallowed her aspirin, then she lay down with a sigh.

'I think I'll go home,' she said rather weakly. 'I don't think this place is healthy.'

'I'd like to come with you,' Frances told her, feeling suddenly homesick.

'Oh, you can't do that!' exclaimed Lady Shore. 'Who's to look after the child?'

'She's not a child.'

'No, but she still is to me. Oh, dear! I'm terribly anxious.'

'Well, supposing I promise to stop till the summer?' said Frances.

Lady Shore opened her aching eyes.

'But what's going to happen then?'

'Sufficient unto the day is the Sidonia thereof,' soothed Frances; 'and now go to sleep.'

3

A week later Lady Shore returned to England. Frances felt unsettled and lonely. A gulf was opening between her and Sidonia, the gulf of interests not shared. It was no good, Frances continued to feel angry at Sidonia's latest departure. They had made up their quarrel, but to Frances, at all events, there remained a growing irritation. She did not pretend to be a judge of singing, and she did not admire Sidonia's voice. She supposed it might sound all right in an opera-house, but found it overwhelming out of one. She had never been really fond of grand opera. She informed Sidonia of this one day, without any adequate reason.

'I suppose you'll aspire to Wagner rôles?'

'Well, rather! I want to sing "Isolde".'

'When you do I shall go to sleep in the stalls, that's the way Wagner affects me.'

A moment later she wished she hadn't said it, Sidonia looked so surprised. She refrained from comment, but her looks said plainly:

'And I thought you were such an intelligent woman.'

But Frances felt nervous and rather wound up, she blundered on with her subject.

'It's not only the music, it's the singers. I can never get beyond their figures.'

'But if, as you say, you sleep peacefully through it, figures can't matter very much.'

'Yes, they do, there's an intermediate stage. I suppose I'm not spiritual enough. I ought not to want to laugh at Siegfried when he finds Brünnhilde on her mountain, but she's usually so much like a mountain herself, that his doubts regarding the lady's sex strike me as being funny. As a matter of fact I don't like grand opera.'

'Well, why should you?' smiled Sidonia.

But Frances frowned; Sidonia ought to want her to like it. In everything she had done hitherto Frances had been asked to take an interest. Yet she could hardly blame the girl, she had set herself so resolutely against the singing. She had said a good many hurtful things, and what had she gained? Why, nothing. Sidonia still sang and would go on singing, at all events for a time; in the end it might even be her career, one never knew with Sidonia. She took it for granted that Frances disapproved and apparently was content to leave it at that. Frances said: 'I'll have to be going home soon. I only came out for five months.'

'Yes, I know. I've been thinking of that,' said Sidonia. 'I suppose you'll stay on until the summer?'

No protest, no urging Frances to remain, just a calm acceptance of the fact that their lives had begun to run on separate lines.

'When you do go, Frances, I shall live with the Ferraris, I've spoken to Liza about it. She's willing to let me pay for my board, so that I'll feel quite free. In any case, I shall join them this summer. I'm going to Alassio with the summer school.'

'I see. And when do you propose to leave Florence?'

'At the end of June, as far as I know.'

Frances was silent for a moment, then she said:

'All right—I'll make my plans accordingly.'

CHAPTER NINETEEN

I

THE country began to blush with spring. The hillsides
and gardens surrounding Florence were heavy with
almond blossom. To Florence itself came rioting colour;
anemonies, crimson, purple and pink; hyacinths, lilac,
daffodils, violets, and the slim, striped cups of sweet-
smelling freesia. The shops were a blaze of flowers. Under
the arches of the Mercato Nuovo all the blossoms of the
earth seemed to be collected. They lay there together in
great, generous bundles, their gorgeous bodies contrasting
sharply with the grey of the time-worn stones. Sidonia
thought that they looked like slave girls displaying their
charms for sale.

The Porcellino sat smiling complacently, a spring smile,
a youthful smile for his age, almost the smile of a sucking-
pig. Sidonia could have sworn that this smile of his had a
way of changing with the seasons. She had grown to love
the old bronze boar, he was so enduring and faithful. His
sides were worn smooth by the legs of children, generations
of whom had climbed on to his back, and clung there
triumphant and fearless. He was theirs and they knew it,
his back was for them, for the future citizens of Florence.
But occasionally Sidonia felt that his welcome was extended
to her as well. He seemed at such times to be trying to
speak, trying to say something friendly. She could never
resist laying her hand on his neck, she always wanted to
touch him. One day she secretly kissed his nose, and left a
rose in his mouth.

This spring he sat in front of his market, like a monarch
awaiting homage. Behind him and stretching on either side

were the flowers of his Tuscan kingdom. Sidonia bought prodigal armfuls of these, she felt that she could never get enough. A kind of flower madness possessed her, she literally wallowed in them. It was wonderful weather, the sky deep blue, the river a soft, turbid yellow. The spirit of Florence was in a gay mood, you could hear it laughing down the streets. People greeted each other with new spring voices and smiled with new spring smiles. Sidonia was never to forget that spring in which she was so gloriously happy, so full of the splendid vitality of things, so contented to be just herself in Florence. Her mood found expression in her singing; she poured herself out in music.

Then Jensen died. He did it unobtrusively, almost apologetically. One week he was teaching the students as usual, and the next week he was dead. He had not even had an expensive illness; there had hardly been time for him to give much trouble—it was all very like Einar Jensen.

Sidonia received Miss Lotter's letter on her return from a singing lesson. She was feeling particularly joyful that morning, the lesson had gone so well.

Miss Lotter wrote because she was wounded and longed to wound in return. That was the way she took sorrow, poor soul, it made her feel desperate and angry. The letter began abruptly:

'I think I ought to tell you that Professor Jensen died a fortnight ago. I would have written sooner, but have been ill myself, and am only now able to write. His death has come as a great shock to us all, as I'm sure you will understand. He had not been well for some little time, but refused to take care of himself. Everyone thought he was looking ill, though he never mentioned his health. I think—we all do—that your failure grieved him more than he would admit; he seemed to lose interest after he heard that you wished to give up your Scholarship. Not that he failed towards us in any way, it would not have been like him to fail, but all the spirit went out of his teaching, it was rather dreadful to see.

'He caught a severe cold, which he neglected; it led to double pneumonia. I did what I could for them while he was ill; as you know, his wife has been bed-ridden for years. I went every evening, and just towards the end I sat up with him every night. They were not well off, and I wanted to save them what money I could in nurses. It did not last long, he was dead in a week; I was with him when he died. He was patient with me then as he always had been, and wonderfully uncomplaining. As for me, I have lost my only friend, the person I revered most on earth. I do not want to reproach you, Miss Shore, but why, oh! why did you do it? Why did you raise his hopes as you did, only to dash them down?

'It is only fair to tell you that he never complained, never criticized your conduct. But everyone at South Kensington knew how badly he must have felt; you placed him in such a dreadful position before the Board of Directors. He had always had such faith in you, and had worked so hard in your interest. But it was not the humiliation that killed him, he cared very little for public opinion; no, it was his faith in you, Miss Shore; when you broke that you broke Jensen. The others all think as I do in this, we feel that you treated him very badly.

'I am sorry if this letter comes as a shock, but I think it my duty to be frank. No doubt, had you realized the possible consequences, you would not have acted as you did.'

Sidonia re-read the letter three times; she felt stunned and unbelieving. Spring in Florence, the room full of flowers, and Einar Jensen dead! She snatched the glowing flowers from their vases, and opening the window, flung them into the street.

2

As she told Frances afterwards, it was not Jensen's death so much as what must have gone before. His disappointment, his broken faith, his desolate sense of failure; and then Miss Lotter to attend his last illness—Miss Lotter with him when he died. Sidonia pictured him helpless in bed, while

Miss Lotter fussed and dictated. She had always had such a heavy tread; it must have driven Jensen mad. And then her smile, with those difficult teeth that held her underlip so firmly; she could see that smile bending over Jensen, coaxing him to drink his medicine, and her silly voice, timid yet self-assertive, she could hear it going on and on:

'Can I turn your pillow, Professor? Are you easier?—Come now, you must take this Bengers—let me help you, don't try to move yourself.—Can't I do something to make you more comfortable?—Shall I give them any message at the school?'

Eternal questions, eternal solicitude, eternal brave, toothy smile. Eyes always welling with large, weak tears, voice always just a little too cheerful. And the bed-ridden man lying there saying nothing, perhaps even grateful to Miss Lotter; and his bed-ridden wife not knitting any more, or worse still, knitting on hopefully.

Sidonia could not sleep; always pictures, always memories. 'What will happen when I die? Shall my back grow straight you think?' Had his back grown straight? She lay wondering. Supposing there were now no Einar Jensen, supposing he had just gone out. In that case she would never be able to tell him how deeply sorry she was. She longed intensely to hear his voice. He would probably say: 'It not your fault. You had to be yourself; I never blamed.' Yes, that was the sort of thing Jensen would say.—If only she could hear him say it!

She could not sing. The lessons were put off; she wanted to indulge her sorrow. She could not go out because of the flowers, because it was spring in Florence. Her grief was as complete as her previous disregard. She reproached herself for what she had done, and for much that was purely imaginary. When Jensen did this, when Jensen said that, she had not done or said the right thing. In a thousand little ways she had failed towards him; her work had often been careless. Sometimes she had argued and taken her own line; sometimes she had sulked and done nothing; and always Jensen had been so patient—and then, his terrible faith. When she spoke of his faith she would burst into tears, unable to endure the thought of it.

Frances listened to much of this in silence, feeling that words were useless. Sidonia turned to her by instinct, as she might have done when she was a child.

'Don't talk, Frances, just let me talk to you; it helps me to tell you about it.' Or, 'I never knew how much Jensen mattered till he died. Do you think it's always like that?'

They would sit hand in hand in the soft spring evenings looking out towards the river, watching the lights as they blinked from the windows of the Borgo San Jacopo. Sidonia would say:

'Jensen never saw Florence. He saw so little that was beautiful.' And tears of genuine regret would well up and run slowly down her face.

Frances knew that this grief would pass; Sidonia was only twenty-three and Jensen had only been her teacher. At twenty-three grief dare not last, Nature is too much in need of our forces for purely physical affairs.

3

Frances picked up a queer old book one day in a second-hand book-shop. The book was in English, which attracted her attention, and she glanced through it with curiosity. It appeared to be a kind of simple treatise on the different theories held in the East regarding reincarnation; she finally bought the book for two lire after bargaining with the sales-man. She never quite knew what had made her buy it, unless it were the thought of Sidonia. Sidonia liked that sort of thing, it might distract her perhaps.

That afternoon Frances opened the book and began to read it herself. She found it extremely uninteresting, all save one chapter, part of which held her attention. She read:

'According to an Eastern tradition, whose origin is lost in antiquity, there are certain spirits who incarnate seven times only on Earth. The seventh incarnation of such a spirit is known as "The Final Path", but among those in the West who hold this theory it is sometimes referred to as "The Saturday Life".

'People who are living a "Saturday Life" are said to have no new experiences, but to spend it entirely in a last rehearsal of experiences previously gained. They are said to exhibit remarkable talent for a number of different things; but since they have many memories to revive, they can never concentrate for long on one. This also applies to their relations with people, which are generally unsatisfactory.

'Their lives are influenced from time to time by the people they have met in past incarnations; but those who are leading a "Saturday Life" cannot tarry too long with old friends; even though their affections be stirred, they can only shake hands and pass on.'

Frances glanced across at Sidonia, where she stood staring out of the window.

'There's something here that may interest you, Sidonia. Have you ever heard of a Saturday Life?'

Sidonia shook her head. She did not turn round.

'Well, read this,' said Frances, holding out the book.

Sidonia took it listlessly.

'What is it? Where did you get it?'

'I found it in a shop in the Via Ghibellina.'

Sidonia read the passage indicated, then she sat down and read it again. When she looked up her eyes were glowing with suppressed excitement.

'Of course, I don't believe in that sort of thing,' Frances said hastily.

'But supposing it were true?' Sidonia murmured. 'Supposing it were really true?'

She was staring in front of her with parted lips, her face flushed ever so slightly. The dull, blurred look of grief had gone, for the moment at all events. Frances said:

'Yes—if it were true, it would certainly help to explain—'

Sidonia came over and stood in front of her.

'It would explain *me*!' she said solemnly. Then suddenly a smile, as it were of relief, began to spread over her face. 'Nothing that's happened would be my fault. It couldn't be, could it, Frances?'

Frances hesitated.

'No—I *suppose* not—I suppose you'd be a victim, in a way.'

'I'd be serving a kind of Saturday Lifer. It sounds like a convict, doesn't it?'

'Well, you would be something very like a convict, chained to your previous experiences.'

A short silence ensued, then Sidonia said:

'If it were true, then I couldn't help Jensen; I had to do just what I've done. I had to hurt him and mourn him afterwards. He was part of my Saturday Life.'

Frances frowned.

'Of course, it's all rubbish, still it might be a dangerous theory. One feels that one ought to improve on things, not just go on making the same old mistakes.'

'Perhaps we have to digest our mistakes, so as to improve on them during some spiritual existence.'

'Um-m,' said Frances, polishing her eyeglass, 'we'll have all Eternity to do it in, that's some comfort.'

'I like the Saturday Life idea,' said Sidonia thoughtfully, 'though it makes me feel rather afraid.'

'Afraid of what?'

'I'm not perfectly sure, afraid of myself, perhaps. Afraid of anything very big and vital that might get bound up with me.'

'Well, I wouldn't worry, not on the strength of this silly old book.'

'As for that,' sighed Sidonia, 'I can't stop worrying since I heard of Jensen's death. I sometimes think I'll never sing again, all the joy's gone out of my music. And as for my lessons, I honestly feel incapable of going on with them. Frances, I mean it, I think it's over; I know I'll never sing again.'

Frances said nothing. Two weeks later Sidonia had resumed her lessons.

4

Gradually, as the spring turned to summer, Sidonia's

work absorbed her once more. The edges began to wear off her grief, and she found herself able to think of Jensen, to speak of him without tears. She was rather surprised and a little remorseful; she had thought that a grief like hers would last for the best part of a lifetime. And yet here it was, in a few weeks only, growing more tolerable every day. Not that she forgot Jensen, she would never forget him. But Jensen would soon have slipped into the place sometimes reserved for carefully-pressed flowers—rosemary for remembrance.

Frances was glad that this should be so, not only for Sidonia, but for herself as well; she longed to get back to England. She felt she could now leave Sidonia safely. She went to Cook's to inquire about tickets, to note down joyfully the hours of trains; she felt like a man setting out on an adventure, only her adventure was a little house in Young Street and a Queen Anne square that was home.

'I'll look after Sidonia,' said Liza. 'You can go back to your dirty old London, Sidonia will stay here with me.'

'And you needn't expect to see me for ages,' broke in Sidonia. 'I shan't come back to England till I'm fit to make my début. If you and mother are pining for a sight of me you'll have to come out to Florence.'

'But surely you'll come back for the holidays sometimes?'

'There won't be any holidays,' said Sidonia.

CHAPTER TWENTY

I

THE entire Ferrari household and ten of their pupils left Florence at the end of June. The muster at the station was a thing once seen never to be forgotten. Mountains of luggage were stacked about the platform, all bearing the Ferrari special label. Six servants led by six turbulent dogs were dragged up and down at intervals. A number of old pets had been left behind to make way for more recent acquisitions, who, as Liza explained, still felt rather strange, and must therefore accompany the family. 'You beasts must learn to be unselfish,' she had remarked on her final round of inspection.

From several stout, padlocked travelling hampers came sounds of indignant protest. Liza glanced once in their direction with a smile. There was Geppe's tame hare, who drummed with his feet and devoured green carpets, mistaking them for grass. According to Liza, this latter activity pointed to something far beyond instinct. There was Gilbert, the lemur, who belonged to Ferrari, and who wished to travel on his master's shoulder with a tail curled round his neck like a boa; Gilbert was shaking his hamper in fury. From another hamper came the doleful remonstrance of a cat with a litter of kittens; while Nannie Carmen's last born, being dragged towards the van, bleated loudly and butted with round, plush-covered stumps, at the legs of the long-suffering porter. There was also a pair of love-birds, whose small, persistent quarrelling could be heard through the cover of their elegant, dome-topped cage. A white rat or two, a dormouse and a slow-worm were disposed about the children's persons.

The eight children and the baby, three nurses and a governess stood lined up in front of the train. First came Maurice the eldest and tallest child, the others followed according to age. A little in front, like commanding officers, stood the three neat nurses and the governess. This military formation, Ferrari's own idea, was always carefully adhered to. The children were hatless, with their bare feet in sandals, the rest of them was dressed in spotless piqué.

Maurice was munching a thick bar of chocolate, Pietrino an apple, Olivia a pear. All the children were eating something, even the baby had a sponge cake; it was one of Liza Ferrari's health-rules that the children should eat before a journey. She liked them to eat on the journey as well, though two of them suffered from train sickness.

Liza surveyed her munching offspring with quiet, maternal pride. She was wearing a voluminous white cape over her white crêpe gown. She took no part in the general uproar, which she did not attempt to stem. She reminded Sidonia of a tall, white lighthouse in the midst of a surging sea.

Olivia snatched Pietrino's apple, he leant across and snatched her pear. The military line remained unbroken, but a violent altercation ensued:

'*Cattiva* te!'

'You know you've had two apples!'

'I have not! Bugiarda—liar!'

'Ghiotto! You're greedy like the Pecorella.'

'I'm not a sheep!'

'Well you're like one!'

'I'm *not*.'

'Basta, bambini,' commanded the governess, as the doors of the train were unlocked.

Ferrari, suddenly coming to life, began to wave his arms. He was dressed in his usual white clothes, and wore sandals like the children.

'Now then, get your places! Par içi, mademoiselle,' to a middle-aged French girl in a dust coat. 'Bambini, avanti!' The children broke line and scrambled into a carriage; after them hustled several dogs and a red-faced, perspiring nurse.

'Come along all of you, *do* come along! Now, pupils, don't get left behind.' He ran up and down the train giving orders; he was hatless and his white hair bristled.

The pupils consisted of several Italians, Sidonia and the middle-aged French girl, a young Welsh tenor and his delicate wife, a small Polish Jew with a large baritone voice, and two German sisters, who clung to their handbags with a dogged, Teutonic grip. On the linen covers of these cheap handbags were embroidered affectionate wishes from the Fatherland. In all, the party that left for Alassio, where Ferrari had taken two villas, consisted of thirty-one talkative souls, not including the dogs.

Frances, rather silent, a little depressed in spite of the near advent of England, grasped Sidonia's hand.

'Well—good-bye, be good, and take great care of yourself.'

Sidonia smiled and nodded from the window.

'Is everyone in?' yelled Ferrari.

A nurse shot out of the train like a rocket.

'Mia bambola!' wailed a voice.

'Leave it, leave it!' Ferrari commanded. 'We'll buy a new doll at Alassio.'

The nurse shot back without the doll, and the train began to move.

'Auf wiedersehen!'

'Good-bye!'

'Au revoir!'

'Addio! Addio!'

It was like the Tower of Babel. They waved and smiled at Frances and their friends where they stood on the receding platform. The train moved faster; Sidonia's face came to the window for a moment.

'My love to mother! Good-bye, darling!' She waved her hand and was gone.

Frances turned away; she must go straight back to the hotel and do her packing. It had been such a business getting Sidonia off, but now she must begin to think of herself; she was leaving for England the next morning. The hotel seemed strange without Sidonia. Frances took out the green case from Cook's that held her books of tickets. On the last of these appeared the word 'London', it looked almost unfamiliar. She had been away for nearly seven months. She knew she was longing to get home, yet now that England had come within reach she was sorry to be leaving Florence. She looked round the little sitting-room, and then at Sidonia's piano, that greedily usurped so much space; at any moment now the men might arrive to take it away. She had always disapproved of the piano, yet now she did not want it to go. She felt thoroughly tired and contrary, and inclined to be sentimental over things that had no real importance.

She folded and packed through the whole afternoon, stopping at last with a backache. She almost expected to hear Sidonia's voice coming from the communicating room.

She began to consider Sidonia. What a curious creature she was; how she had grieved over Einar Jensen! But it had not lasted; she was happy again, or so it seemed to Frances. 'And a good thing, too,' Frances told herself. 'She couldn't have kept it up for long, not that kind of desperate grief. It had to pass, it was like a storm—everything is with Sidonia!' Then she remembered the queer old book—of course, it was all perfect nonsense. 'The Saturday Life', she murmured thoughtfully, 'a preposterous idea, still—I wonder——?'

CHAPTER TWENTY-ONE

I

Two years of life at the Villa Ferrari, two brimming, delightful years! Sidonia looked round her at the terraced garden. Summer was coming once again to Bellosguardo. She stood there under the great ilex tree that seemed to protect the house. A kindly tree, a kindly house; both had given her hospitality and more—they had given her love, she felt. She stroked the tree with lingering fingers. Her thoughts hovered over the past two years, as a flight of migratory swallows might hover over some place of kind harbourage before bidding it farewell. What clever, broadminded people she had met; one always met such people at the Villa. They had become her friends, her companions; she knew that she would miss them terribly. These people believed in her voice, her career; they admired her beauty and said so openly, as people did in Italy, happy to praise. In the streets of Florence the humbler folk who knew her by sight would turn to stare: 'Guarda, guarda, la bella Inglese!' 'Guarda che bella biondina!' And Sidonia would feel glad that they found her good to look upon—glad that they delighted in the colour of her hair. She would smile to herself and walk proudly.

In all the two years she had never gone home, never left Florence except in the summer. Lady Shore and Frances had come out twice, but only for two or three weeks. Liza had once suggested a visit to Rome, but Sidonia had shaken her head.

'No, Liza, Florence is enough for me. Some day perhaps I'll go farther afield, but not yet, I don't want to go yet.'

The spell of Florence had held her fast, she had grown to

love its every corner. She and Liza would drive down together in the little carozza with its fringed linen top, so suggestive of a perambulator. The coachman, looking too big for the box, would whoop to the small plump ponies. The brake would squeak, the carozza would sway on to two wheels going round corners; but finally, by the grace of God, they would find themselves in the Tornabuoni. They would potter about in and out of the shops and lunch at Rigarno's, where Mamma Rigarno, very fat, very proud and perspiring profusely, made celestial omelettes in front of your eyes, while Papà Rigarno pretended to help her, and il figlio Rigarno served.

Then home again in the cool of the evening, if it happened to be spring, sunset and twilight contesting for Florence like knights for the favour of a much-loved lady, while a low-swung moon looked on. The barking of dogs, the cries of children as the carriage swung in at the gates; the screams of the macaw, the bleating of the kid (there was always a kid for the collar and chain, old Nanny Carmen saw to that); Ferrari's voice booming somewhere in the garden; the sound of several tunes being played at once; the clang of the noisy, embarrassing bell—it had all grown familiar, grown to be part of Sidonia's life, the life of the Villa Ferrari.

She was one of them now, an important spoke in the busy family wheel. An ingenious, yet very simple wheel, for ever revolving round Liza's ideals. Every ideal had a rule attached, by which the household was bound; and every rule was specially devised to make something or someone free! Many things were forbidden, but even more were gently insisted upon. You must wear as few clothes as convention permitted, and sometimes even fewer. You must worship the elements of sun and air, and avoid all animal food. It was wrong to tolerate the use of furs once you realized the horrors of trapping. It was wrong to vaccinate yourself or your children, because vivisection was wrong. You must not see anything indecent in Nature, if you did so you had a prurient mind; things were as they were, God had made them so. Who were you to know better than God? No baby was found under a gooseberry bush or brought in the doctor's bag;

156

then why say it was? If you lied to your children they would naturally grow up liars. The mystery of birth was a wonderful thing, every child must be taught to respect it. The moment a child asked intelligent questions you must tell it the whole truth at once. The very fact that the child had asked meant that it was old enough to know.

Beyond the rules that were necessary adjuncts to Liza's scheme of life she believed that no child, and indeed no adult, should ever be checked in anything; give them plenty of God's good air and sunshine and go on hoping for the best. The world was divided into three large sections: the good, the bad and the fools. There was, fortunately, plenty of room for them all; therefore, why interfere? But be kind. Nothing mattered so much as kindness; like faith, it could sometimes move mountains. Be kind to the good, and they would soon become better; be kind to the bad, and they might become good. As for the fools, they were more of a problem, but even so not quite hopeless. People who made a practice of repeating to themselves the magical words 'Be kind!' were never likely to do much harm. Naturally not, for to harm anything was obviously most *unkind*!

You never trod on a worm in your path, you carried it on to the border; you never trod on a human soul by doing it a vital wrong. Worms and souls, they were all God's property, as well as numerous intermediate things, such as horses and dogs, and cattle and chickens, and even mosquitoes and fleas. Could you create a flea? Could you resurrect a flea? Very well, then, why presume to kill it? If the flea was alive it was meant to live. If it bit you it wasn't its fault or yours, though it might be uncomfortable for you.

Be kind, be kind! Be kind to the plants, they might feel, one never could tell. If you cut their flowers you should do it skilfully, thus helping them to grow others. Never drop flowers in the dusty road and leave them to wither there, alone. Never let ignorant florists plunge wire into their delicate bodies. Never wear flowers against your own body, most flowers disliked it and died. Never hurt anything if it could be avoided, it spoilt the harmony of God's design.

Be kind, be kind! The Ferraris were kind; eccentric, but oh, so kind! The Villa Sant' Antonio was as full of kindness as a gold mine of precious metal. The Ferraris' kindness broke all bounds and went flooding out over the surrounding country. They belonged to those people who must always help something. They were born helpers, helping was necessary to their welfare, as well as to the welfare of the helped. The peasant whose crops had died of drought, a woman whose baby had broken out in sores, a mangy cat, an overloaded mule, these things and their like belonged to the Ferraris, because of the help they claimed. People laughed a little, but took what they gave. There were even some people who criticized their clothes, or rather their lack of them. But Liza would say:

'Let them criticize. Everyone has a right to think and say exactly what they like in this world. If no one took any notice of them slanders would injure no one.'

This expressed her mental attitude very exactly, a mental attitude reflected physically by her great placidity of movement. She would walk through her house and her terraced gardens with a firm, unhurried tread. She never hurried, she never worried. She was quite impervious to household cares while never neglecting her household. Her large and carefully-kept white hands held a thousand little strands together, and one big strand; the impulsive Ferrari, who was always knotting himself up. Sidonia, with all her moods and crazes, her changing and violent emotions, was soon gathered up into those strong, white hands, and held there kindly but firmly. She knew quite well what had happened to her, but was glad to let it happen. She felt like a little craft safely tethered behind a white sailing frigate. For the two years that followed Jensen's death she wanted to feel secure.

She had lately had a lesson every day, and now she knew several Wagner rôles. Her voice had submitted like herself; it was under perfect control. It had mellowed, too, grown more mature, as Sidonia's figure had done; no longer a tall, thin slip of a girl, she was now a robust young goddess. The lines of her body were round and generous, Liza said it was better so:

'There must be meat on the bone, my dear, a voice needs perpetual feeding.'

2

Good years, kind years of bountiful growth, drawing all too quickly to a close. Sidonia gazed out across the garden and her eyes were wide with regret. It was nearly June; in three days she would leave all this and go back once more to England. She would go with letters of introduction to important musical people; with one special letter to Ferrari's old friend, Saunders, the impresario. This would be an impulsive letter:

'Our pupil, Sidonia Shore—a wonderful voice in our opinion, and the girl herself very intelligent—lovely timbre and splendid compass—she should make her name in Wagner some day. If she is in anything like good form when you hear her, I think you will agree with all I have said.'

Sidonia knew beforehand the sort of thing he would write. Liza would contribute her bit; a calm, considered comment at the very end, more valuable, probably, than all the rest.

She did not feel nervous of meeting Saunders, though they said he was very disagreeable. She had perfect confidence in her own ability, he was almost certain to do something for her. She stood there visualizing her future, a brilliant operatic career: 'Sidonia Shore will appear as "Isolde".' 'Sidonia Shore will sing in *Tannhäuser*.' She could conceive of no more splendid fulfilment, no more complete self-expression.

3

Liza and Ferrari came out arm in arm. They stood at the top of the marble steps looking down on their flowering garden. He pointed to a fig-tree thickly covered with little, hard green marbles, which would presently swell and ripen into purple figs.

'See how that old tree bears,' he said. 'Everything is fruitful this year.'

They looked at each other, smiling gently—Liza was once more great with child. Her face expressed neither fear nor joy, only a vast contentment. Now, when she walked, she placed her feet with a slow, considered care. She moved with reverence, as a priest might move carrying the Blessed Sacrament.

She and Ferrari came down the steps; he seemed quite a small man beside her. The face that he turned towards his wife had a wondering expression in the eyes; he had never grown used to this oft-repeated miracle, it continued to fill him with awe. It led him to curb his impetuous actions, to moderate his great voice. Liza paused to rest in her walk, her hour was drawing very near.

'Oughtn't you to lie down?' inquired Sidonia anxiously as she joined them.

Liza shook her head.

'Listen, Sidonia, I've got so many things to say.'

'We must give you our final words of advice,' broke in Ferrari impressively.

'Remember,' said Liza, walking on slowly, 'to keep your breath under control. Don't let the breath get over the notes, makes the notes sit on the breath.'

'And when you sing for Saunders, my dear, give it him good and strong!' Ferrari chuckled. 'I know old Saunders, he doesn't think a voice is a voice if you don't blow the top of his head off.'

They made her walk between them, each taking an arm, while they counselled and cautioned and encouraged. She might not get her audition until the autumn, in which case she must practice with very great care, and above all not overdo it. Remember, she would be quite alone now—no Liza and no Ferrari. There must be no smoking and no late nights, and, of course, no wrapping up of her throat, no matter how cold the wind.

'And for goodness' sake don't eat asparagus!' Liza reminded.

'Or ices,' said Ferrari.

'Or oysters,' cautioned Liza.

'Or nuts,' said Ferrari.

'Or anything really nice!' laughed Sidonia.

Maurice came over the lawn and joined them; a tall youth now with down on his lip. He would soon be going to the Conservatoire at Milan to study his violin. He walked along at his mother's side, but his glance kept straying to Sidonia. They sat for a while in the pergola, through the arches of which they could just glimpse Florence where she lay in the sunshine below. Sidonia felt suddenly heavy at heart. 'Firenze bella!' she murmured.

Maurice sighed. His expressive eyes rested on Sidonia's face.

'I'm so much in love,' he remarked quite simply. 'I'm so much in love with Sidonia.'

Nobody smiled; Liza's eyes filled with tears as he turned and left the pergola.

'My boy is unhappy; he's only a child, but I hate to see him unhappy.'

Ferrari took her hand.

'Only growing pains, my Liza; believe me, only growing pains.'

Sidonia stretched out her arms impulsively.

'Dio! I think I'm in love with you all, from Umberto here down to Ascanio!'

They laughed at that.

'And long may you remain so,' they told her, kissing her by turns.

'I shall come back,' said Sidonia wistfully. 'Darlings, I shall come back.'

'Who knows?' murmured Liza.

'I do—I know. Darlings, I *must* come back!'

They sat on until the sun went down in a hot, red disk behind the cyprus trees; then the three of them turned towards the house, walking solemnly hand in hand.

CHAPTER TWENTY-TWO

I

SIDONIA's emotions upon her home-coming were mixed and rather distressing. For one thing she felt intensely cold; it was raining and blowing a gale. She decided that she had never known what sunshine could mean until she had to do without it. She looked from the car at the drenched, muddy streets, at the drenched and lugubrious people. No one was talking, much less smiling; their English faces seemed to her dull and sodden, like the rain-soaked garments they wore. Frances had come alone to the station, Lady Shore had a cold. Sidonia glanced at Frances from time to time, but she got scant consolation from her profile; Frances looked stiff and a little aloof in her mannish, tailor-made clothes. Not that she did not feel glad to see Frances, Frances was a dear old thing, but after Liza she seemed rather queer, almost a little unfamiliar.

The Queen Anne house was another shock, it had grown so appallingly small. The hall was narrow and so were the stairs; even the drawing-room had shrunk. Upstairs in her bed lay Lady Shore, clad in a Jaeger nightgown. She welcomed Sidonia with husky croaks:

'Darling, you mustn't kiss me!'

Sidonia did not very much want to kiss her, yet she felt a little aggrieved. From his cage in the window Horus gasped and sneezed in horrid imitation. The room smelt of Elliman's and eucalyptus; Lady Shore smelt of both these things, with a tinge of cinnamon thrown in.

Frances said:

'Prudence, you've forgotten your medicine!' and proceeded to pour out a dose.

Lady Shore said:

'So I have.—You've grown fatter, Sidonia.'

Sidonia said nothing at all.

In her own little bedroom she found Blake unpacking, Blake grown incredibly old. The maid looked up with a garment in her hand.

'Don't seem to be much of this thing,' she remarked. 'Don't seem to be over-much of nothing!'

Sidonia snatched the dress hastily away.

'I'll unpack for myself; don't you bother, Blake.'

Whereupon Blake rose stiffly from her knees, with the face of one deeply offended.

They had roast beef and horse-radish sauce for dinner. It made Sidonia feel sick; she had not eaten meat for nearly two years, and this meat was bleeding profusely. She nibbled a watery boiled potato and some sea-weed known as 'spring greens'.

'Aren't you hungry?' Frances inquired.

'It's not that, I'm a vegetarian, you know.'

'But, good heavens! We've got no vegetables in England. I do hope you're not going to starve.'

Lady Shore had two poached eggs on a tray and a table-spoonful of whisky. The combination of whisky and eggs made Sidonia turn away her head. Frances would not release the tray until she had minutely examined each thing on it, she even picked up the butter dish and smelt its contents suspiciously.

'Is this the fresh butter I sent in to-day? Ah, I thought not! Well, this won't do for her ladyship, take it down and get the fresh.'

By the time the tray was on its way upstairs the beef on Frances' plate had congealed; Sidonia stared at the hardening grease with an interest that was positively morbid. In another ten minutes a hand-bell rang. Frances jumped up once again.

'That must be your mother, she's ready for her tonic. I'll be back in a second, Sidonia.'

But she did not come back for quite a long time, and Sidonia tackled pudding alone—a decoction of stale bread and treacle and figs, that made a gritty noise when you chewed it. The dessert, for which the whole table was cleared, then carefully swept and garnished, consisted of three apples and two unripe bananas. There were also some brazil nuts in a dish by themselves; they manfully refused to be cracked. Sidonia sighed, not from sorrow but from greed; she felt excessively hungry. It seemed incredible, she thought, but there it was; after two years at the Villa Ferrari she detested this English food.

Dinner over, they went up and sat with Lady Shore. She spent the evening in sucking jujubes and blowing something into her nose. This something, however, she never allowed to remain there; no sooner was it in than she seized her handkerchief and blew it out again. This performance appealed intensely to Horus, he literally shrieked with laughter. In the end Frances had to cover him up, where-upon he reproduced the atomizer sound from underneath his baize. As well as she could for her streaming cold Lady Shore surveyed her daughter.

'You're certainly much more robust,' she said. 'You've certainly grown much fatter.'

She seemed incapable of getting beyond this change in Sidonia's appearance; that, together with the cold in her head, entirely monopolized her mind. Sidonia sought vainly for something to say, for topics of conversation. She looked appealingly at Frances once or twice, but Frances was pre-occupied.

'Did I give you your aspirin at five? Yes, of course I did, how stupid!' She was ringing the bell for a fresh hot-water bottle.

Sidonia stretched her arms and yawned.

'I think I'll turn in, Mummy dear. Good night, Frances; I'm half asleep after the journey.'

2

For about ten days she longed to run away, but of course she only settled in. She revenged herself for feeling perpetually cold by having fires lit all over the house. The pitch of the drawing-room piano was down, she got them to come and raise it; then she engaged an accompanist and started to practise her singing. She went through her rôles, *enormous* rôles they seemed to Lady Shore. She practised her scales, interminable scales, and then the Ferrari exercises. Lady Shore lay and groaned in her bed, the groans were not solely on account of her cold. The housemaid gave notice because of the fires, and the cook complained of overwork because of Sidonia's vegetarian requirements. Ptah made another discordant note; he disliked Sidonia's singing. The sound seemed to give him an acute ear-ache, he was always trying to hide. On the other hand, Horus joined in with zest, and this distracted Sidonia.

'Will nobody cover that devil?' she demanded in a voice of exasperation.

She began to go out to a number of parties at which she would be asked to sing—friends of the Ferraris, musical people, who often invited her alone. Wherever she sang they praised her voice, her style, her excellent training. She should go very far, only wait until Saunders heard her. Saunders was away in Germany, it seemed, and would not be back until September; but he wrote in answer to Sidonia's letter enclosing Ferrari's introduction. The date he appointed for Sidonia's audition was September 21st; he would try her voice in the opera-house at half-past three precisely.

Sidonia sighed as she read his letter, it was such a long time to wait. She would so much have liked to know her fate before the summer holidays. Would they expect her to go to the seaside? She felt almost certain that they would. Lady Shore was about again now and the air was heavy with plans. Sidonia wanted to stop alone in London, but to this Lady Shore objected. Sidonia might get ill, the house might be burgled, it might even be burnt down. She stared apologetically at her daughter while clinging firmly to her point. Her eyes seemed to say:

'I'm a tiresome old woman, but please try to like me a little.'

Lady Shore looked older; her voice was older and so

were her eyes and hands. She was gradually allowing old age to intrude, too lazy to keep him at bay. She took it for granted that Sidonia's new friends did not want Sidonia's mother.

'I'm not really musical, never was,' she would say. 'I'm just a dusty old bookworm.'

But she fretted a little nevertheless; rather late in the day she found herself wishing that she counted for more with her daughter.

'But what can I do?' she inquired of Frances.

'Nothing,' said Frances briefly.

And she could do nothing. Sidonia was a woman, with a life and ambitions of her own. Ferrari's friends had taken her up, they began to lionize her a little. She was popular, very much in request; she was scarcely ever at home; she even talked of taking a studio and setting up house for herself. Then one day she suddenly pitied Lady Shore. She pitied her for nothing in particular, unless it was for the way her hands were resting limply on her lap. Yes, she felt certain that it must have been those hands, so inadequate, so obviously ageing. They seemed to cry out to the youth in her, making it feel abashed.

'Mother.'

'Yes, dear?'

'I've been out a lot lately, but you do understand, don't you, darling?'

'Of course I do. You're young, Sidonia—and beautiful,' she added shyly.

'But we never seem to go anywhere together.'

'That's so; but your friends are not of my generation, they don't want me.' There was not a trace of resentment in the voice, Sidonia wished that there had been.

Then Sidonia said a ridiculous thing, she said it because of those hands. No sooner was it out than she wished she had not spoken, foreseeing all kinds of complications. She said:

'But don't any of *your* friends want *me*?'

Lady Shore looked up in surprise.

'Of course they do. They're always asking me to bring my clever daughter to see them, especially people like the

Wilsons and the Seaforths who have known you ever since you were a child.'

Sidonia hesitated for a moment; she knew she was being unwise, but she went on:

'Then why not take me to see them?'

'Oh, would you really come, Sidonia?'

Sidonia nodded. After all, why not? It would bore her but it would be kind, and Liza believed in kindness. She need only go to see a few old friends, she ought to have gone already.

'I'm going to the Seaforths' this afternoon, if you'd come——' ventured Lady Shore timidly.

Sidonia got up and kissed her.

'Of course I'll come,' she said, feeling self-righteous.

And that was where she met David.

CHAPTER TWENTY-THREE

I

THE Seaforths lived in a large, dingy house on the other side of Kensington Gardens. According to their note-paper their address was Hyde Park, but if you were poor or thrifty or honest you directed your taxi to Bayswater.

Mrs. Seaforth was imposing. She was massive and blonde, and affected the princess fringe of her youth. She was always a little over-trimmed and her favourite stones were tur-quoises. General Seaforth remained so much in the back-ground that one never quite knew what he looked like.

When Lady Shore and Sidonia arrived they found the drawing-room crowded. Most of the men were a little bald; most of the women wore painstaking clothes and bought their hats at Whiteley's. The silver tea set was decorative and huge, and so was the tray that it stood on; both were excessively badly polished, perhaps on account of their hugeness. The conversation was very polite, dealing strictly with generalities; as the hostess was constantly shuffling her guests, there was small chance for anything else. In the midst of these incongruous surroundings David Morgan was passing tea and cakes. He was rather solemn and stately about it; he suggested Apollo turned waiter. He stood still in front of Sidonia with a plate, and they eyed each other gravely. He was so unexpected, she was so unexpected, that neither of them spoke for a moment; then—

'Cake?' inquired David.

'No, thanks,' said Sidonia, who was eating a bread-and-butter finger.

After that he became considerably less helpful; he just sat and stared at Sidonia, and she stared back without pride, without shame. They were not unlike inquisitive children. He had nobody with him, not even a mother to explain his presence at the party. This was natural enough, for his mother was dead, but he had inherited her sense of duty. The Seaforths had been old friends of his parents, hence the claim that they had on himself; he always visited them four times a year at about the change of the seasons.

He was tall, quite six-foot-two, thought Sidonia, and his shoulders were flat and broad. His waist and flanks were excessively slim, his close-cropped hair waved a little. His eyes were grey, not intelligent, but kind, his features blunt and regular. His clean-shaven face would have looked well in bronze. He had a deep cleft in his chin.

Mrs. Seaforth, intent on yet one more shuffle, brought Sidonia and David together. They smiled at each other; they had waited for this, it appeared to them natural and inevitable. He was silent for a moment, stroking his hair, then he said:

'Do you like polo? Would you care to have vouchers for Ranelagh? I can always let you have some.'

She had heard something very like this before. Joe Poulsen had once said: 'Do you play golf?' How dull and uninteresting it had sounded. But this did not sound in the least the same, because of the man who was speaking.

She had heard of Ranelagh, everyone had, but Lady Shore never went there; nor for that matter did Ferrari's friends. She hesitated, uncertain.

'It's rather jolly if we get some fine weather.'

She thought his voice sounded eager.

'I'm sure it is.'

'But I'd like you to come when I'm playing,' he told her with naïve self-importance.

'Oh, do you play polo?'

It seemed that he did. Mrs. Seaforth had overheard the question.

'Good gracious! He played in America last year, he's one of our best players.'

David blushed.

'Oh, I say! But you will come, Miss Shore?'

'I shall love to,' she told him truthfully.

They sat and talked for an hour and a half; they said nothing at all arresting. Sidonia could never remember very clearly what they had talked about. But while they talked they gazed at each other, their words a screen for their eyes. When at last Lady Shore made a move to go he obtained her permission to call.

'And I'll send you those vouchers to-night,' he said. 'Come on Tuesday, Miss Shore, if you can.'

2

On Tuesday she saw David Morgan play polo; she went with Lady Shore. They got chairs in the front row against the wooden barrier, and Sidonia thought that he saw her. Most young men look well in polo clothes, they flatter the masculine figure, and David's was as near perfection as a figure could very well be. He swooped at the ball, bending gracefully forward over his pony's shoulder. He dashed across the ground at breakneck speed; he swerved, he swung round, he checked. His left hand rested lightly on the bridle with the ease of perfect control; his right hand wielded his polo stick with deadly and unerring precision. Sidonia thought him a goodly sight, as indeed he was. People discussed him.

'Morgan's in form.'

'Yes, by Jove! He is a fine player!'

'He did the trick in the States last year.'

'I believe so; I wish I'd been there.'

David changed ponies. Now he rode a grey, a hot-headed little beast. It reared twice before it settled down to the game, and as it did so Sidonia was conscious of a queer tight feeling in her throat. They were off! The ball struck the low wooden barrier close to Sidonia's feet. After it pounded David Morgan, his eye intent on it. He checked his impetuous pony with a jerk. His aim was vigorous and true; the ball sped away in the direction of the goal, but was quickly intercepted. David was flushed and Sidonia heard him swearing gently to himself. There was just one moment when their eyes could have met, but David did not look up. Had he known she was there? He must have known, she was sure that he had seen her earlier. But if so he was not thinking of her, he was thinking only of the game; and this, for some inexplicable reason, pleased her.

All the way home she analysed that emotion, she compared it to its predecessors. As a child her dancing had delighted her, then her talent of improvising. Later, her sculpture had thrilled her at times, and her singing, yes, that always thrilled her. She had found old Frances quite exciting but that had been ages ago. In any case, none of those emotions had been the same; their quality had been different. What she had felt this afternoon was more humble yet more exalted; it had seemed to thrust her down and down, and then to sweep her triumphantly upwards.

3

David came and dined quietly two days later; they had not asked anyone to meet him.

'Just treat me like one of the family,' he had said; 'I rather like family parties.'

He was very respectful to Lady Shore; when she spoke he listened attentively, his manners were perfect towards the old, in which category he evidently placed her. With Frances he seemed rather less at his ease; he was very painstaking with her, and once or twice as the evening went on Sidonia caught him looking at her curiously. The expression on his face was a little amused, and she thought, though she could not be perfectly sure, that it was also just a little pitiful.

'What do you think of him?' she asked Frances afterwards.

'I think he's a very nice young man.'

'Is that all?'

'Well, no—he's very good-looking.'

'Is that all?'

'I think so,' said Frances.

He came very often. He suggested plans, things that

would give Sidonia pleasure—a box at the theatre, lunch at the Berkeley, tea at his flat on Hay Hill. Lady Shore liked him when she thought of him at all, which was only when she happened to be with him; Frances thought of him rather more often; Sidonia thought of nothing else.

4

It all happened quite naturally, quite without a hitch; events moved as though on roller skates. He explained to Lady Shore, having got her alone, that he had an estate in Essex, and moreover that the property had been in his family ever since the sixteenth century. He told her further that he was an orphan, having no brothers or sisters; that his income was rather more than sufficient, and that he wished to settle down.

'But mind you,' said David, 'I've never been wild, not wild as men go, Lady Shore.'

She listened politely, rather bewildered as to what these confidences meant. She supposed that having no mother of his own he was glad to find an elderly woman in whom he could sometimes confide. When he finished by humbly begging permission to propose at once to Sidonia she stared in amazement, first at the idea that her permission was required, and then at what she conceived to be the suddenness of his request.

'My dear young man, of course you may propose, but I don't think Sidonia likes men. She's got her career——'

'I know,' said David, 'I'm thinking of her career.'

'Then you're interested in opera and that sort of thing?'

He hesitated a moment.

'Well, to tell you the truth, I was thinking of marriage,' he said gravely.

5

That afternoon he took Sidonia to the Zoological Gardens, he was a Fellow of the Society. Of course, he had not meant to propose to her in so unromantic a spot, but somehow, while they were watching the seals being fed, he found himself taking her hand. She saw what was coming and drew him away, the seals smelt so abominably fishy. He proposed as they walked past the jackals' cage; a few yards farther on she accepted him. In the taxi going home he glanced out of the window—Regent's Park seemed fairly deserted—so he took her in his arms and kissed her lips, and she lay there kissing him back.

CHAPTER TWENTY-FOUR

I

SIDONIA began to monopolize Frances again; she wanted to talk about David. Of course, Frances did not understand him; still, she was better than no one. Frances listened, but said very little; Sidonia wished to talk, not to be talked to, which perhaps was just as well. Her sentences circled round his name like moths round candle-light: 'David says —David thinks—David likes—David hates—David approves—David disapproves——' It went on all day long.

David wished to be married in September, it was now the first of July. There could be no going away for any of them that summer, as Sidonia must get her trousseau.

'But surely, my dear,' protested Frances, 'you can't need three months to do that?'

'Well, you see David thinks it's rather important, he doesn't want me to hurry over it; then I've got to get nearly everything new; David doesn't much like my clothes.'

'Why not?'

'I don't know, he thinks they're too Italian, and I think myself that they're rather Ferrari-ish; one couldn't help getting a little like Liza when one lived in the house with her.'

She announced one day that she meant to let her hair grow.

'David thinks it looks rather odd.'

'But, my dear, you've had it like this all your life!'

'All my life? I've had no life until now.'

She neglected her singing, there was so little time and she had so many other things to see to.

'What about your audition?' murmured Frances one day.

Sidonia looked rather worried.

'I've not quite decided yet what I shall do—it's so awkward its coming in September.'

'What does David say?'

'Well, naturally, Frances, he doesn't much like the idea of the stage.'

'But your voice——'

'Oh, of course, he likes that all right, but he wants to keep it for himself. And, after all,' she went on reflectively, 'I suppose it's natural enough—I can't see David as a *prima donna's* husband holding my cloak and my flowers, can you? It's a rotten sort of stunt for a man.'

'Ah, well,' said Frances, 'there are charity concerts; you'll be able to sing at those.'

But Sidonia did not smile.

'And there'll be my own home, I don't think my voice will be wasted.'

Frances stared at her honestly amazed.

'But—I don't understand one bit, Sidonia. Do you mean to say that you'll give up your career? Aren't you afraid you'll regret it?'

Sidonia smiled gently, a charming smile if just a little patronizing.

'Regret? With David? Why, he *is* my career! The trouble is you've never been in love.'

'No, that's true enough, still I should have thought——'

'Oh, no you wouldn't, not if you had David!'

The honeymoon caused a lot of discussion; Sidonia thought somewhere in England would be nice. A man like David always felt so dull abroad. David hated not understanding what they said, and still more trying to make them understand him. And then there was the food. David liked a big breakfast; he'd never hold out on coffee and rolls, and the bacon was vile out of England.'

'Why not go to Florence?' suggested Frances. 'You love it, and they're used to English people there.'

There was silence for a moment, Sidonia looked embarrassed, she fidgeted a little with her hands. Then she said:

'Frances, you do know I love the Ferraris? You do know I love Liza, don't you?'

'Yes, of course, how could you do anything else? They've been wonderful friends to you.'

'I know they have, and they're perfect dears, I was marvellously happy with them. But I don't think they'd quite go with David, somehow; David wouldn't understand them.'

'They might not understand him either,' said Frances.

'No, that's just it, they probably wouldn't.'

2

Frances was very much in request, David was always needing her. Lady Shore was too vague to make a good chaperone, late for every appointment; but Frances was quite a reliable soul, David could depend on Frances. He had very strict ideas in regard to his future wife; he would take Sidonia out alone in the daytime, but preferred to have Frances after dark. The moment the street lamps were lit he grew prim; from then on they must always be three. Frances, good-natured, but frankly bored, played watch-dog at David's behest. He struck her as being a pompous sort of lover, but Sidonia assured her that he was not.

'He's only a little old-fashioned, Frances; it's rather a relief after all the ultra-modern people. But David's not pompous, good Lord! You don't know him.' She laughed a little to herself. 'In any case I simply adore him, so what on earth does it matter!'

What did matter, and matter very much to Frances, was Sidonia's mentality, which seemed to be rapidly descending to the level of a schoolgirl's. She had noticed that David's outlook in some things was still distinctly Etonian. Perhaps this mental condition was infectious, and if so she hoped that the infection would be temporary. But as time went on the disease increased; Sidonia began to brag about it.

'I just let go and depend on David. I'm rather proud of myself. When you think how I've slaved over things all my life it's wonderful that I can let go, I think it shows strength of character.'

'Um-m, I don't quite see that.'

'Oh, don't you? I do. David says a woman's strength is her weakness.'

These sort of remarks, more frequent every day, left Frances feeling dreadfully inadequate. There were so many things that she longed to say, things that she felt should be said, but whenever she tried to approach them with tact Sidonia would flare up immediately.

'You ask me whether we suit each other; that's only because you don't like him! You think he's stupid; well, what if he is? That's just precisely why I want him. David's a rest, and I need a rest. I'm sick to death of clever people!'

'But, Sidonia, now don't fly off at a tangent—I know he's a nice young man, I know he's honest and good and all that —but you haven't a taste in common!'

'We've got the one thing that counts in common——'

'And that is?'

'Love!' said Sidonia.

Frances was silent. Presently she said:

'Have you ever told David about "The Saturday Life"?'

Sidonia frowned.

'No, he hates that sort of thing, he thinks it's rather un-wholesome. I'm not sure he isn't right, it's all so exotic, it's —well—un-English, isn't it?'

'I suppose it is; but then so is Christianity, that didn't begin in Essex!'

'Are you laughing at David?'

'No, I'm only wondering——'

'David says that everyone wonders too much. He says that religion's quite simple.'

'Do you think it's simple? You never used to.'

'I never thought anything simple, but since I've known David I'm beginning to see that a man thinks only of essentials. The details are what muddle women up so, women think too much about details.'

It was not only trying, it was rather distressing; Sidonia was so very thorough. She simplified life down to the merest unit, simplified it down to David. She wiped out all that had gone before, like a child that sponges a tiresome sum from its slate with illicit enjoyment. Her memory became conveniently short. She decided to be married at St. Mary Abbott's.

'It's rather a dear old church,' she said one day, 'there's a dignity about it.'

'But you used to dislike it!' said Frances, bewildered.

'Did I? I don't remember that. David simply adores the chimes; they are rather jolly, aren't they?'

3

David wished that Frances would dress a little better, he thought her clothes so unbecoming. He liked a woman to wear soft, clinging things, even if she were past her youth. He thought that Frances looked rather odd, especially in the evenings. He disliked her eyeglass, it made people stare. Couldn't Sidonia persuade her to wear pince-nez? He was charming about Frances, he took an interest in her, but his interest was rather regretful. He seemed for some reason to pity her deeply.

'Poor old thing, it's damned hard luck!'

But when Sidonia questioned him regarding the hard luck he refused quite gently to explain.

'We must always be awfully kind to her,' he said, 'ask her to The Hall, and all that. I expect she'll enjoy it, though when one comes to think of it, it must be jolly hard on her to see us so happy.'

'I don't think she minds.'

'Oh, you bet she does! I'm sorry for the poor old pelican.'

Sidonia laughed. It was not a very flattering description of Frances, but then David meant it kindly—and, indeed, he had meant it very kindly, it was David's expression of sympathy. He tried to express this sympathy for Frances in a hundred little ways.

'I don't want the poor thing to feel left out,' he was always explaining to Sidonia.

Whenever he brought Sidonia flowers he brought Parma violets for Frances; not a buttonhole that she might have worn, but a large round blob with its leg in silver paper. He embarrassed her by constant small attentions until she dreaded to leave her chair. Whenever she moved he would bound to his feet.

'Let me—can I get you something?'

He had a great talent for opening doors; he was always opening them for Frances. Wherever she went, whatever she did, she was conscious that he watched with an anxious eye, the eye of one longing to be kind. He longed to be kind to Lady Shore too, but she was much less accessible. She wandered through the maze of the betrothal with the face of a straying somnambulist. If she saw things these days she did so in a dream, and no one attempted to wake her. It was Frances who ordered the wedding-cake, Frances who sent out the invitations. Frances who arranged for a full choral service at David's special request. Sidonia chose her own wedding-dress, but Frances attended all the fittings. The dress was of ivory satin, very simple, the train was of cloth of silver. David produced a wonderful veil of priceless old Honiton lace. This was a family heirloom, it seemed; the Morgan brides always wore it. He also produced a sporting best man, and brought him to call on Lady Shore.

'You will like old Bobbie,' David told Sidonia, 'he's one of the best, *ab-so-lutely*!'

Sir Robert Tattenham was plump and breezy, yet he suggested David. They were different in build, they were different in face, but somehow they did not seem different. Of course, they had many tastes in common—both played polo, both rode to hounds, neither of them ever missed a match at Lord's, both had been to Eton and Oxford. Their tailor was the same though their clothes were different—Sir Robert affected checks—but not in these minor details alone did their resemblance reside. It was deeper than that; a brotherhood of mind, a kind of twin outlook on life. When you knew them both well, when you met them together, this brotherhood of mind almost hypnotized you into thinking that they must look alike.

Sir Robert insisted that things were quite simple, ambiguities bored him. There were good and bad people, well-born and base-born, rich folk and poor folk, manly men and freaks. There was also 'cricket' and the opposite. His manner was polished towards Lady Shore, admiring but respectful towards Sidonia. With Frances he became just a trifle self-assertive, the fault of her collar and tie. Like David he had the door-opening habit, the watchful, well-meaning eye.

He stayed for the whole of one afternoon, and finally left with David. Once out of the house he grew somewhat shy, because he admired Sidonia. He wanted to say quite a number of things; she reminded him of a young chestnut filly that he had acquired quite recently. He thought her a fine, upstanding creature, with good ankles and plenty of line; he envied David his honeymoon, and decided that the children, when they came, would be strong—Sidonia looked to him like a first-class breeder.

'Don't you think I'm a lucky man?' inquired David.

'Rather!' replied Sir Robert.

'Don't you think we'll hit it off well together?'

'Rather!' replied Sir Robert.

After that they were silent, engrossed in their thoughts, which their breeding forbade them to mention. They dined together at the Carlton Club and discussed the food—*not* Sidonia.

CHAPTER TWENTY-FIVE

I

SIDONIA was married on September 21st, the day appointed for her audition with Saunders. She only remembered this afterwards; Saunders must have waited in vain.

The church was filled with nicely-dressed people, the chancel with nicely-placed lilies. Sidonia was given away by her mother, there being no male relation. Up the long nave wobbled Lady Shore, her mauve toque a little awry; her anxious eyes straining painfully in front of her, her lips close set in the will to be efficient. At her side walked the tall and serene Sidonia under the Morgan veil; she was holding a gold-mounted ivory Prayer Book, the gift of the bridegroom to the bride.

David was waiting for her calmly, with Sir Robert close to his elbow. David's trousers were grey with the classical crease, his black morning-coat was neatly braided and he wore a white carnation in his buttonhole. His face was a little paler than usual, but otherwise he showed no emotion; he looked tall and manly and thoroughly reliable, in spite of his too handsome profile. He met Sidonia with a grave little smile, and they turned and stood together.

The service began. Through the stained glass windows came the sun, throwing shifting, harlequin patterns across the carpet in the chancel. The lilies smelt of weddings and funerals, the chancel smelt slightly of furniture polish and of musty books on the choir stalls. The clergy, in spite of their surplices, suggested a man-of-war; they might have been dressed in trim white ducks, so neat and efficient they seemed. They moved with the quiet and disciplined tread of men accustomed to duty. They were very well groomed, from their neatly-parted hair down to their polished boots.

The wedding guests sat or stood or knelt, punctilious, very attentive; old friends of Sir Godfrey and Lady Shore, old friends of the Morgan family. Most of them felt intensely depressed in spite of the cheerful words of the choir that had heralded in the bride. One or two women had tears in their eyes, one or two men looked embarrassed; for the rest, their faces were set in the mould that is specially reserved for such occasions.

It was all very neat, very British, very proper, in spite of the vicar's exhortations. It was all very like the cut of David's coat, irreproachable, expensive and good; it was all very full of superfluous people among whom only two people counted; it was all very full of time-honoured words, man's words, that he printed for his own delectation and believed in for his own peace of mind. But David's cropped head was dutifully bowed—he was young and kind and in earnest. He was probably praying inarticulate prayers to the God who belonged to weddings. Sidonia's head was bowed because David's head was bowed, her hands clasped the unaccustomed Prayer Book. It was really a great and desperate adventure dressed up in ridiculous clothes; an adventure of the body, but also of the soul, an adventure concerning the ages that had gone, the ages that were yet to come.

In a front pew knelt Frances, feeling suddenly old, because they were both so young.

2

The organ boomed out; they would soon be coming, they were in the vestry now signing their names. Ah, here they were. What a splendid couple, the handsomest pair in England! Women craned forward to look at the bride. How was she feeling? Elated? Shy? Nervous? Some of them thought of their own wedding-day. They began to whisper:
'God bless them!'
'Amen.'

'Did you see her look up? How pretty that was, she smiled up into his face.'

'I don't like her dress.'

'Oh, don't you? Why not?'

'I think it looks rather stiff.'

'I wonder if she'll let her hair grow now she's married?'

'I wouldn't be surprised, men don't like short hair.'

'But isn't she lovely?'

'Oh, perfectly lovely! And he's got the kindest face.'

'This sort of thing always take me back.'

'I know, one feels quite sentimental.'

A medley of sentiment and commonplace of memories and speculations. The organ booming the newly-married into the street, into life. Sidonia very proud, a little self-centred; David very large and protective. 'My wife!' 'My husband!' They would say that now, whenever it came in useful; and sometimes—just at first—for the sound of the words, because they were in love with each other.

More sentiment, more memories, more speculations and some curiosity thrown in, as the people in the street crowded close to the porch, irresistibly drawn by a wedding. The chimes that David was said to adore clashing down the High Street, Kensington. The policeman on point duty holding up the traffic to let the wedding party pass in their motors. Inquisitive faces on the tops of buses. A beggar selling boot-laces, looking pathetic, hoping to profit by the occasion; and the clash of David's jubilant chimes splitting the air with their clamour.

3

The Queen Anne house was full to overflowing. Barker's had stretched a new awning from its door and red carpet over its steps. Its discreet interior was humming with voices, humming with congratulations. Everyone was shaking hands with the bride, and secretly pitying Lady Shore for the loss of her only daughter. David, smiling, charmingly courteous, especially to the old ladies; Sir Robert making decorous jokes and handing glasses of champagne. Then no more

Sidonia; she had gone to change. What would her travelling dress be like? Then Sidonia again, all in pale grey this time —and the motor throbbing at the door.

People flocking down from the drawing-room—wedding guests—the invited. People crushing close to the steps— shabby—the uninvited. The policeman's voice:

'Keep back there, please!'

Then a woman's voice:

"Ere she comes! Look, Willie, there's the bride, isn't she pretty!'

'Keep back there, please!'

'Good-bye—good-bye——'

'God bless you! Good luck—good-bye!'

The traditional slipper thrown by Sir Robert, the traditional storm of rice and confetti. Sidonia's face at the motor window for a moment, then David's, smiling. And soon the bustle of departing guests, all saying the usual things.

4

Frances and Lady Shore stood in the hall; the house was untidy but quiet. Lady Shore's hair, rebelling at last, had escaped on to her cheek. She was feeling much too tired to push it back; it tickled, and she let it tickle. Frances, still neat but looking rather worn, brushed some confetti off her coat. They turned and stared at each other wearily, divining each other's thoughts.

'Yes,' said Frances, as if it were an answer, 'this sort of thing does make one feel old.'

Lady Shore nodded, and more hair came down.

'We're not very young any more, are we, Frances?'

'It's not only that,' said Frances thoughtfully, 'I think it's Sidonia and David. They got into the car with a kind of frisk; they reminded me somehow of overgrown lambs! It made me feel—oh, I don't know.'

CHAPTER TWENTY-SIX

I

THE Queen Anne house was extraordinarily peaceful; it seemed to be smiling to itself. It lived in the pleasant, dim light of sunblinds, soothed by a warm September. Sidonia's little room was tidied and left with a dust-sheet over the bed. The attic, once the cause of such hot dispute, received Sir Godfrey's papers again, and Lady Shore began the pleasant task of cataloguing all her books.

'I've wanted to do this for years,' she said happily, taking down an armful of volumes, 'but somehow I've never had time before. Oh, well, the child's settled at last!'

Frances, her head tied up in a cloth because the books were so dusty, continued to examine their title-pages, making voluminous notes.

'I feel so much younger,' continued Lady Shore. 'Sidonia's been a great anxiety!'

Frances was silent, she did not look round, she was deeply engrossed in her work.

At one o'clock they retired to the bathroom and washed the grime from their hands; at a quarter past one they sat down to lunch, placing their chairs side by side. They were hungry. They ate cold beef and pickles, rice pudding and Gruyère cheese. After lunch they returned to the study again and catalogued books until dinner. During the evening Lady Shore said:

'Why not stay the night, Frances? You look tired to death. I'll tell them to make up Sidonia's bed; it's fairly comfortable, I think.'

'I ought to get home——' said Frances doubtfully; but she slept in Sidonia's bed.

They worked at the books for a week or two; they enjoyed their work, they felt quietly pleased. Frances admired her own neat catalogue and showed it to Lady Shore. It was very elaborate—red and black ink—there were many little flourishes and scrolls.

'Pretty good, don't you think?' inquired Frances.

'Quite perfect, my dear. What should I do without you?' Frances laughed.

'The Lord only knows. Well, here's your catalogue, it's finished.'

Then Lady Shore said an extraordinary thing, she said it with a gleam in her eye:

'Why shouldn't we go to a cinema, Frances? Wouldn't it be rather fun?'

Frances was taken aback for a moment, she had never known her friend go to cinemas. Then she laughed again.

'Yes, why not? Do let's, we might go this afternoon.'

They went to the Marble Arch Pavilion because the film sounded exciting. They sat and watched desperate, hairbreadth escapes with the thrill of two elderly children.

'I can't think why we've never done this before,' said Lady Shore reflectively.

'Nor I,' agreed Frances, 'it's so little trouble, and really it is rather interesting.'

They continued to discuss the film during tea, which they had at Stewart's in Piccadilly.

'It's a change to go out to food sometimes,' remarked Lady Shore, eating a bun.

'*I* think so—we ought to lunch out now and then; you don't get a bad lunch here.'

'Or at Barker's; they've got a good restaurant at Barker's. I lunched there once when you were in Florence.'

'I've never tried Barker's—but Derry and Toms—or I know an Italian restaurant.'

'I don't like Italian food.'

'Oh, I forgot. You and I might make a real splash one day, Prudence, and lunch at the Ritz or the Berkeley!'

They smiled at each other across the table.

'I think I'd like that,' said Lady Shore.

They discovered, quite suddenly, that the drawing-room looked shabby and required new chintz covers and curtains. They spent a long morning at Storey's in the High Street examining Queen Anne chintzes. The chintz that they finally selected was bright, reflecting their cheerful mood—masses of prim little red and pink roses in prim little clusters of leaves. When it made its appearance about two weeks later they stood and admired the effect.

'This *is* a lovely old house!' said Frances, looking round the drawing-room with affection.

'Yes. I've been thinking—I've been wondering lately—Frances, why don't we share it?'

Frances shook her head.

'No, I don't think that would do, we're not young enough any more; we ought to have started a mutual home at least ten years ago.'

'But there was Sidonia ten years ago.'

'Yes, of course—there was Sidonia.'

'I miss her,' said Lady Shore hastily.

'Naturally,' Frances agreed.

Three days later Lady Shore said:

'That furniture up in Sidonia's room, I think it's rather inadequate. If she ever wanted to come for a night—or if you were staying, Frances——'

They paid another visit to Storey's, this time to the antique department, and somehow or another they purchased oak. They had meant to buy Chippendale, or perhaps Queen Anne, but Frances had always liked old oak. The room now had curtains of blue brocade and a velvet pile carpet to match. The new-old oak looked well, they decided. They were glad they had chosen that blue brocade.

'I think I'd like to build another bathroom on that flat roof half-way up the stairs.' Lady Shore's voice was all innocence.

'Do you think you really need it?' inquired Frances. But yet again, they found themselves at Storey's, this time in the building department.

The new bathroom was tiled, and when it was finished Frances had the first bath.

'You must christen it for luck,' insisted Lady Shore, 'and mind you turn on the shower.'

3

Lady Shore said that she needed a rest, Egyptology could be very tiring; she was not going to do any more work just yet, she was going to enjoy herself. She developed a passion for matinées, followed by tea at Stewart's. Occasionally now she would go out at night, dining with old friends, accompanied by Frances; they were generally asked together. Nearly every Sunday afternoon they went to the Albert Hall concert, unless they deserted Landon Ronald in favour of Henry J. Wood. Frances preferred Landon Ronald's conducting, Lady Shore Henry J's. They both said they did not understand music, but enjoyed a good-natured argument all the same. If Frances sometimes dozed while the concert was in progress, she generally managed to wake up in time to appear quite passably intelligent.

They both felt so well, in spite of the weather; they thought they would escape influenza.

'How right we are to go out more, Frances.'

'Yes, one ought to keep in touch with things, it makes one feel more alive.'

'It's not only that,' said Lady Shore happily, 'it seems to enlarge one's mind.'

4

Frances came back with some goldfish one day, the water from their bowl splashing over her skirt. She could not conceive what had made her buy them at the fishmonger's shop in the High Street; they had looked so pretty, perhaps it had been that, they had also looked very uncomfortable. She ordered a large aquarium for them and a packet of ants' eggs at Barker's. They had trouble in deciding where to put the aquarium; it had to be fairly high up, for Ptah the Second, unregenerate, though ageing, sat watching the goldfish lustfully. In the end they hid them out of his sight on top of a Chippendale cabinet. Frances or Lady Shore changed the water daily—sometimes, between the two of them it got changed twice, but perhaps the goldfish understood.

The days seemed always to be full of pleasant things; nothing that counted for very much, of course, but small, entertaining trifles. They thought they were getting disgracefully frivolous, but found that they thoroughly enjoyed it. Lady Shore dropped her afternoon's At Home (Frances said they were too old-fashioned), and gave instead some regular parties at which everybody played bridge. Quite often now there were people to dinner, sometimes at the little house in Young Street and sometimes at Lady Shore's— quiet folk, old family friends, but pleasant because of that. Lady Shore consulted the catalogues that wine merchants pushed through the letter box. She herself preferred water or lemonade, but Frances enjoyed a good glass of wine and so did the family friends. She tried to remember what Godfrey had said concerning old port and sherry—the port should be dry and the sherry sweet? Or was it the other way round?

She and Frances bought rather expensive flowers; flowers cheered up the house, they said. Lady Shore ordered two new evening dresses and took more interest in her hair; Blake had discovered an improved type of net, guaranteed not to tear easily. On special occasions a man came from Wilson's, after which Lady Shore did not know her own head, but Frances approved of the effect; and once, only once in a reckless moment, Lady Shore had her hair waved.

They basked in a kind of Indian summer that emanated entirely from themselves. No mere external weather had the power to depress them; they defied it, and went out just the same. They discussed Sidonia very often, of course, but placidly, happily, smiling a little; telling each other how much they missed her, but always smiling as they said it. In the evenings they would turn to remembering things— Sidonia's childhood, her crazes, her amusing remarks about this or that, the time she had danced stark naked. They might grow a little doubtful, a little bewildered, just a little bit ill at ease; but when this happened they decided they felt tired, it was time that they went to bed; and Frances, nothing loth, would be easily persuaded to remain and sleep the night.

CHAPTER TWENTY-SEVEN

I

Lady Shore was the first guest to visit Sidonia at The Old Hall after the honeymoon. A house party was gathered together in her honour, David had insisted on this. Lady Shore had begged to be asked alone, or if not alone, then with Frances; but David was firm.

'She's your mother, Sidonia; we must ask people to meet her. And I'd rather she came without Frances this time, Frances can come later on.'

Lady Shore felt even shyer with the married Sidonia than she had with the single; and as David and his wife were now one flesh, she found herself shy with him also. The house was huge and the weather very cold. David said it was always cold in Essex, that was why Essex was healthy. There were many servants and many guests, and Blake proved extremely inadequate; she spent her time criticizing the staff and complaining that they gave themselves airs.

Sidonia was very kind to her mother, but of course she was dreadfully busy; David took up the best part of her time, and then there was the large house party. Lady Shore envied the perfect self-possession that marked her daughter's manner, the ease with which she entertained her guests, her way of appearing to ignore the servants while never erring in politeness.

David insisted that his mother-in-law was the privileged guest of honour, but her privileges, she found, were regulated by him; he believed in taking care of the old. Thus when Lady Shore would beg to be left at home David said she needed fresh air; when she felt like a walk he said that it might rain, and insisted on her staying at home. He ordered her breakfast to be taken to her room, though she liked coming down to breakfast; he even decided what wraps she should wear, having first consulted a reliable thermometer outside his dressing-room window.

'Isn't he darling to you, Mummy?' said Sidonia, beaming fondly at David.

'Very darling indeed,' replied Lady Shore, trying to sound properly grateful.

At the end of ten days she returned home feeling rather depressed and discouraged.

'It's all so big, and they're both so big,' she complained to Frances that evening.

2

They had barely begun to settle down again when Frances received *her* summons.

'You must stay for three weeks at least,' wrote Sidonia, 'I've such tons of things that I want to show you,' and she added, 'David says so too.'

Frances packed with unusual care, going doubtfully over her clothes; she felt, somehow, that they would look all wrong, that they would not suit The Old Hall. Sidonia was at the station to meet her with an open runabout. David, it appeared, disliked closed cars, he said they were always so stuffy. He was waiting in the drive when they arrived and greeted Frances cordially.

'So glad to see you, Frances; it's good of you to come. I hope you don't mind our being quiet?'

There was no house party in honour of Frances, David had said that he thought on the whole she had better be asked alone.

'She looks a bit unlike other people; the bumpkins down here might think her rather freakish, and I don't want that for old Frances.'

Sidonia agreed that they did not want that, and added that Frances would enjoy herself more if she came down quietly as one of the family.

Frances was not given much time for her luncheon,

Sidonia wanted to go out; David had quickly retired to the gunroom to prepare for some slaying on the morrow. Sidonia wished to show Frances the grounds, which were not, she said, looking their best. They began by making a tour of the greenhouses, of which there appeared to be acres. The greenhouses had one distinct advantage, they were at least beautifully warm. Frances envied the bold, pink peaches basking there so complacently.

'I can't pick you more than one, darling,' said Sidonia; 'David likes a few of them kept for dessert, and the rest go up to Covent Garden.'

They passed on slowly from house to house, Frances dutifully admiring. The Malmaison houses made a wonderful show, with their opulent, paper-collared inmates. Every now and then they chanced on a man squirting dark brown water over something; it smelt quite extraordinarily unlike the flowers that would presumably result. The tour of the greenhouses finished at last, they began to walk round the gardens. There was nothing to see, of course, it being winter, but Sidonia expatiated upon every flower that might or might not appear later. She called them all by their Latin names, even to the humble violet. Some of the names she read from labels, but quite a good many she seemed to know by heart. At last she turned to Frances with a smile:

'Now I'll take you to see my chickens. I've got some splendid Sebrights and Houdans, but I think you'll like the Cochins best; I do, they're so amusing.'

They crossed two paddocks, extremely damp, not to say boggy in places, then a spinny, then a narrow plank over a stream, and finally arrived at an open space on which stood the poultry farm. Frances' shoes were sticking to her stockings, held there by Essex mud, but Sidonia was wearing thick greased boots to which she pointed with pride.

'You've got such unsuitable shoes on, Frances; I thought you went in for heavier soles, those things are perfectly useless.'

Frances sighed; she knew they were useless, but then she had bought them specially; she had thought them sufficiently ladylike to meet with David's approval. They stood by the elaborate poultry houses and gazed at their elaborate inmates, while Sidonia expounded her theories on breeding, with many technical details.

'The male bird influences the colour, Frances, he also influences the comb. A second year male bird gets animal food mixed with cayenne pepper.'

'Good heavens! Why?' inquired Frances, who associated chickens with garbage.

'It promotes proper vigour,' Sidonia told her. 'And of course it assists fertility.'

She babbled on about cockerels and pullets, sterile and fertile eggs, until Frances felt that never again could she look her boiled egg in the face.

'How on earth has she learnt it all?' she thought. 'She's only been here five weeks!'

The light was waning, it grew even colder. Frances began to shiver.

'Not cold, are you?' said Sidonia incredulously.

'A tiny bit,' Frances admitted.

Sidonia looked the picture of health; her cheeks were glowing, her hands were quite warm when Frances leant forward to feel them. However, they turned in the direction of the house, which Frances felt was a concession.

Sidonia took Frances up to her bedroom.

'Do stay with me while I change,' she pleaded. 'David doesn't like these tweed things worn indoors. Have you brought a tea-gown with you?'

'My dear, I never wear tea-gowns, you know that. Have you forgotten me, Sidonia?'

'Oh no, nor you do.' She began to laugh, 'You are an old joke, aren't you, darling?'

'If I don't change my shoes soon I'll be a corpse!' said Frances a little crossly.

'Take them off here, they can dry by the fire. I never catch cold from damp stockings.'

Frances obeyed her reluctantly, then she looked about the room. It was large with long french windows, added by latter-day Morgans. The windows were out of keeping with the house and so was the Georgian furniture; an enormous wardrobe, an enormous bed over which was suspended a blue satin tester. The carpet was faded Aubusson, a delicate thing of beauty, but a crewel-work firescreen stood by the grate, and the screen had refused to fade. Over the marble mantelpiece hung a portrait of David's mother. Frances looked at these relics and then at Sidonia; they did not seem to belong to each other, they could never belong, she felt.

'I had an idea that you'd have a different bedroom—an Italian bedroom,' she ventured.

Sidonia smiled.

'I bet you did! Well, I may change this room some day. At the moment I rather love it as it is, it looks so homely and safe.'

'Safe?'

'Yes, safe. I can't explain, and you wouldn't understand me if I could. Anyhow, David loves these old things, they all belonged to his mother.'

The maid was helping her into a tea-gown, a thing of soft swirls and folds. It fell away from her strong young throat, showing the family string of pearls that David's mother had worn. Sidonia surveyed herself in the glass with a little contented smile. Frances thought how happy she looked, happy and very much at peace.

They went downstairs arm in arm to tea. Sidonia pressed Frances' hand.

'You do love me still just a little bit, don't you?' inquired Sidonia softly.

Frances laughed. 'Yes, fraud—I do.'

'I'm not a fraud, Frances.'

'Oh, yes you are!'

'Well, I don't mean to be—I never *mean* to be,' said Sidonia rather sadly.

She grew confidential over tea.

'I'll tell you about our bedroom,' she said, 'I'll tell you why I haven't changed it. David thinks that the bedroom of married people is always—well, rather sacred. He feels that one ought not to move the things that loving people have loved; he thinks that it's rather like a church, hallowed by time and all that.'

'I see,' said Frances, and then she added, 'I think that's rather nice of your David.'

3

The three of them dined in solemn state; the food was solemn, the servants were solemn, and so was David—when he looked at Frances. He went out of his way to be attentive to her.

'Do have some more wine, you look quite fagged. Can't you eat a little more meat?'

'Have you chucked your vegetarianism?' inquired Frances of Sidonia, who was eating mutton with obvious gusto.

'I've stopped all that rot!' said David quickly, 'Sidonia's not Nebuchadnezzar! She was looking distinctly anaemic when we married, and look at her now, she's a picture!'

After dinner Sidonia sat on his knee and ruffled his short, crisp hair.

'Plague of my life!' he exclaimed. *'Don't do that!'* But his voice expressed only pleasure. Then they settled down firmly to petting each other and continued throughout the evening.

David engaged had been pompous and stiff, but David married was quite different. Of course, neither he nor Sidonia counted Frances, she was just one of the family.

'You mustn't mind us,' David told her fatuously. 'We're feeling so silly to-night.'

'Oh, she doesn't mind,' affirmed Sidonia. 'You don't mind, do you, darling?'

Frances sat smiling the vacant smile of the great unwanted Third; she had never felt quite so large in her life, she seemed to be filling the room. She was so much there, and she could not get away, she could not get rid of herself. She tried to look unobservant but pleased, and only succeeded in looking embarrassed.

'Frances is feeling prim!' laughed Sidonia.

'What rot! I'm feeling nothing of the sort.'

'Oh, yes you are, I can see it in your face. But isn't my David a sweetheart?'

'Of course he is,' said Frances weakly, her voice sounding quite idiotic.

They began to talk a lingo of their own, rather suggestive of the nursery. It was also suggestive of those endearments lavished on pampered dogs. They grew more playful as the evening went on.

'I'm going to kiss Frances!' announced David, teasing.

'Let him kiss you at once!' commanded Sidonia.

'And don't look so shy,' laughed David.

In the end he performed a feat of strength by carrying Sidonia up to bed.

'Some weight!' he remarked as he staggered upstairs. 'Some weight, but I like hefty women.'

4

Once in their room he became very grave.

'I do pity Frances, Sidonia.'

'I can't think why.'

'Oh, can't you, dear? Just think of all she's missed, married life and all that sort of thing. It's damned hard luck on a woman—no man, no kids, no home of her own! No wonder she looks so withered and dried up.'

'But does she?'

'Good Lord! as dry as a bone. You can't expect anything else.'

'I don't think Frances has ever wanted to marry.'

'What rubbish! Of course she has. I bet she's longing to marry even now. It's damned hard luck, I think!' Presently he began again: 'I've been thinking over Frances' type just lately; you know, the middle-aged virgin! I've noticed that they tend to get rather unsexed, at all events late in life.' He rubbed his chin gently, his face looked puzzled. 'It's very curious,' he continued, 'but we have an example of the same thing in does—I believe that does have been known to grow horns when their breeding activities are over.'

Sidonia laughed. 'How awful! I hope Frances won't grow two little horns.'

'Of course not, don't be silly,' said David, 'I was only speaking metaphorically.' He considered a moment, puckering his brow, then he looked at Sidonia solemnly. 'But I tell you what, she may grow some hairs!'

'Grow *hairs?*'

'Yes, the long, lonely sort, on her chin—I've seen that happen before now!'

CHAPTER TWENTY-EIGHT

I

THE weather was bad, but David felt that Frances should see the country.

'It's so good for her to get out of herself, it's more wholesome,' he told Sidonia.

There were Norman churches all over the place in addition to Jacobean houses. One need not consider distance with a car, which of course was such a blessing! David generously gave up his shooting in order to please 'Poor old Frances', every afternoon they drove to some new place that David felt she ought to visit. After a week of this intensive sight-seeing Frances developed neuralgia. By the end of a fortnight she had ceased to remember the name of a single church; they had all begun to look so much alike, and so had the Jacobean houses. She made one or two bad mistakes in the evenings when David discussed their drives. He would say:

'That's a fine old church at Puddle.'

And she would very probably reply:

'Yes, isn't it; I love its queer, wooden steeple.'

David would look pained.

'No, no! Not that one, that's at Rochford, not Puddle! Puddle's got a Norman tower, you know, an exceptionally fine example.'

At last she protested feebly to Sidonia.

'Don't let's motor to-day, it's going to rain.'

'I don't think so, we'll put the hood up if it does; we're not salt, a little rain won't hurt us.'

'But I feel a bit tired.'

'Well—of course if you don't want to—but David says

you're looking ten years younger; he says it's the open air.'

They went in the end, and in David's new car, a Bentley just down from London. He said you could do sixty miles an hour and not know you were doing more than ten. He lent Frances one of his motor coats and wrapped it round her himself.

'You won't mind if I speed a bit?' he inquired. 'We want to let her stretch her legs.'

Frances thought that they had speeded for two weeks, but she nodded and smiled agreeably.

'Will you be an angel and sit at the back? I want to sit by David and see how the car goes,' said Sidonia.

'Of course,' agreed Frances.

David admired his new car immensely, it made him feel extra kind. He insisted on tucking Frances up in rugs until she resembled a cocoon.

'Now you'll keep beautifully warm,' he told her, giving a few final tucks.

He decided to run across to Plumbury Heath, just a matter of a hundred miles. A couple of hours might do it, he bragged, provided the roads were clear. He drove down the drive and out through the gates with very suspicious caution; then they struck the high road to Plumbury Heath and the Bentley 'stretched her legs'.

Sidonia was all right, she had on a cap that buttoned under her chin; she craned forward with one hand clinging to the car in very obvious delight. David crouched loosely over the wheel with his hat jammed low on his head. He occasionally rested an elbow on the siren, otherwise he appeared to be in trance. They dashed over cross-roads and passed danger signs with a splendid disregard for such trifles; but Frances supposed that he must drive well, since she still remained alive.

The Bentley had looked such a comfortable car as it stood there purring in the drive, but Frances began to realize that something was radically wrong with the back seat. It was hard, it was narrow, it was also very slippery. It evidently did not like Frances at all, for it kept trying to dislodge her;

and her legs were so firmly bound up in rugs that she could not retaliate. She had thought that at least the day was windless, but now it appeared to be blowing a gale. David and Sidonia had a wind-screen, of course, Frances had only the wind. There was also a quantity of unexpected dust, that got in under her eyeglass. She vainly tried to release her legs, as she did so her toque blew backwards. She left her legs to attend to her head, her eyeglass dropped out and, caught by the wind, streamed gaily over her shoulder. She clutched at it crossly, frowning as she did so. At that moment David glanced round.

'All right?' he inquired in a hurried bawl; his eyes were watering a little.

'Quite all right!' yelled Frances, clinging to her toque. She did wish he would look at the road again instead of being polite!

2

They made the Heath in two hours and a half. David said it was a jolly fine record considering the twisty road. They went to tea at The Lion Hotel. Frances felt numbed and hazy. Her eyes were half closed from wind and dust, her hair was a mass of frayed-out ends, her legs were stiff from sitting so long tucked up in David's rugs. He helped her down.

'Some car!' he remarked. She nodded, speechless for the moment. 'I say, I'm afraid you're tired, though,' said David with genuine anxiety in his voice. He insisted on getting her a glass of port. 'You're tired,' he kept on repeating.

She would so much rather have had a cup of tea, but David would not allow it; he declared that port wine prevented chills, and for the sake of peace she drank it. David and Sidonia ate enormously, they might have been playing a game of Rugger from the amount of food they consumed. Sidonia had kept fairly neat and quite warm.

'It's the warmth from the engine,' she explained, 'and then we've got a wind-screen in front; we must have one fixed at the back.'

Whenever their eyes could be divorced from their tea they both looked anxiously at Frances.

'I'm all right, I like speeding,' she lied irritably at last. 'I thoroughly enjoyed the drive.'

David smiled.

'No, you don't like speeding. We're a couple of selfish pigs.'

'Yes, I do.'

But he only shook his head.

'It's been rather too much for you, I'm afraid. Shall I get you another glass of port?'

3

Sidonia sat on the back seat going home, and David took Frances beside him.

'You'll feel more confidence here,' he told her; 'you'll be able to see the driver.'

In spite of Frances' angry protests, he drove home at twenty miles an hour. Very occasionally they touched twenty-five, but when they did this he slowed down. They got back some time after 11 p.m., not having stopped for dinner. David ordered cold supper to be brought, and brought as quickly as possible.

'You must eat. I'm afraid you're in for a chill. I feel we've been most inconsiderate.'

Frances was only too anxious to eat, she was literally starving with hunger. She made an extremely hearty meal, but David was not quite satisfied; he watched her every mouthful, declaring the while that she only picked at her food.

'Now you turn in with a nice hot-water bottle and get a night's rest,' he said kindly.

She was only too thankful to escape to her room. He made her feel such a fool!

4

The one or two neighbours that Frances met struck her

as being very dull; but Sidonia did not seem to find them so, she said they were jolly people. She was learning to ride side-saddle in order to please David. The Master in those parts objected to a woman with a leg on either side of her horse.

'And I think he's quite right,' David told Frances. 'It never looks well, somehow.'

Frances had come down hoping for some hunting, but she did not mention this fact; however, David did.

'Got your habit with you? I can give you a topping mount on Wednesday. It's a good meet too, our best country. Not that the hunting's up to much round here; still, it's better than nothing.'

Frances shook her head.

'I haven't ridden side-saddle for years and years, I don't think I'd stick on now; in any case, I haven't got a habit, but I brought my breeches with me——'

David shook his head.

'Can't be done, old thing. Absolutely can't be done!' he said playfully.

Frances' visit was drawing to a close. She wished she could have got some hunting, but perhaps she might get some shooting instead, she was quite a respectable shot. Since the trial of his Bentley David had ceased to suggest more motor excursions.

'If you'd really like to go out with the guns just tell David so,' urged Sidonia.

Frances screwed up her courage to ask him one evening when she found him alone in the gun-room.

'Anything here that would fit me?' she inquired.

He turned round with a puzzled expression.

'Fit you? What kind of thing?'

'Well, a gun of course! I didn't mean ready-made clothing.' Her voice was flippant with nervousness.

'Oh, a gun——' said David slowly.

'I wouldn't mind having a shot if you'll have me. I used to shoot quite well at one time.'

'It's a tiring business,' David told her. 'Are you quite sure you'd stay the course?' His voice was gentle, but she saw at once how intensely the idea bored him.

'Perhaps not,' she said dryly, 'I'm only a woman.'

'Exactly,' agreed David in relief.

There was nothing to feel angry about, yet she did feel extremely angry—angry with him for being so male, angry with herself for minding his aggressive masculinity.

'You don't want to shoot,' he was saying persuasively, 'it's a beastly job for a woman. Fox hunting's different, it's not so intimate—the killing business, I mean.' He paused and surveyed her with questioning eyes. 'It's a beastly business!' he repeated.

'For me, but not for you!' Her voice sounded foolish, trembling with irritation.

'Oh, I'm different,' he told her, lighting a cigar. 'A man does those things to keep hard and fit, he's a slaying animal by nature; it probably comes from primitive times, when he killed to feed his women.'

'And now he does it for the pure joy of slaughter?'

'Oh, no, for the joy of sport.'

'It's exactly the same thing.'

'Perhaps,' he admitted, 'that's why I don't want you to do it.'

She was not being clever, she had given him an opening; she struggled to cover her slip.

'Mayn't a woman feel primitive sometimes? She existed as well as the man, you know, in the days when they shared a cave——'

He looked at her steadily.

'No, Frances, she may not. Woman has evolved much farther than man in some things; she's become the beacon that we all try to follow; she dare not retrogress.'

Frances smiled a little.

'Platitudes, David.'

'Platitudes if you like, but platitudes are not always worthless, they often spring from some fundamental truth. What I've just said is true.'

'Then you think?'

'I think that you ought to have married. Why haven't you married, my dear?'

He stood there surveying her critically, but his eyes were

not altogether unsympathetic. She thought: 'Supposing I tried to explain?' and began to laugh softly to herself.

'Bless you!' she said, 'I've never wanted to marry.'

'All women do,' he told her.

'Not being a woman, how can you know?'

'Because I'm a man, I suppose.'

This answer was so illogical, so naïvely opinionated, that Frances, in spite of her irritation, could not find it in her heart to retort. There were so many obvious things she could say, that she curbed her inclination to say them. She looked at him smoking his excellent cigar; why disturb such sublime contentment? His brown shoes shone like mahogany his well-worn tweeds were distinctly of the kind that took pride in remembering their tailor. His hair looked so crisp and healthy and young, his grey eyes so clear and untroubled. So far he had met no problems in life, and therefore for him there were none. Quite suddenly her irritation left her. She felt very miserably old and wise in the presence of his overwhelming youth. He reminded her, somehow, of a reckless boy, a boy filled with dreadful confidence. She said:

'It's not all so simple as that; some problems are quite difficult to solve.'

'Oh, I don't know, Frances—don't try to solve them. Just get on a nice, safe, well-laid track and run along, that's my motto.'

'Some of us don't fit any track. What's to be done then, David?'

He frowned.

'There's the right gauge for everyone born, only some people won't try to find it. Some people like to think they're misfits, it makes them feel more unusual.'

'Do you really think that?'

'I honestly do. I can't believe that God makes mistakes.'

'But mayn't He vary the pattern sometimes?'

'He might if He wished, but He doesn't.'

Frances was silent for a moment, then she said:

'Do you think Sidonia is the usual pattern?'

His answer came glibly:

'Yes, why not? I think she may have been a bit cranky before we married; but marriage has normalized her of course, it always normalizes women. After all, it is their natural vocation, you can't deny that, can you? Frances, may I ask a very personal question?'

She assented.

'Well then, honestly, are you really happy?'

'No, of course not, nobody is.'

'Ah, there you are!' he said triumphantly.

'But I might have been still more unhappy if I'd married.'

He shook his head, looking very wise.

'Not you!'

'You think not?'

'I'm sure of it.'

She lit a cigarette, inhaling deeply. The corners of her mouth twitched a little, but she managed to keep her face properly grave while David's eyes were upon her.

'You smoke much too much,' he told her reproachfully, 'it's shockingly bad for your nerves.'

CHAPTER TWENTY-NINE

I

FRANCES had left by an early train and Sidonia sat reading alone in the drawing-room. She wondered if David, who had gone out hunting, would get home in time for tea. She yawned; a most uninteresting book—she could not keep her mind on the plot. After a little she gave it up and drew her chair closer to the fire. She began to consider Frances' visit. It had not, she felt, been a great success, but that had not been David's fault, nor had Frances been really to blame. Only poor old Frances hadn't quite fitted in—she *was* a misfit, poor old Frances! Sidonia stared into the crackling logs. How fond she had been of Frances once—for a short time very devoted. She had loved and admired those things in her that now seemed a little ridiculous. She had even been jealous of her mother, she remembered, jealous of her hold on Frances.

'I would have liked to take her away from mother,' she mused, smiling to herself incredulously. 'Thank God, I didn't succeed in doing that; what a mess I'd be in now! I might have had Frances round my neck, and David would have grown to hate her. I might have grown to hate her too in time—poor old Frances, she's rather dictatorial.'

She let her mind drift away from the present, it went slipping back and back.

'Only happy people would dare to do this,' she murmured contentedly.

She tried to recall her first conscious memory. She thought she remembered her perambulator, and a vigorous protest that she had made on re-entering if after a walk in the park. She was sure she could remember disliking the strap that they buckled to keep her in; she could almost recapture the spirit of her fury—tucked-up fists and small, thumping heels. After that a medley of odds and ends, not unlike Blake's old rag-bag. Her mother's stray lock—she had tweaked it one day, and her mother's glasses had fallen off and been broken against the fender. Very faint memories of a pale little man with a hesitating voice, her father. Brioche bread for tea, the nursery milk jug, the handle of which was a thieving cat in pink china. Blake darning socks by the nursery fire. A canary who had sat with his feathers ruffled up and finally died, no one quite knew why. The alphabet, laboriously learned with Blake. The urge to draw things, the urge to write things, the excitement of rhyming words. Her governess, Miss Thomas—Miss Thomas used to cry when she had tried her too sorely. Slate pencils, the smooth, pale kind that you chewed; delightful new pencil boxes. A series of Bibles and prayer books and hymnals; bought with saved-up pocket money these, during spells of religiosity. The period when she had wanted to dance all day long, and dance naked. Miss Valery's school, one or two of the children she had liked but quickly forgotten. Miss Valery herself—'She's not Greek, she's Greece!' And that one particular note on the piano that invariably failed to sound. Sidonia smiled, remembering the school; it had grown quite celebrated now—one often saw Valery pupils appearing at the West End theatres these days. Tunes— the lure of little haunting tunes that your fingers itched to play. Mr. Willowby-Smith's impatience because you could not read music. The first struggling effort to model in wax, the thrill of partial achievement. The dispute that had arisen over the attic. The School of Art, Miss Lotter— Jensen.

'Jensen!' She spoke his name half aloud, 'Jensen, Einar Jensen!' A little shadow, too faint for sorrow, crept over her mind for a moment.

Jensen had chopped his speech so queerly—Jensen had known great hopes, great faith. Florence, her singing, the Villa Ferrari; Liza, Umberto, the children. Then all in a moment the first sharp knowledge of grief that had come with a Florentine spring—flowers—there had been such cruelty in flowers that Jensen would never see. The nights, when tossing wide awake on her bed, she had longed for nothing in the world but one thing, the sound of his voice—forgiving. The slipping of grief into deep regret, of regret into gentle remembrance. The two years that followed—her voice, her ambitions—the merging of herself in the life of the villa, in those dear, cranky, great-hearted people. Maurice in love—Ferrari had smiled and had called his love 'growing pains'. The terraced garden with its glimpse of Florence—Mamma Rigarno and her omelettes—shopping with Liza in the Tornabuoni—driving back in the evenings, 'E-e-e yup! E-e-e yup!' The coachman urging his ponies. A fig-tree that grew in the villa garden, it had been quite heavy with little green figs that would later turn to purple. Liza, majestic, treading with slow care—Liza once more great with child. Then England, a cold, detestable country. Then David, and England suddenly transformed into a splendid and gallant place where David had made his home. And after David nothing but David; the peace, the marvel of that! Liza had written so kindly on their marriage, Ferrari had written too. They had not been angry about her singing; Liza had said that creating a child was finer than creating a rôle. Darling Liza! That had been so like her; seeing it all as the means to an end. 'But,' thought Sidonia, 'I'd be jealous of a child—I'd be jealous on David's behalf.'

Her mind concentrated itself on David, suddenly curious about him. What manner of creature was he? Strange how little she really knew him while loving him as she did. Did any two people really know each other? Wasn't there always a secret something that they instinctively withheld? She knew certain obvious things about David—his good looks, his magnificent figure; her sculptor's eye rejoiced in his figure as it had always done. She knew that he was not a clever man, that subtleties tended to bore him, that he saw right and wrong as black or white, while of course she admitted of grey. She knew that he was inclined to judge people by their ability or inability to fall in with his own views on life, that she had been David's great exception, David's perilous adventure.

Perilous—was she a perilous adventure? Her thoughts paused, suddenly uneasy. A log fell into the grate with a crash; she got up and put it back. She crossed to the window and looked out at the garden, dripping now under rain. It was David's garden and therefore her garden; their garden for years and years. But one never knew, she might die young; on the other hand, she might live to be very old. She and David might walk in their garden arm in arm because they were growing feeble. They might say:

'Look, that's the mulberry tree we planted. How quickly mulberries grow!'

But the mulberry tree would not have grown quickly, it would have taken nearly a lifetime. A lifetime; a lifetime might mean anything—a moment, an hour, or she and David growing distressingly old. Would it be distressing to grow old with David? It must always be distressing to grow old; but she and David loved each other; they would kiss each other for each new wrinkle, and yet—it might be a very long business—time for the mulberry tree to grow. Supposing the days should seem over long? Inconceivable, of course; still, supposing—could two deeply-loving and devoted people tolerate outside interests? Could one or both, perhaps, find a solace in some new activity of mind?

'No, no!' she exclaimed with sudden fear. 'Love—that would always be enough!'

Oh, but she was grateful to David Morgan who had opened the gates of life, who had taught her the sweetness of secret things, who had made her completely woman. She began to dwell on their hours of love, on his kisses, his moments of deep tenderness, on her own glad and eager response.

'It is enough!' she said, clasping her hands. 'Not only enough, but *all*.'

2

He stole up very quietly behind her.

'Dreaming?' he inquired gently.

She turned and flung her arms round his neck.

'Yes, dreaming of you,' she said.

She rested her cheek against his sleeve. His sleeve was wet from the rain. Little drops of moisture clung to his cheeks; he smelt of damp earth and saddle leather, of the countryside, clean and vital.

'We had a topping good run to-day!'

She smiled, scarcely hearing his words. She laid her hands on his rain-soaked shoulders, then slowly she let them trail down his side till they clasped his strong, slim flanks.

'Aren't you a beautiful fellow!' she said softly. 'Aren't you a lovely man, David!'

They stood quite still and gazed at each other; then he caught her to him roughly. She yielded herself, triumphant, reckless with the urge that he called into being.

CHAPTER THIRTY

I

I T was August, eight months later, when Lady Shore heard that Sidonia was going to have a child. She handed the letter over to Frances with a startled expression in her eyes.

'She seems very calm about it,' said Frances, 'but that may be a good sign with her. I see that she doesn't want you to go down until the very last moment.'

'A child—Sidonia is going to have a child!' murmured Lady Shore, biting her thumbnail. 'I can't get used to the idea somehow; it seems so unlike Sidonia.'

'These things do happen, you know,' smiled Frances.

'Yes, but do they happen to Sidonia?'

'Well, apparently they do.'

'Oh, dear!' sighed Lady Shore drearily. 'I wish my Godfrey were alive.'

'I can't see what use he'd be just now, he wasn't a mid-wife, darling.'

'I know, but Godfrey was always so calm—he'd have been a great support to me.'

'Don't worry, Prudence, it's a natural phenomenon; you had a child once yourself.'

'So I had, but that seems ages ago. Ring the bell for Blake, will you, Frances?'

Blake answered the bell in her own good time.

'I'm ironing, me-lady,' she announced on entering, 'my iron will be getting cold.'

Lady Shore looked at her with entreaty.

'Never mind the ironing to-day, it doesn't matter. Miss Sidonia is going to have a baby.'

'There now!' said Blake, somewhat mollified. 'I thought it was overdue!'

'Blake——'

'Yes, me-lady?'

'You were with me in Egypt when Miss Sidonia was born.'

'I was that; I'm not likely to forget it either, the mosquitoes was something awful!'

Lady Shore pushed back the hair from her brow.

'I can't remember the mosquitoes.'

'Not remember the mosquitoes that bit you that bad at the actual moment of birth?'

'Never mind the mosquitoes! I was rather ill, wasn't I?'

''Orribly ill!' said Blake.

'Can you recall the sort of things we did? Did we take any special precautions?'

Blake pondered.

'We stopped them donkey boys from chattering under your window——we ordered a new mosquito net, only it came too late——we sent Sir Godfrey out of the 'ouse to stop him getting in the way——'

'Yes, yes, but I mean important things.'

'You was 'orribly sick while carrying, me-lady!' said Blake, on a ghoulish note.

'Oh, well, thank you, Blake. You'd better do your ironing —no doubt we shall manage between us.'

'We must 'ope,' remarked Blake as a parting shot, 'that Miss Sidonia won't miscarry.'

'Good heavens, why should she?'

Blake looked back round the door:

'Them very tall women——' she said cryptically.

Lady Shore sighed and folded her hands.

'I *must* be practical, Frances. I feel that the moment has now arrived when I'll need all my presence of mind.'

'Well, you've got several months in which to prepare. I shall make you take hypophosphites.'

'Life—new life,' said Lady Shore softly, 'it's a very wonderful thing. Godfrey and I, Sidonia and David, and now this small, unborn other. It goes on link by link in the chain, right down the ages, Frances; always the same and yet always different. I wonder so much what it means.'

2

A week before Christmas came a letter from David begging Lady Shore to come at once. His writing was that of a careless schoolboy, his spelling distinctly erratic. He wrote: 'I may be foolish to be anxious, but I'd like to have you here now; apart from which you have every right to be present to welcome your first grandchild. As one cannot be sure when the thing may happen, I don't want you to delay. I must say at once that I don't like the nurse, nor have I much confidence in our doctor. Sidonia is quite extraordinarily brave, but certain of her symptoms, according to the books, are not at all reassuring. I've been reading up the subject very carefully lately, and I don't like several things about her. The doctor tells me that all is well, but I cannot agree with him. Of course, my Aunt Alice had thirteen children; but then, she wasn't Sidonia. If you write to Sidonia don't mention what I've said, and be very careful when you see her; the last thing we ought to do is to frighten the poor child, whatever we may feel ourselves. She has not seen this letter, so once again—be very careful.'

Lady Shore rang every bell in the house, and finally Blake appeared.

'Pack up my things at once,' said Lady Shore, 'we shall leave by an afternoon train.'

Frances was sent for and came post-haste; the panic was very infectious.

'Where's my Chavasse? I've lost him again!' exclaimed Lady Shore, hanging over the banisters.

'Do you mean Chavasse's *Advice to a Mother?*' inquired Frances, looking up.

'Yes, and his *Advice to a Wife*.'

'I saw them last on your study table.'

'Well, I've looked, and they're not there now!'

'Are you sure?'

214

'Quite sure; I couldn't have missed them, they're covered in light brown paper.'

Frances turned and went into the study. The books were the first things she saw.

'Here they are,' she called; 'they're just where I told you, right on the front of your table.'

'Thank God!' murmured Lady Shore fervently as she hurried back into her bedroom.

Her face was wearing an inspired expression, as though she expected help from on high.

'If you'll go away and just leave things to me we may catch that train,' snapped Blake.

She omitted to say 'me-lady', there was really no time for trifles, and Lady Shore did not notice the omission; at the moment they were just two anxious old women, the one cross the other abstracted.

'Why didn't he send a telegram!' murmured Lady Shore for the twentieth time.

'Because he's a man,' said Blake satirically. 'They cause all the trouble and then lose their 'eads. I wonder 'ow we can abide them.'

'Don't pack my Chavasse!' exclaimed Lady Shore, concentrating her attention for a moment.

'Why not?' inquired Blake in an injured voice.

'Because I want to read him in the train.'

Blake sneered.

'I don't hold with all that stuff. Nature's nature and books is books, and they've nothing to do with each other.'

'Don't be so silly,' said Lady Shore sharply, 'everyone reads Chavasse.'

She thrust the books into her dressing-case and began to pin on her toque. Blake slammed the lid of the trunk with a bang and closed the hasp with a snap.

'Has the car come yet?' fussed Lady Shore. 'Won't *anyone* get this trunk taken down?'

The train they caught to Chelmsford was not an express, so that Lady Shore had time in which to think. Frances had found her an empty carriage, and she decided to take Blake in with her, in case she felt inclined to voice her own misgivings. As the train moved off Lady Shore put on her glasses and turned to Chavasse for comfort; unfortunately, she opened the book at random, and her eye lit on: 'Swelling of the ankles.' She read for fifteen minutes or so, then looked across at Blake.

'This is too awful!'

'What is?' inquired Blake.

'The things that *can* happen in childbirth.'

Blake sniffed.

'I don't believe in them books; the Lord knows His business all right.'

'I dare say He does, but just listen to this.'

Blake listened but remained unconvinced.

'You was much worse than that.'

'Oh, no, surely not.'

'Yes, indeed, you nearly slipped through our fingers.'

'Did I suffer very much? It's a curious thing, but I can't remember very clearly.'

'I 'ope I'll never be asked to witness anything like it again,' said Blake; 'if you've forgotten you're a marvel!'

'But on the whole women come through all right.' Lady Shore spoke to comfort herself.

'Some do and some don't. We must 'ope for the best. Miss Sidonia's no different from the rest.'

'She's always been strong, though,' persisted Lady Shore, but Blake only shook her head.

'The delicate kind often comes off the best, they has the easiest confinements, so I've heard.'

Lady Shore took off her glasses in despair and tried to doze in her corner, while Blake looked stolidly out of the window with a face quite devoid of expression.

'Good gracious! We've forgotten the spirit lamp!' exclaimed Lady Shore, starting up.

Blake continued to stare out of the window.

'They'll 'ave all such things,' she mumbled.

'But suppose they haven't? That spirit lamp might have come in very useful.'

As Blake did not answer she sank back again and resolutely closed her eyes. She managed to stay in a fitful doze until they arrived at Chelmsford.

4

David was anxiously waiting on the platform as the train drew into the station. His face lighted up when he saw Lady Shore, and he hurried her off to the car; he had specially hired a closed motor, he said, in case she should feel the cold.

'Thank God you've come, Mother!'

He seldom called her mother, and she turned to look at him more closely. His eyes were rather sunken, she thought, and his face decidedly thinner. He looked like a man barely over an illness, and Lady Shore's heart misgave her.

'How is she?' she inquired as soon as they were in the car. David shook his head slowly.

'Not well. Of course, she thinks she's all right, and I haven't undeceived her; but between ourselves I don't like her symptoms, I think they're rather disquieting.'

'What symptoms don't you like?'

'Well, her right ankle's puffy.'

'Oh, dear!' said Lady Shore, remembering Chavasse. 'No, indeed, that isn't a good symptom!'

'Then she's sleepy all the time,' David went on, 'yet she's dreadfully nervy and irritable. The doctor down here is obviously a fool; I've got Sir Thomas French for the confinement.'

'Has the nurse arrived yet?'

'Yes, she came two days ago—I told you about her in my letter. Sidonia likes her, she says she's sensible; but in my opinion she's too sensible, she's got no intuition and that's jolly bad; she judges too much by appearances.'

They were silent for a time, then he moved a little nearer

and groped for Lady Shore's hand. He held it during the rest of the drive, like a child much in need of comfort.

'I'm terribly anxious!' he burst out presently. 'I never thought it *could* be like this. I can't sleep at night for thinking of Sidonia, and of all she's going through for my sake.' His voice shook a little, he stared out of the window and his grip on Lady Shore's hand tightened. 'She's so damnably plucky!' he muttered unsteadily, 'she's so plucky that it's awful to see her!'

Lady Shore stared at his agitated profile, she thought that he looked almost old. It was clear that David was quite unnerved, no doubt from so many sleepless nights. His voice was changed too, no longer self-assertive as she was accustomed to hear it; and it suddenly dawned on Lady Shore that their rôles were completely reversed. David had liked looking after her, but now he longed to be looked after; David had liked reassuring others, now he wanted to be reassured. His face had grown older, but his heart had grown younger; he was feeling like a badly-scared child. She became very practical all at once.

'You must keep calm, my dear,' she told him gently, 'I feel sure she'll get through all right; after all, it's a constant occurrence in nature. I had Sidonia, and yet here I am. Still, we'll need all our strength to help her, perhaps, so we must keep absolutely calm.'

He turned his worried, grey eyes upon her.

'It *is* such a comfort to have you, Mother; you see, we two love her so, don't we?'

She nodded, afraid to trust herself to speak, so much did this creature touch her. He looked so large to be sitting there clinging to her hand for comfort. The car turned in at the iron gates.

'She mustn't suspect that we've talked about her,' said David, suddenly grown nervous.

'No, of course not, trust me, I'm very discreet. You'll see, it'll be all right.'

Sidonia was waiting for them in the library behind a hospitable tea-table. She got up at once and kissed her mother.

'Hallo, Mummy!' she said cheerfully.

Her eyes were clear, her skin smooth and cool with a faint tinge of colour in the cheeks. Lady Shore had not quite known what to expect, but she certainly had not expected this. Sidonia was looking exceedingly well, though she limped a little when she walked.

'I knocked my ankle last week,' she explained. 'Look, Mummy, it's quite badly swollen.'

Lady Shore stared at Sidonia's ankle and then at Sidonia's husband.

'She *knocked* her right ankle,' she said rather pointedly.

David was silent, but his smile seemed to say.

'Isn't she unendurably plucky!'

'A knock would cause swelling,' went on Lady Shore.

'She didn't knock it hard,' whispered David.

'Don't be an idiot!' snapped Sidonia. 'I'm not engineering an alarming symptom. Ask nurse if you don't believe me.'

He sat down beside her and stroked her hand.

'Of course you're not, sweetheart,' he agreed, but the eyes that he turned to Lady Shore were cloudy with misgiving.

'I never felt better in my life,' went on Sidonia.

'She's a whale for sleep,' put in David significantly.

'Well, of course I am, that's part of my condition. If you'd let me alone it might do me good, but you always come hovering round or something just to see that I'm still alive!' She turned to Lady Shore. 'I'm glad you've come, Mummy, you can look after David a bit. For heaven's sake make him go out hunting, or find him a job in the carpenter's shed, or let him help someone to sweep up the leaves—he's driving me nearly mad!'

'She's a little strung up,' explained David apologetically.

'I'm nothing of the kind,' said Sidonia, 'I'm feeling very

well and I'm going to have a baby; I can't see what there is to fuss about.'

6

The local doctor called after tea, and spent a few minutes with Sidonia.

'She's splendid!' he told Lady Shore as he left. 'Nothing could be more satisfactory.'

'Well, she certainly seems all right,' said Lady Shore, turning bewildered eyes on David.

'Of course she's all right.' The doctor smiled, then he lowered his voice confidentially. 'The prospective father is a little over-anxious, they're like that sometimes with the first.'

The nurse came up, a rosy-cheeked woman with a pleasant, reassuring face.

'I won't telephone to-morrow if she seems all right, doctor, unless of course you wish me to.'

'Use your own judgment about that, nurse; no need to ring up if she's going on well, I leave that entirely to you.'

David glared at the nurse with positive venom. The moment she had gone he turned to Lady Shore.

'There you are! What did I tell you?' he said furiously. 'The woman's a careless idiot!'

7

Sidonia's baby was born on Christmas Day at six o'clock in the morning. Just as the dawn was streaking the sky he clamoured into the world.

David sat hunched on the library chesterfield in his camel's hair dressing-gown; he had flatly refused to lie down in his dressing-room in case he might hear Sidonia moaning. His face was ashen, his eyes red-rimmed, his mouth set in lines of anguish. All night long he had waited like this, ruffling his hair at intervals.

Lady Shore found him still crouching there when she came to tell him the news.

'David, my dear, you've got a son!'

He stood up and stared at her blankly.

'David, you've got a son!' she repeated, holding out congratulatory hands.

He took both her hands like a man in a dream.

'And Sidonia?' he whispered, 'Sidonia?'

'Going on splendidly. You can see her now, it was quite a normal confinement.'

He did not let go of her reassuring hands, and she left them quietly in his.

'Sidonia's given me a son!' he said slowly, and his voice sounded hushed and incredulous.

Then his head dropped forward on to Lady Shore's shoulder and, quite unashamedly, he wept.

CHAPTER THIRTY-ONE

I

EARLY in the new year Frances was sent for to pay her respects to the heir. She found a perfectly normal David waiting at the station with his open Bentley.

'Hallo, Frances! So glad you've come. Sidonia's longing to see you. She wants to show off our gold-medal baby—he's a perfectly stunning fellow!'

As they drove he talked glibly about the confinement.

'As easy as nothing at all,' he told her. 'Sir Thomas said the most normal affair that he'd attended for years.'

'I suppose you were terribly anxious,' said Frances, smiling a little to herself.

'Well, not really. I was a bit worried, of course; but I knew Sidonia would come through all right, she's got a splendid constitution.'

He touched the accelerator slyly with his foot, and the Bentley gave a leap forward.

'Not too fast?' he inquired in a teasing voice.

'No, go on, I like it,' said Frances.

They raced along selfishly for over fifteen minutes, just missing two dogs and a cat, and finally dashed through the open gates and whirled up the drive with a flourish.

'Your nerve's much better, you've been smoking less,' said David, as he helped her out.

2

Sidonia was lying in the huge Georgian bed over which swung the blue satin tester.

'You can go away, David,' she remarked firmly after a moment or two, 'I want to have Frances all to myself; go and smoke a cigar in the library.'

He laughed.

'All right, but don't be too long, and take care of my son and heir!'

As the door swung to on David's broad back Sidonia looked up and smiled.

'*His* son and heir! Did you hear that? I ask you—you'd think *he'd* carried the child for nine months and gone through the confinement at the end. David is funny sometimes!'

The baby was lying in the crook of her arm, a red little creature swathed in flannel. The creases of the packing were still on his face; his eyes were smoke-blue like a kitten's. Frances stood at the foot of the bed and surveyed the pair very gravely.

'Well, Sidonia, how does it feel?'

'Like heaven!' Sidonia told her. 'Look, Frances, he's got red fluff on his head. I had red fluff on my head, mother says. I believe he's going to look just like me.'

The baby doubled up tiny fists and began making tiny noises. He fumbled blindly but greedily.

'He's hungry, the lamb!' Sidonia explained. 'It's his dinner-time and he knows it too; we can go on talking while I nurse him.'

The talking was mostly done by Sidonia, and mostly about the baby. He liked this, disliked that; he loved this one, hated that one—showed a preference already for certain members of the household. He was quieter with his mother than he was with the nurse; he knew his mother when he saw her.

'In fact,' thought Frances, patiently attentive, 'he does all the impossible baby things that first babies have done since the world began.'

Presently Sidonia fished under her pillows.

'Do you remember this, Frances?'

Frances stared at the small brown book that Sidonia was holding out to her.

'Yes,' she said slowly, 'that's surely the book that I found on a second-hand bookstall in Florence—I didn't know you'd kept it.'

'Oh, I kept it all right! I've just read it again, but I don't want David to find it. Poor old darling, he hates all this sort of thing—he's not got much imagination.'

They were silent for a little while after that, then Frances said:

'Your David's all right. He's the tenderest thing on earth, deep down, and a perfect fool about you, I may tell you!'

Sidonia nodded rather absently: her eyes were kept on the baby.

' "The Saturday Life", do you remember, Frances? We thought it might be true.'

'You did, I didn't,' said Frances firmly. 'I don't believe in such rot!'

Sidonia laughed.

'You sound like David! Well, even if it is true, I think it's over—I'm in my last act now, Frances.' She stared at the top of the baby's head. 'There can never be anything after him; he's an end in himself, he's *the* end. I've a feeling that it's always ended like this. And, you know, he was born on a Saturday too, the last day of the week.'

Frances' eyes filled with difficult tears, not because of Sidonia's 'Saturday Life', but because of her beauty, lying there—a woman with a child at her breast.

'Well, so long as you're happy,' she said rather gruffly.

'I'm happy, and I don't feel afraid any more. I used to feel afraid sometimes, you know.' Sidonia paused, then she smiled at Frances. 'I'm going to prove that I'm not afraid. I shall christen him Noel, Godfrey, David, but I've thought of a special name of my own for him; *I* shall always call him Saturday!'

Frances screwed in her tortoiseshell eyeglass and fished for a cigarette.

'Um-m,' she grunted, striking a match. 'All the same, I'd call him Monday, I think, if I were you.'

VIRAGO MODERN CLASSICS

The first Virago Modern Classic, *Frost in May* by Antonia White, was published in 1978. It launched a list dedicated to the celebration of women writers and to the rediscovery and reprinting of their works. Its aim was, and is, to demonstrate the existence of a female tradition in fiction which is both enriching and enjoyable. The Leavisite notion of the 'Great Tradition', and the narrow, academic definition of a 'classic', has meant the neglect of a large number of interesting secondary works of fiction. In calling the series 'Modern Classics' we do not necessarily mean 'great' — although this is often the case. Published with new critical and biographical introductions, books are chosen for many reasons: sometimes for their importance in literary history; sometimes because they illuminate particular aspects of womens' lives, both personal and public. They may be classics of comedy or storytelling; their interest can be historical, feminist, political or literary.

Initially the Virago Modern Classics concentrated on English novels and short stories published in the early decades of this century. As the series has grown it has broadened to include works of fiction from different centuries, different countries, cultures and literary traditions. In 1984 the Victorian Classics were launched; there are separate lists of Irish, Scottish, European, American, Australian and other English-speaking countries; there are books written by Black women, by Catholic and Jewish women, and a few relevant novels by men. There is, too, a companion series of Non-Fiction Classics constituting biography, autobiography, travel, journalism, essays, poetry, letters and diaries.

By the end of 1988 over 300 titles will have been published in these two series, many of which have been suggested by our readers.